FUNNEL VISION

STORM SEEKERS 1

BY

CHRIS KRIDLER

Published by Sky Diary Productions, Rockledge, Florida

Learn more about the author and storm chasing at

ChrisKridler.com

Cover design and photo illustrations by Sky Diary Productions

Paperback ISBN: 978-0-9849139-0-9

First edition

SPRING RISING

J udy tried to fit the windy world within the rectangle framed by her camera's lens — the crumpled-carbon-paper sky, the wrestling clouds, the inexorable tornado. It snaked downward, stirring up and swirling the red earth. For a moment, as she clicked the shutter, she thought she could keep it there, hold it steady so she could study it and understand why it sprang forth, a vine sown in the sky's garden, like the one so many years ago. It had grown in her imagination, that storm of her childhood. Familiar fear prickled at her neck, rebuffed by the stubbornness that would not allow her to turn away.

She longed to freeze the storm's motion, but on a chase, that's not how it worked. Standing beside the rocky road, she looked up and watched as the twister moved out of her frame and closer. She let the Nikon hang loose around her neck so she could lean over the tripod and adjust her video camera. The wind shifted as the edges of the circulation enveloped her. A thousand bits of color snapped and popped through her peripheral vision: the whipping trees, the rippling grass, and a car moving her way, somewhere beyond the dust rushing along the ground and into the funnel's base. The storm would not be confined. She could not hold it there. Part of her wanted to make it safe and small, beautiful in the lens of her camera, but it was never safe. She longed for it to be so safe she could walk up and touch it, remember what happened, contain it and put it away, but then, she wouldn't feel like this. She loved this sensation, wild and vast and uncontained, spawned by the sky, the tornado, the implication of infinity, and the wind caressing her cheek.

JACK HEARD it more than he saw it, the flapping metal octagon whizzing by his ear like some crazed aluminum bird. "Get in the car!" he told Dennis. He grabbed his video camera, tossed the tripod in the back and slipped behind the wheel as he kept an eye on the tornado. He was already rolling the sedan forward as his passenger slammed the door.

Dennis was breathless. "Do you think that stop sign was trying to tell us something? Maybe we should go back."

"That was just an inflow jet." Jack stole a glance at the writhing funnel on their left as he drove the car hard, trying to keep pace. "Do you have any idea how lucky you are right now? You can't bottle this, Dennis. Drink up while you can."

Jack lived for moments like these. Every day without storms the rest of the year beat a dull metronome in his head, the routine of bar-hopping, women, grad school. Sunshine depressed him. This was what he waited for: spring. Storm season. The scientific allure was strong, but for him, there was more to the chase. He wanted to catch what he pursued, to lose himself in that moment when he forgot everything else. He couldn't turn back now.

He dodged another pothole on the gravel road, then aimed his video camera at the swirling plume of dust.

"Let me shoot the video." Dennis, pretending he wasn't worried, took snapshots with a digital camera as the car bumped along. "This is why the mesonet is better. One person drives; the other does the video and the data."

Jack snorted. "This isn't the mesonet. Next week, we'll have the mesonet. This week, you shut up and navigate."

"I'm glad I'm not riding with you next week."

"Yeah, Marcus isn't a mean bastard like me." Jack laughed.

"He's pretty cool for a dweeb, but it's the hail-catcher I'm excited about."

A paunchy undergrad on the five-year plan, Dennis had wavered before capitulating this morning when Jack asked him to be his navigator. Most of the research team saw Jack as intimidating, fearless or unnaturally lucky, and those who had chased with him knew that he would push them to their limit, just to see them squirm.

Jack was aware of his rep. He didn't care. He had seen the sky's spinning gears crank out more tornadoes than he could count, but the first one of the season was one he couldn't miss. The late-April tube kicked up ruddy dirt, Oklahoma style, as it hurried east.

"It's starting to turn," he said, eyeing the now-leaning tornado. The rural highway was turning, too, curving gradually north, its power poles stretching like a necklace to the horizon. He popped his video camera into the dashboard mount so the lens would point out the windshield. "I think it's going to cross the road."

"Then shouldn't you slow down a little?"

"In a minute." Jack smiled, enjoying Dennis's discomfort. He liked to get right to the edge of where he shouldn't be. This was it. He engaged the brakes, and the car crunched to a halt, idling as the tornado ripped through a hedge line a half mile from them, tossing trees in the air.

"Unbelievable," Dennis whispered.

As it crossed the road, it appeared to weaken, but power flashes bore witness to its violence as it hurled down a couple of poles. The grinding column of red and black undulated as it eased east, and small rocks and grass on the fringes of the circulation smacked against Jack's car. The urgent, pattering sound tapped a primal center in his brain, the one that said *flee*, the one he always resisted.

"It's roping out," he said, making sure his camera was centered on the dwindling tornado. Now it was a ghost of its former self, and soon the dust rotating on the ground seemed broken off from the skinny funnel lifting into the clouds. Then there was no more dust.

Dennis squinted out the window. "It's gone."

"There might be another." Jack sighed. One was never good enough.

He pressed the accelerator and noticed another car parked on the left, a couple of miles ahead and facing them, on the other side of the tornado's track.

Dennis noticed it, too. "They had a great view. Looks like another chaser."

"Looks like a woman," Jack said with interest. As they closed the distance, he rummaged in the camera bag between the seats for his cigarettes, then checked the matchbook tucked in the pack. Empty. "Damn it. Do you have any matches?"

"Nope. Doesn't this car have a lighter?"

"I lost the cap, and my laptop's usually plugged into the outlet anyway. Let's ask this girl." As they got closer, Jack could make out golden hair and an attractive figure. "Besides, she's beautiful. I have to talk to her."

"Oh, no, not again," Dennis said.

"We have a second. There's not even a wall cloud yet." Jack pointed to the new rotation developing in the storm, hoping Dennis would accede to his experience and buy his delay tactic.

"Whatever." Defeated, Dennis pulled a cell phone out of his pocket. "I'm calling Marcus for data."

Jack brushed a hand through his short, dark hair. She would like him. They almost always did.

He loved to meet women on the road. He loved to meet women anytime, really, but it was rare to meet a woman who chased storms. She looked as if she belonged out here on the windswept prairie. He pulled up by her small, silver SUV and saw she had dark blond hair with long, thick braids, a pretty, unusual look. She wore close-fitting khakis and a short-sleeved, sky-blue blouse that whipped in the wind, clinging to her curves. The blue matched her eyes, which were dreamy with the storm, still staring up at the clouds — she wasn't breaking away to acknowledge him, wasn't stopping her shot until she was ready. Parked on the shoulder and standing behind a sturdy tripod, she filmed the fading mesocyclone with rapturous attention. A serious 35mm camera hung from her neck. Jack felt a familiar desire, the yen for conquest, along with something else, more unusual, a kind of recognition. She was an elemental force on this elemental day, or was it his adrenaline talking? It almost felt as if lightning were about to strike.

❦

JUDY WAS SO ENGROSSED in shooting the last tendrils of the tornado that she didn't realize the car was there until its trailing dust cloud wafted past her camera. She finished her shot, hit the button and glanced over. Antennas on the roof. Dashboard cam. Chasers. The passenger was on the phone, a bit disheveled and plump, with limp brown hair and a rumpled college T-shirt and jeans. The driver was a different story, in his crisp, white T-shirt and long shorts. He had a great smile, an angular face, spiky black hair and eyes as green as young wheat. A handsome devil, she thought. Impulsively, she grabbed the camera that hung from her neck and snapped his picture, a wide-angle shot that captured the scudding clouds of the storm.

He laughed. "Nice to meet you, too."

"I have to take pictures when I see a good subject," she confessed, slightly embarrassed at being caught. "Those clouds looked incredible behind you."

"A sky like this makes me think anything is possible." His voice was pleasantly deep. "Wasn't that a great tornado?"

"Fantastic!" She was happy to share the thrill of the moment, still high from the storm. Somehow, this man was part of it, and made infinitely more attractive by the association.

"Got any matches?"

It wasn't exactly what she expected him to ask, but Judy held up a finger, silently telling him to wait while she opened her passenger door, leaned in and sifted through the glove compartment. She pulled out a glossy white matchbook embossed with red foil hearts and the names "Hank and

Emily," then walked back around her car and tossed it to him. "Keep them."

He caught the book with one hand and glanced at it, then ripped out a match and lit his cigarette before turning to her again. "You Emily?"

"No, I picked that up at a wedding."

"Not your wedding, then?"

She laughed. "Oh, no."

"Thank god. Want one?" He held up the pack of smokes.

"No, thanks. I just like to play with matches."

"Lucky for me."

His passenger got off the phone. "We have to go *now*, Jack. Marcus says this circulation's really getting its act together. It's about to do it again."

"OK, OK," Jack said, turning toward the passenger to impale him with a pointed glare. Then he looked out his window at Judy and winked. "We'll meet again." He flashed her another smile as he drove off.

"I certainly hope so," she said to herself. He looked like trouble. Like the tornado, possibly irresistible trouble.

The dust kicked up by the car formed little sparkling clouds that tumbled and fell back to Earth.

A WEEK without tornadoes passed like a glacier when you were stuck on the road. Jack tried to speed it along with beer, but beer just slowed it down.

At the hotel bar, he let the Oklahoma tornado and the pretty girl play in his head like a movie reel. Now, they were last week's memory, and he tried unsuccessfully to use them to blot out today's poor chase.

The early-season low had sped off to the east, and the next system, which had looked so promising, was falling apart all around them — had fallen apart, in fact, as the research team chased it that afternoon. With the downturn in the weather sank his mood. Not willing to endure Marcus's godawful snoring in the room, not motivated enough to work on his dissertation, and not sociable enough to join the others at the all-night trucker cafe by the highway, he chose the bar instead.

One dangling, bubbled globe of amber glass saved it from shadow, mocking his memory of the prairie light, the way the golden rays shot beneath the storm at sunset. The cell had collapsed with the day, leaving only fragments of structure, rain, and not a hint of the slim tornado, which had fizzled almost as soon as it touched down.

The dark wood of the bar absorbed most of the lamp's sickly glow, except for a little glimmering in his clear, square ashtray and the dew on his brown bottle. A few dust motes drifted, stirred by the beige, plastic fan bolted to the wall next to the shelves of liquor. It was too cool for it, since the front had moved through, but its blades made a futile attempt to keep the air moving in a smoky bar from which smoke had no escape. It was not unlike the general air of oppression in this town, one of so many built along a strip with a Pizza Hut and a Dairy Queen and a sign on the outskirts from the last century claiming bright hopes for the next, only the next was here, and the chamber-of-commerce colors were peeling. Nebraska. The Good Life, as the border crossings kept reminding them.

He lit another cigarette, contributing to the noxious weather of the bar, the clouds wafting from his lips and dissipating. After four days of touring, this was their first real storm. It was a weak start for their research, which after all the thousands of miles came down to giving people without basements a few more minutes to lug a mattress and the babies into a closet and huddle beneath the big, square cushion and pray it all isn't ripped away in one screaming inhalation of nature. They were barely speed bumps for the tornadoes, he thought. They weren't like him and the others, rolling ahead of the beast, dancing around its claws. That was the romantic version, anyway. The others waited for fate, and sometimes, they died.

What time was it? 11:21 p.m., the digital clock next to the whiskeys said. The red numbers glittered in the walls of the glass vessels, the dreamy brown liquids looking back at him. He could almost see the watery outlines of his taut, narrow face. And something else. Another face reflected.

He looked to his left, around the corner of the L-shaped bar, and saw a woman there, staring at him. She had brown eyes and brown hair streaked with blond, curly in the everlasting fashion of the Plains, a couple of decades behind. Soon, it would be hip again, and she would never know as the global style rotated on its pointless axis.

"Are you one of those storm watchers?" Her voice sounded raspy. A cigarette stub glowed in the ashtray next to her. God, did he sound like that? She shifted closer, into the light. She was not as young as she first appeared.

"Yes, I am." He knew they were obvious wherever they went. If it wasn't a blatant logo on a T-shirt, it was the fleet of cars with instruments sprouting out of the roofs, like deformed bike racks.

"It came right past our farm today," she said. "We lost a fence, but it wasn't too bad. I've seen worse." She wore a white blouse and a brown overall dress with ruffles. Was everything brown here? Restaurant uniform. Waitress. Wedding ring.

"You're out kind of late," he said. "I mean, if you have to milk the cows in the morning."

"Oh," she said with a slow smile, nice teeth, moving to sit next to him at the corner, "I work too late to milk cows, even if we had some."

"You on a break?" he asked, knowing she wasn't.

"The Wagon House closed already. Sometimes I need to wind down." She took a sip of her drink. It was red. Vodka-cranberry, he guessed. He tried to stick with beer on the road, unless he was sweet-talking a girl. Beer was cheaper, and he didn't feel as shitty in the morning.

"Bartender, another for the lady." He pointed to his nearly empty bottle, too, and the pale mole-man snapped into slow-motion action.

Her eyes sparkled under the curls and the poufy bangs, still damp from the rain outside. "Tell me about chasing those storms. Why do you do that? It's so dangerous."

"Not if you know what you're doing." He touched her arm lightly as if he were sharing a confidence, enjoying the feeling of playing her. He sensed she might provide the distraction that today's storms could not. She was attractive enough, and by all the signs, willing. She probably only had a few years on him — he was nearly thirty — but a hard life made it look like more.

"I'm Jack." He offered his hand and clasped hers warmly, lingering a little. She flushed. The amber light spilled through the air between them and smoldered weakly in her brown eyes. Whiskey light. He heard a roll of thunder far away, the melancholy clatter of the decaying storm. He took a pull from his fresh, cold bottle and started to tell the tale as outsiders liked to hear it.

❦

"FUCKING STORM CHASERS," Greg said to Judy, looking out the window of the hardware store upon the land that Dorothy forgot. Her younger cousin had a push broom in his hands, idle, as he gazed at three sport-utility vehicles in various states of hail-dentedness parked at the library across the street. They had a lot of antennas, but Judy knew they weren't university researchers. Not enough gear, and too many tacky lights. Their license plates didn't have the Kansas clouds hers did.

"If it weren't for all the duct tape they buy, you and Uncle Ray would be out of business," she teased, drinking in the thin sunlight of early spring. Down the street, she could see it glint off the statue of the Great Pioneer in the circle at the heart of Pancake. Home. Beneath the warm, sweet calm, though, she felt a whisper of unease, a need to get out there and into the prairie wind, to find the storm she sought.

This weekend was shaping up nicely. A strong system promised to kick into the Plains from the Four Corners, but she had Eliza Hendricks's wedding to shoot. It would kill her to miss a good outbreak. She'd love to get on the road again.

Oh, hell, the system was two days away. No use fretting. It was the weather. Anything could happen.

She glanced over her shoulder at old Ms. Reynolds in the back of the store. The wizened little woman was flipping through seed packets, shaking one and holding it up to the green-tinged fluorescent lights before rejecting it and moving on to the next.

Across the street, three men in T-shirts and jeans emerged from the library, one carrying a road atlas. They walked to the biggest of the cars, pulled another map from its cavernous interior and unfolded it on the hood, chatting all the while. One of them, a lanky, curly-haired guy in a baseball cap, laughed, and Judy could hear the joy in the sound.

Members of her tribe.

"I wish I were chasing." She said it without thinking.

"See? You're a sympathizer," Greg scoffed, going back to his sweeping. He was as close to a rebel as this town would allow — shaggy dark hair with white streaks; a tiny mustache; a glinting, silver, dagger-shaped earring; and a tattoo on one arm that said "Wheat Me," just visible under the short sleeve of his Hale Hardware polo shirt. He was going nights to the community college to be a computer technician.

"Maybe I'm an artist." Judy wouldn't confess it to Greg, but she was a chaser first. She always wanted to be chasing. She sold storm video to TV news or through a stock agency when she wasn't shooting weddings and portraits, removing acne scars and tooth stains with Photoshop, even inserting lost loved ones for an extra fee. Resurrection wasn't cheap.

"They bring the storms with them," Greg said. "They're like plague rats."

"Watch out, then. I think one of them is about to infect you."

The curly-haired guy walked toward Hale Hardware. The jingle of the door heralded his entrance. He nodded at them, a bit bashfully, then wandered into the aisles. Judy watched him, evaluating his sloping nose and slender figure and deciding she approved. As he picked up a roll of duct tape and strode to the front, she had to giggle.

"What?" Puzzlement creased his forehead.

"Duct tape," she said.

"It is inherently funny, isn't it? Like it has something to do with ducks." He smiled at her. "Robinson. I mean, that's me. Robinson."

"I'm Judy." She stuck out her hand and he shook it. "Not much to chase today, huh?"

"Not yet. I wouldn't worry."

"I'm not worried. I just wish I were out there, too."

His brown eyes lit up. "You're a chaser?"

"At least some of the time. In real life, I'm a photographer. I'm supposed to shoot a wedding Saturday."

"Oooo, not good," Robinson said. "I think that's going to be the big day. We were just checking some of the models."

Greg cleared his throat. "You going to buy that?"

"Um, yeah." Robinson set the roll of duct tape on the counter, pulled a Superman wallet out of his back pocket and plunked down some bills.

"That's my cousin, Greg," Judy said. "He doesn't like storm chasers."

Greg blanched at her tattle and fished some change out of the register.

Robinson laughed at his expression. "He must like *you*. I mean ... who wouldn't? I mean, because you're related." He cleared his throat. Endearingly awkward.

She smiled awkwardly in return. *You have no idea. I'm a pain in the ass,* she thought, as Greg began to quiz Robinson about the various uses of duct tape. It was no picnic growing up on the Yellow Brick Road, shadowed by Dorothy's tornado. Her parents had even named her for the actress who played the girlish hero. Now her folks lived on an Arizona golf course, scarecrows forgotten, while Shannon, her prettier, scattered younger sister, drifted from job to job in Oklahoma City. And

Judy still wore her Dorothy braids, in a shade of straw, her skin sun-warmed from all the time she spent outside in her garden or on the Plains, trying to find the sweet spot between tornadoes and the steel-reinforced concrete bunker in her head.

It was as if Judy were the only one who could bear to live with reminders of the twister that came through when she was fourteen. For her, being here among the signs — the still-stunted trees, the empty lots, the stark new buildings where old houses once stood — was almost a compulsion. She got her degree in Lawrence, tried a few classes at the Kansas City Art Institute, but was drawn back to Pancake. She lived and worked in the house on Main Street that her parents bought after the tornado and later sold to her.

Gone in an instant, the tornado was always there. Memories surfaced with a fierce, pricking force: eight dead, including Greg's mother — her Aunt Kate — and their boxy houses on the west end of town reduced to splinters. The families' anguish was almost too much to take. Her father worked endlessly. Her mother made martinis, and when she was out of olives, drank straight gin. Or beer. Or whatever was available. Judy lost herself in the search for her pictures, the albums she'd put together of the family reunions and the nature hikes and their long-lost cats. The negatives were waterlogged or just plain gone, launched on an updraft into some Missouri back yard.

She noticed Greg and Robinson staring at her.

"What are you thinking about?" Greg asked.

She paused. Not Aunt Kate. Don't bring up Aunt Kate.

"Cats."

"Them's good eatin'," Greg said.

Robinson laughed. "My dog would agree. I miss him. One of my buddies is watching him while I'm out here."

"What kind of dog?" Judy asked.

"A mutt. A lovable little guy. He rides along at home. Only slightly scared of thunder."

"Where are you from?"

"I drove out from Maryland."

"That's a long way to come."

"Not for tornadoes. But I envy your commute. Here." He reached into his wallet and fished out a wrinkled business card. "If you think you can get away, give me a call. We can always use a native guide."

"I'll even bring my own duct tape."

"We would also accept a duck, but only if he has gas money."

"You guys staying in town?"

"I think so. Maybe you could join us for dinner later? You can text if you don't want to call. I know some people can't deal with the sound of the human voice anymore. I don't mean you, though, I mean — I mean, I'm sure — anyway, call me." He was flustered. Awkward, again. Robinson smiled, touched the brim of his cap, turned on his heel and was jingling out the door in a moment.

It was as if a light had left the room. She couldn't believe she'd actually run into a chaser at home. She had more in common with him than she did with everyone else in Pancake.

She'd probably end up like Ms. Reynolds, still browsing by herself in the back of the store, shopping for more and better chemicals to further mutate the botanical freak show she called a yard. Why did Judy stay? Maybe it was people like her cousin, or the sunflower farms, or the windmill park on the edge of town. More than anything, she thought, it was her quest to pin the thing down, that desire, that strange yearning to be back in the moment when the tornado tore apart their peaceful lives. It was in all of her photos, her quest to capture the ephemeral light and energy and darkness of that moment in the storm when nature brought everything together into a laser-fine point of undeniable power. It was in the painting on her living-room wall, the mural she couldn't finish, the fine strokes of gold and green and blue and bruised purple that were the boundless, mysterious Kansas horizon. If she could just get that right, or snap that perfect photo, or hone that fiery point within herself, maybe she would understand.

ROBINSON'S FACE, lit by the pink neon of The Filling Station, shone with bliss as he took another lick of his caramel-drizzled soft-serve vanilla cone.

"I told you it was the best ice cream in town," said Judy, who sat next to him atop one of the picnic tables outside the old gas station-turned-cafe. They'd compared chases for an hour before ordering their ice cream, and now they were among the last customers of the night. The evening was getting dark and chilly.

"I'm so glad you did," he said. "I'm nuts about ice cream. The rest of the guys don't know what they're missing. Too bad you skipped dinner."

"Deadlines. One of my clients wanted to review the portraits I shot for his press kit, and this was the only time I could get it done, especially with that wedding coming up."

"Do you work a lot?"

"When you work for yourself, you never get time off. My boss is a bitch." Judy smiled.

"I don't believe that," Robinson said. "I work for myself, and my boss is awesome. Lets me take Fridays off, buys me gourmet coffee every day and loves puppies."

Judy laughed. "What do you do?"

"Writing. Web design. Graphics and that sort of thing."

As if to prove her point, the phone in her sweatshirt pocket buzzed. He looked in its general direction and held out his hand. "Want me to get it?" he asked playfully. "That's the third time."

She grimaced and pulled out the phone. "Guess I'd better ... Hello, this is Judy."

"It's Madeline Hendricks. We have a problem." Uh-oh. The bride's mother.

"What's wrong, Mrs. Hendricks? I'm all set to go for Saturday."

"Eliza isn't."

"What do you mean?" Judy looked at Robinson and shrugged.

"She's missing in action. She went after Rick this morning when he didn't come home from his bachelor party and hasn't been back since."

Judy wasn't sure why the mother of the bride had called her. "What can I do for you, Mrs. Hendricks?"

"If she calls you, please call me right away."

"It seems unlikely, but I'll be happy to call you, Mrs. Hendricks. I'm sure she's OK." Judy and Eliza had gone to school together, but their friendship was casual at best. She suspected her old friend had sought her out more for the friend discount than for any lasting warm regards.

"What was that?" Robinson asked as she disconnected the call and dipped her tiny spoon into her melting mint chocolate chip.

"Girl trouble."

"You ... you have girl trouble?" His brow creased, and Judy chuckled to see what he was thinking.

"No, the bride I'm supposed to shoot Saturday is having troubles, apparently."

"There's something about being a bride that turns women into alien, fire-breathing creatures," he said, starting to crunch into the sugar cone.

"Not all of them. I've met a few calm ones."

"My sister Tess was a raging beast. She sold her car to pay for her wedding, because my parents refused to fork out the ridiculous amount she demanded. Then she started bicycling to work, lost thirty pounds, then lost her husband. Or he lost her, to be more precise. She left him after two years."

"As long as she's happy?" Judy wasn't sure what to make of this.

"Very much so. Now an avowed divorcee, dating a successful plumber."

"Maybe people aren't meant to be together forever," Judy said, feeling the black truth of it, based on her own pathetic experiences. The phone buzzed again. She looked at it. Eliza. "I should get this."

"Please do," Robinson said, amused.

"Eliza, is that you?"

"Judy, I'm sorry," came the rapid-fire syllables of her friend. "I'll pay the cancellation fee, but you won't have a wedding to shoot on Saturday."

"You're not getting married?"

"Oh, I'm married, all right." Eliza laughed. "Just not to Rick. The asshole didn't just rent two strippers for his party; he rented them for two days of intimate interaction. I found him and his buddies passed out at a roach motel in Wichita. I told him he could go to hell."

"But you married — I mean —"

"You know I've always had a thing for Ed."

"Ed Pusher?" He owned a gas station at the western extreme of town.

"We're in Vegas. Don't tell my mother."

"She called me specifically and asked me to call her. I said I would."

"I'll text her that I'm OK and call her tomorrow. Judy, I'm so excited!"

Obviously. Excited and crazy. "You promise you'll text her? Your mother actually looks at texts?"

"Yeah, it's the only way she can communicate with my brother."

"OK, Eliza. Take care of yourself." Judy heard laughter on the other end. It sounded like a party.

"You know it, sweetie. See you next week."

Judy ended the call and looked numbly at the phone. "Holy cow," she muttered.

"Is something wrong?" Robinson looked concerned. Nice guy, that. And then, she realized, nothing at all was wrong. She felt a smile take over her face.

"Guess who gets to go chasing on Saturday?"

◣

THERE WAS nothing a storm chaser liked better than a whirlwind wedding, especially if it set her free to chase an early-season cyclone.

As the bottom dropped out of the low-pressure system

pushing into the Plains, Judy Hale Photography went mobile. She was happy as she packed her boxy car with cameras and set out on Saturday morning in Robinson's caravan of chasers, while the first bright, white cumulus clouds began to pop up to the west.

"I like the look of that line," Robinson's voice crackled over the ham radio. His yellow SUV, one of the three she'd seen outside the hardware store, rolled behind her silver one. The other two were in front. Ahead of them was the vast, green prairie.

"I love the smell of Kansas in storm season," she replied on the radio, as waving wheat and windmills showed there was warm, moist air streaming from the southeast into the caldron of atmospheric ingredients beginning to mix to the west. Farms, cows and the occasional tree or town zipped by as they pressed west on a minor highway.

It turns out they weren't total strangers to her, the rest of the guys, but chasers she knew lightly from the online world. She'd learned last night that Robinson had chased some of the same tornadoes she had, and they had seen each other's storm photos on the web.

In the lead car, the one with the spin lights and spotlights, was Bruce, the sort of guy who was always in the lead, whether he should be or not. He owned three car dealerships in Dallas. A little burly and a little geeky, with thinning, spiky brown hair, a goatee and a funny laugh that recalled cartoon squirrels, he always made the right forecast, even when he was wrong. Obviously, it was God who was mistaken.

Driving behind him was his best friend, redheaded, soft-spoken and mustachioed Whit, on vacation from his Weather Service job in Texas. He quietly diverted Bruce from his worst mistakes and played practical jokes on him at every opportunity. This morning, it was canned whipped cream all over

Bruce's impeccable black tank of a sport-utility vehicle, topped by at least three jars' worth of scattered maraschino cherries. When Bruce emerged from his room at the Super 8, a dozen grackles were wing-deep in the mess, slipping as they tried to nail the bright red orbs oozing through the snowy peaks of whipped cream.

Bruce had wailed and flailed his arms at the offending birds while the others laughed and, of course, shot video. They knew he would get over it. After all, it was a chase day, and potentially a good one. They had already paged through data sites on the web to find the best potential convergence of low pressure, dewpoints, cold front and dryline. West it would be, probably in the northern Texas panhandle. They would check data again farther down the road, just to see what curves the wind would throw.

"Judy, you got your ears on?" Robinson said over the radio, employing a mock drawl. Though Maryland was technically below the Mason-Dixon line, he wasn't really a Southern boy.

"Still on," she said.

"What camera gear did you bring?"

"Two digital SLRs, one old film camera just in case, and an HD video camera."

"Geez," Robinson said. "We'd better see some tornadoes, then."

"Stop it!" Bruce's command came over the channel. "Don't jinx it."

Whit broke in. "There's no jinxing. There's only science. The sky will tell its own story." His measured Texas twang quieted them. They felt that subtle tension, the faint vibration of nature's spring coiling all around them. They had no influence over the energies gathering, like the magical forces in a storybook, often unpredictable, sometimes vengeful, sometimes blessed, always puissant. Wind. The power of the invisible.

Judy, her window open, her thick braids flapping, took a deep breath of the sweet-smelling air, mercifully upwind from feed lots at the moment. There was nothing like that crazy feeling of hope and awe, borne on breezes and blue sky, kissed with spring fever. Maybe somewhere out there was the perfect picture, the one she knew she had inside her, the one that would transcend all her doubts.

She pumped up the Propellerheads in her CD player, not quite enough to drown out the occasional chatter on the radio, and then steered with her right hand while grasping a yellow gadget in her left. She held the digital psychrometer out the window, using her fingers to shade the sensor so sunlight wouldn't skew the reading, then pulled it in and hit the dewpoint button. Temp seventy-nine, dewpoint sixty-eight. Not bad at all for this late morning, early in May. As the air heated under the intensifying sun this afternoon, the atmosphere should have all the fuel it needed. All it lacked was a spark. Where they were headed, the match, they hoped, would soon be lit.

❧

"MARCUS!" Jack bellowed at the milling team, all atlases and laptops and suitcases, an anthill of confusion swirling around him in the parking lot. He coughed, then took a draw on his cigarette. Looked around again. "Is the van ready?" He hoped Marcus would reveal himself.

They'd had a couple of days off, given the break in the weather, and had mobilized last night to take a strategic position, a hotel on I-40 in the eastern panhandle of Texas.

Once, this had been Route 66 or thereabouts, but there were no leisurely road travelers here now. Trucks roared by on the nearby Interstate as the twenty-five or so students and researchers readied their fleet of cars, bristling with instruments. This was the mobile mesonet that would attempt to surround whatever storm they found today. And they would find one. Jack was sure of it. He was too superstitious to say the *T* word, though it came to mind unbidden — tornadoes. Tornadoes. He had seen dozens but never enough.

It was a little cool and cloudy here, but the satellite showed it was clear north and west, and dewpoints and temperatures were already starting to climb east of the dryline.

He heard a rumble and turned to see the white van pull up and crunch to a halt next to him in the gravel parking lot, nearly flattening his toes, which were already threatening to squish out of his worn but beloved generic black high-tops.

"Jesus, Marcus." Jack was too tired to be really alarmed. He hadn't been sleeping much, and when he did, in his dreams, he never got to the tornado in time.

Marcus hopped out of the van. He was a topsy-turvy mirror of Jack. Where Jack had short-cropped dark hair, Marcus's was curly and long. Where Jack had a clean storm T-shirt and long shorts, Marcus had a wrinkled red flannel shirt and stained khaki pants, along with glasses perpetually perched on the end of his nose. Jack was clean-shaven; Marcus had a two-day-old beard. Marcus was what Jack had left behind, young, in his second year of grad school, and not too sure of what he was doing. He was a sergeant in this army. Jack, who was working on his Ph.D., was a captain. The generals would be in the lead van, deploying the soldiers according to their own forecasts, radar feeds, satellite downloads and nowcasts they got from the storm lab, back home in Oklahoma.

"We need gas," Marcus said.

"Well, get it. Keep the receipt," Jack reminded him.

Marcus hopped into the van's driver's seat and roared off, across the access road. He had a sweet job. He was driving the hail-catcher, whose roof was affixed with a net that funneled hailstones into a dry-ice-lined cooler on the van's floor. Hail was Marcus's specialty. But despite two years of driving in research projects like this one, Marcus had never seen a tornado. His strange luck had become a running joke among the crew.

Jack would be in one of the cars — on the business end of the storm, he hoped. Usually, that's where he was told to go. He had an uncanny eye for developing tornadoes and knew just when to slip through the curtains of rain and hail to take readings and videotape the show.

He wasn't sure who was driving him today. Oh, Giselle. She sauntered toward him, tossing her short chestnut hair. She was French, an undergrad, here on some sort of research exchange. Whatever. He narrowed his eyes at her as she approached. Too aggressive, he thought. Not driven, not the way he was. Just aggressive. She'd insisted on being his driver. He wondered, with momentary alarm, do they drive on the right side of the road in France?

"Oh, Jack!" She was painfully flirtatious. "Are we going to see a tornado today?"

"If you want to see a hose, that can be arranged."

"A hose? Oh." She laughed. "I understand. Your word for tornado."

Believe that if you want, he thought. God, he needed to get his mind in the game.

"Jack Andreas!"

Now it was his turn to be summoned. He followed the voice to the field control van. At one of the desks in the back, fiftyish, eternally tan Professor Malik, looking official and handsome in his white storm center polo shirt, was grinning from ear to ear as he paged through screens of data on two laptop computers.

"Got something, Mr. Wizard?" Jack asked.

"Look at the profiles for north of here," Malik said.

The weather balloon data already showed favorable temperatures and winds, changing direction with elevation. As the low tracked east, the surface winds would back even more. A stacked spiral. A supercell merry-go-round.

"We need a good one," Jack said, not trusting their luck.

"Don't worry. We're due. Tell them to grab a sandwich. We have to get into position. We'll leave in twenty minutes."

◥

"WE'RE in the land of cell phone death," Robinson whispered.

He and Judy stood side by side on the edge of a dirt road, a few feet from a barbed-wire fence, looking out over the endless land that surrounded them. They had their feet planted in amber-grass earth that rose gently away from the road, providing a limitless view of the flat plain beyond. The late afternoon sun shone warmly on their faces. The breeze ruffled Robinson's wavy hair. The only sounds were the murmuring of Bruce and Whit, across the way behind them, and the persistent, portentous southeast wind softly whistling through the scrubby vegetation and wire fences. The back of Judy's neck prickled.

The quiet was saturated with subtle sensation, the magnificent breathing of nature. To the west, the architects of the sky had begun to build their towers.

The cumulus clouds there were getting ambitious. Amid the fluffy field of white, one would throw a pile of hard swells billowing up toward the blue, and there they would collapse and stew before popping upward again. They were bumping their heads against the cap, the layer of warm air that might or might not let them through. The afternoon had become warm, full of energy straining for release.

This bleak expanse was the prairie, and yet beyond, where even wheat seemed impossible, where the idea of hills was something forgotten in the back of a drawer in a beaten-up desk in the dusty office of a gas station that hadn't been open in decades. This was where the edges of land and sky met, where tumbleweeds rolled, where cows lowed with foolish innocence, snorting and mooing and stampeding before every roaring storm.

Here, in the desolate flats of the Oklahoma panhandle, on the other side of this lonely road, gadget freak Bruce couldn't get a cell signal to save his life. Or to help them get online, load satellite data and choose which way to go. They had driven a few hours to get here, including stops for food and data; then, by turns, drove in circles and waited in spots like this for another two hours, searching for signs of hope. Sometimes the best setups produce no storms at all, and they were worried the cap might win. But those clouds, those towering clouds, were tantalizing. They lined up all along the dryline, from the northwest to the hazy, distant southwest. The towers, as they so often do, were building on a boundary between two air masses. The latest surface map they saw, about an hour ago, confirmed that dewpoints west of that line were in the forties — twenty degrees less than here.

Judy raised her Nikon and snapped a couple of wide-angle pictures, including the road for perspective. She loved capturing this moment, the beauty of the possible.

They were close to the conjunction of the warm front and the low-pressure center. A secondary low was developing to the south, however, and it wasn't clear yet where the best action would be. They had picked a favorable area, Judy knew, but now things were starting to happen. Their choices were crucial. Wait too long, and any storm that formed might be unreachable. Act too soon, and they could pick the wrong one.

"Bruce," Whit said, getting impatient. "Let's just go to the next town."

"No, I can do this!" Bruce's voice had that squirrelly pitch. "Let me just move the antenna around. Besides, the next town is twenty-five miles away. I knew I shouldn't have dumped the WeatherWorx this year."

Robinson, who had glanced backward at this exchange, sighed and looked forward again, toward the western prairie. "I don't think radar is necessary at this point. We just need to go visual and pray for a popper," he said quietly to Judy, his arms folded against his flat, narrow chest.

"We may need to go farther south, though," she said. "The towers look more persistent down there."

In the hazy distance, the clouds appeared harder, pushier.

Whit materialized at her elbow. "Judy, I think you're right." Exasperation was evident in his voice. "Tell Bruce. He won't listen to me right now."

Judy and Robinson exchanged glances. Then Judy stepped off the mound of dirt and crossed the road to the big, black beast of a car. She leaned against the driver's side and looked into the open window. Bruce was inside, tinkering with his laptop, which was mounted in front of the passenger seat.

"Bruce, would you look at something for me?" She had a hint of persuasion in her voice, about all she possessed. Her sister had cornered most of the charm.

He looked up, startled, as if he'd just been awakened. They didn't know each other very well yet, but her gentle query shook him out of his frustrated obsession with the recalcitrant hotspot. Sometimes it helped to be just acquaintances. People were more likely to remember their manners.

"Um, sure," he said. She stepped back so he could open the door and get out. "What is it?"

"I'm wondering what you think of those towers down there." She pointed to the southwest as she led the way across the road.

He stepped up next to her and the others and gazed that way, scratching his tiny beard. Side by side, they looked, their eyes beginning to drill down to the obvious, a point in the line where a cell was just now breaking the cap. Even as they watched, it began to burst upward. Within minutes, it was blossoming into a cauliflower mass of thermal violence.

"Holy crap," Bruce said under his breath. Then, more declarative: "You know, guys, I think we should go south."

Even this far north, perhaps fifty miles away, they could see the hard bubbles of rapidly growing convection swelling fast. It was exploding.

Robinson and Whit smiled, but not so Bruce could see. "Good idea," Robinson said, already turning toward the cars with the others.

"This is really going to be a chase, though," Whit said as he trotted across the road. "Let me look at the GPS. I'll radio you the best route. We've got to haul."

Judy felt the adrenaline iceberg melting in her brain and gushing warm into her imagination. What would they see today? Where would they end up? She never knew. That was part of the appeal.

At least they would be moving, she thought, as she double-checked her laptop on the passenger seat and popped a video camera into the dashboard mount. She wasn't as patient as some chasers and preferred to go to where the action might be, rather than wait for it. Sometimes it cost her. But right now, there was no clearer beacon than the burgeoning storm to the southwest.

She was sure, just before she turned the ignition, that she heard the first, low rumble of distant thunder.

BRAD TREAT SAT at the wheel of the rented Thor's Tours van and tried to figure out what to do.

He was in Canyon, parked outside a Fuel & Flee, a name that seemed to invite drive-off thieves. His tourists, seven of them, were inside the convenience store. He'd told them that eating burritos was good luck. That much he knew from reading the chaser message boards online. Unfortunately, he was still a little fuzzy about the rest of it. It didn't matter. If those people could find tornadoes, especially all those other tour groups cashing in, why couldn't he? And if tourists, suckered by the seemingly easy chases on television, were willing to pay, hell, he'd find them a goddamn storm. It was Tornado Alley, for Christ's sake, and if he didn't, well, nobody can really predict the weather, right? They'd all signed waivers from harm. He hoped cluelessness was covered as well.

Brad had a rudimentary idea of what he was doing after a

year of chasing, when his father paid for him to go on a storm tour as a last-ditch attempt to get him interested in something. He'd always been entrepreneurial in school, when he'd majored in business — late-night poker games, jungle-juice rent parties and, of course, the porn lending library in the trunk of his Camaro, which he liked to call his Fookmobile. At twenty-three, he was just old enough to rent the white van, now adorned with magnetic decals of a pudgy, angry, cartoon god hurling lightning above the blocky words THOR'S TOURS. The mascot didn't look much like Brad, who was six foot two, thin, clean-shaven, with a neat, dark haircut and thick eyebrows that rose in the middle, as if he were always asking a question.

The Storm Prediction Center's website gave him his first target each day. Rather than refining that target, he drove to the middle of the risk area. This morning, that was Amarillo — convenient, since they'd spent the night there at a Motel 6. Then he would tell everyone he had to get more data, and they would drive to what he said was a better vantage point. This morning, he sort of randomly picked south of Amarillo, thinking that at least he'd have a better view, away from the truck stops and elevated highways. While the tourists were hiking in Palo Duro Canyon, he called his girlfriend, Willa, at home in Fort Worth, and she went online to read him the latest forecasts by local weather service offices. Later, she would check for warnings and call him if she saw any.

He knew vaguely that the dryline was a good place to be. His only worry right now was that, above him, the sky was a bright, cloudless blue. At 4 p.m., all the clouds were somewhere east of him. He wasn't sure, but he thought maybe that was bad. Some of them were starting to look big. Movement caught his eye. A dust devil whirled through the gravel parking lot next to the store, tossing dirt and candy wrappers in a cyclonic swirl. Ugh. Desert air.

The three women and four men emerged from the store, and he motioned for them to hop in the open doors. "We have to get east," he told them.

"I was wondering when we might do that," said Noel, crossing his arms as he settled in the passenger seat next to Brad. The balding, baseball-capped tourist was a second-string TV meteorologist from Georgia, and Brad didn't like him a bit. Even though Noel didn't know that much about storm chasing, he knew weather, and he gave the impression that he knew quite a bit more than Brad did. But Brad was driving the van, and he had to put on a good show.

"Sometimes, you have to wait to be in the best place at the best time," Brad said to the tourists as they climbed in.

"Are we going to see a tornado?" one of the women asked from the back. She was about Brad's age, pink-haired, tattooed, with thick, black eye makeup, and she wore platform-heeled sandals even in what he thought of as snake-ridden farm fields. He had taken to calling her Pinky, since it was easier for him to remember nicknames than real ones. They seemed to like it, except for Noel. He couldn't forget Noel, even if he tried.

"Who knows what the day will bring? We're in the middle of a moderate risk." Brad liked using the Storm Prediction Center's terminology. It sounded good. "Anything could happen. Who knows?"

"As long as you know," Noel said under his breath.

Brad's brow furrowed. He turned up the radio as they started moving. Van Halen was playing.

"This is just like *Twister!*" Pinky said.

Brad frowned at the mention of the movie, wondering if

he'd ever see that many tornadoes in one day. He'd be happy
to find one first.

❧

PROFESSOR MALIK LOOKED CLOSELY at the two slim
laptops on the desk in front of him. This was their mobile
command center — more of a souped-up truck than a van,
really, about the size of an ambulance. In front, senior Travis
was driving, and in the passenger seat, grad student Micki
helped navigate. They and their caravan were headed west on
the Interstate.

Malik worked opposite a rack of blinking computer equipment and monitors, including gear for the wireless data
network they were using this year. On his laptops' screens,
the radar was starting to light up like a Christmas tree all
along the dryline, mostly green, with the first hints of more
intense yellow and red. Multiple cells blossomed along a
north-south line, east of Amarillo.

Seated at another computer on the desk just in front of
Malik, bouncing with the van's movement, was Samuel
Rainier. A professor who often did projects with the severe
storms lab, he had been chasing storms for decades, when he
wasn't tending to his horse ranch. His silver-white hair flowed
to his shoulders, and he wore a striped white shirt, a
turquoise bolo tie, blue jeans and cowboy boots. The screen in
front of him was split between a diagram of weather balloon
data and a tracking map that showed the other mesonet cars
as bright green dots, lined up behind them on the highway.
Now, however, he was more interested in what the eyes in the
sky could tell him. He stroked his close-trimmed moustache

and beard as he got out of his chair to look over Malik's shoulder.

His gaze flitted from Malik's radar screen to the other monitor, which showed a satellite loop of the Texas panhandle, all data streaming in through a satellite Internet link. Nearly circular discs of white blossomed against a black landscape on the screen, some now with hard-looking buttons in the middle, evidence of overshooting tops — vigorous updrafts pushing through each storm's anvil, knocking against the lid of the troposphere. Every once in a while, Rainier would turn and peer through the windshield at the storms lining up on the horizon. They were getting bigger in the window, their anvils blowing eastward, white discs cutting into the blue sky. Soon the caravan would be under their shadow. They had to make their choice.

"Let's head for tail-end Charlie," Malik said, pointing to the southern end of the line on his radar image. "There's great moisture convergence there, and the winds are backed beautifully."

"That's always a safe choice, but this one is looking pretty mean," Rainier said, indicating not the southernmost storm but the one just north of it. "With the upper-air support this afternoon, it could really go nuts."

"Either one might benefit," Malik said. "We can at least head that way. Regardless, we have to go south. Micki, what's the best route?"

Though she had a computer running GPS software mounted on the dash, Micki was already paging through her Texas gazetteer. Lipstick was the only makeup she wore, and it gleamed red as she pursed her lips. "We can go south on Route 70," she said, pushing a strand of long, brown hair behind her right ear as she traced a finger along the route with her left hand. "That will give us some west and east options later on." She presented the open page of the atlas to the men.

"Fine, fine," Malik said, stepping forward to pick up a speaker attached to one of the radios mounted above Rainier's desk. As always, he was Field Control. "FC to all teams. We're heading south on route 70 at Jericho. Stay alert for rogue deer."

"And rogue tornadoes," Jack's voice came back over the radio.

Micki giggled.

"If anyone'll find a tornado," Travis said with an Arkansas lilt, "it'll be Jack."

IN THE CAR that carried Jack, driver Giselle sang French songs to him. She started out with folk tunes. Then she moved on to sappy pop songs. He didn't know French, but they sounded sappy to him. Translations of American hits, he thought.

"How do you know all this stuff?" he asked, not really caring but needing something to take his mind off a sudden craving for a cigarette as the cars of the mesonet took the exit, one by one. He wasn't supposed to smoke in the government cars. He got a good look at the storms and their anvils as they turned, and he stared out the passenger window at the billowing monsters while she chattered.

"I used to sing at weddings," she said in that accent. "I still do, sometimes. Most people here think these songs sound better in French. But you, no?" She laughed lightly.

He tried to expunge from his mind the image of Giselle in a maid outfit, singing the theme from *Titanic* in French.

The sight of the storms helped. He could almost shut her out.

The problem was, of course, that Giselle was female, young, and pretty, and her personality didn't matter much once she closed her mouth. He couldn't stand her, yet he was attracted to her as she tossed her reddish hair and sang her little ditties, wiggling her titties — stop it, he told himself, stop it.

He'd been like this with women forever. There had been a few aberrations, beautiful, exceptional women he'd stayed with for six months, a year. Part of the pleasure in having them in the first place was their initial resistance. Usually, it was too simple. Women responded to overt attraction. That and confidence. Men who never got laid didn't realize how easy it was to ask for more.

But these few women, these women who had held his attention for more than a night, or a week, they had something that resonated in him. They acted like they didn't need him. Then, when he won them over, when they made it clear they did need him, they still had an independent streak that kept him guessing — usually a mask for a vulnerability that, when explored, opened into a chasm of childhood darkness he barely had the guts to look into. It raised too many memories of the years without his mother, the thousand reasons he found not to be with his dictatorial father. Yet he was drawn to the pull of the vacuum, the little core of darkness at their heart, until he was overcome with the emotional equivalent of vertigo and decided to leave and look again for a woman so whole, or so delicious, that she would satisfy the hunger that made him keep searching.

Most were good enough for a taste, even if they didn't sate his appetite. And now, like a film critic who'd seen too many movies, he was jaded by even the most light and pleasurable entertainment. Too often, he couldn't wait to get out of the theater.

This, the spectacular sky, was the only kind of show he could rely on. They were getting closer to the line of storms; or rather, the line of storms was moving closer to them. He took advantage of a swell in the cellular signal to pull down a radar image on the laptop. The two southern storms were starting to look interesting. So was one to the north. Huh. When they lined up like this, southern storms tended to cut off the incoming moisture, starving cells to the north. But the big one north of the interstate was becoming dominant, and the two cells immediately below it were choking. Farther south were the two Malik and Rainier had apparently chosen as their babies, and why not? They also were starting to crank, still pulsing a little, but gaining strength. Their team likely would have to zigzag west again to meet the storms at some point, but for now, they had a good view as they headed south.

To his right, he could see the anvils cutting into the sky — hard, crisp circles against the hazy blue. The two southern storms looked damn good to his eyes, as well as in the radar readings, and soon, his eyes would be his best weapons. Only they would see the subtle changes that revealed the strengthening or weakening of the updraft, or the best way to get at the base and, hopefully, the tornado.

"Jack, are you even listening?"

"Giselle, are you even looking?" he replied. "This is the best classroom you'll ever get, not those rooms back at the university. Not that school in France. This is it. This is what it's all about." He pointed out the window. "Have you ever seen anything like that before?"

"They are very big clouds. They look more cruel than the ones in Toulouse."

"Everything in America is more cruel, baby," he said, as the car ate up the road and now dipped and rose through the blocky, weathered geography that was the hallmark of the Caprock. "Do you mind if I smoke?"

Giselle waved a hand at him. "Please, darling, go ahead. It will make me feel more like home."

❦

JUDY, Robinson, Whit and Bruce were driving their cars fast, south and west, trying to catch up with what was clearly becoming a kick-ass storm. Their only blessing, Judy thought, was that they didn't have to try to catch it from the west or the north, with all the baseball-size hail such an approach could entail.

No, at least it was before them, probably slowly moving their way, and they should be upon it in a half hour or so. They needed to get into a place where the anvil blown off the top of the storm would block the sun, like the gods' own visor, so they could see what was going on underneath the base. Now, the sun was in their eyes. One thing was clear: The cell was getting big, mean and ugly, in the most beautiful way possible. Judy's video camera rolled, capturing the approach and the radio chatter as they got closer.

"I keep wondering if we need to go farther south than this one," Bruce said. By now, they had dropped into the Texas panhandle and had just cruised through Spearman, where they topped off their gas tanks and managed to get a cellular signal. "There are a couple below I-40 that look really good."

"This one does, too," Whit said. "Those others are unreachable."

"But will the storms just to the south kill this one?" Robinson asked.

Judy picked up the ham radio speaker. "They haven't so far. In fact, they look like they're wimping out."

It was strange, but true. There was clearly good inflow into their storm — southeasterly winds increased by the minute as it fed greedily on the moisture — and the towers to the immediate south looked kind of crappy. There was a threat that all these storms could join into a big, messy line, but on radar and visually, they were still distinct and eminently chaseable.

"I hope this thing drops a tornado before dark," Bruce said. "I have to get home tonight."

"*What?*" Robinson practically shouted. "Didn't you tell me earlier not to jinx us? Aren't you violating every superstition in the book? Knock on wood, somebody. Don't say the *T*-word, for god's sake."

"Why on Earth do you have to get home tonight?" Judy asked.

She heard Whit chuckling over the speaker. "His wife asked all his in-laws over for a picnic tomorrow, and he promised he would be there."

"Ugh," said Robinson. "That's a nasty drive no matter where we end up tonight. You're not going to get any sleep at all if you have to get all the way to the metroplex."

"Robinson," Whit said, "aren't you the one who drove more than twenty hours straight to OKC on your way out here?"

"Uh, yeah," he said, "but I was doing it for storms, not a woman."

"She's an actress, you know." Bruce's tone implied that his

spouse was a higher life form. "She does all my car commercials."

"Hear that, Robinson?" Judy couldn't resist. "For the right woman, you probably would drive all night, too."

"Maybe. But I think the right woman would want to drive with me."

"Most women wouldn't be caught dead chasing storms," Whit said. "I mean, present company excepted. Not that you would be caught dead. I mean, my ex-wife hated it when I chased storms, and I just figured that women, um—" He paused. "Somebody shut off my radio, please."

"I wish I could," Robinson came back. "Let's just leave it at the fact that Judy is extraordinary."

She laughed. "Oh, there are dozens of us, it's just that you guys are too busy comparing your gear to notice."

"Ouch!" Robinson was funny. And flirtatious. Though most chasers were men, Judy rarely found such flirting on the road. There was usually an invisible line they didn't cross; we're all chasers here, not boys and girls. But all was not equal. Often great as friends, the guys were also clannish with their connections, very boys' own. Their personalities varied widely — geeks, daredevils, drunks, monks — and she hadn't clicked with one yet. She blamed herself for not being able to make the connection. She'd like to share her passion. Maybe another chaser would understand her deep need to experience the storm. Robinson? She hardly knew him. Or that guy from the Oklahoma tornado — Jack, his friend called him. She might never meet him again. She banished the foolish notion, but it crept back into her heart with a flutter.

Some women were known in the chaser community for their brains or talent or artistry, and a few were known for being Mrs. You Name The Chaser. At twenty-nine, she suspected she wouldn't have to worry about it. Her hopes of finding a stormy soulmate had withered. She'd dated a couple of guys in college and her hometown but had gone without steady company for almost two years. She had trouble forging a lasting rapport with men, and they didn't understand her priorities. They always wanted to go out when she had to shoot a wedding or, worse, when she wanted to chase storms. And once they got into her house and saw her moody photos all over the walls, and that half-finished mural in the living room, and the piles of books everywhere, they started to hesitate, sensing trouble. She could almost hear the cogs in their brains clicking as they churned out their analysis: *She thinks too much.*

"Look!" Whit said. "The sun is starting to give us a break. Does that look like a wall cloud?"

The sun's intensity gave way behind the wispy shield of the white anvil above them. They got their first good look at the storm's base. There was a ragged but distinct lowering.

"We'll have to get closer," Robinson said. "I can't tell if it's rotating. But I sure would call that a wall cloud, or my name isn't Robinson Crusoe."

"Your name isn't Robinson Crusoe," Bruce said, sounding annoyed.

"Which one of us is Friday?" Judy asked.

"Maybe it's that pretty girl driving behind me," said Robinson, whose car was in front of Judy's now.

She really didn't know what to say. There was a palpable pause.

"Smooth, aren't I?" He sounded embarrassed.

"Eyes forward," Bruce said.

"Oh, they're always looking forward," Robinson replied. "I

have an extra pair in the back of my head, where my brain should be."

"Look at the striations in this thing," breathed Whit, his voice full of awe. The storm's rotation was visible in the grand patterns that spiraled through its bubbling walls.

They all began to forget their other issues, their pasts, their tomorrows as they sped forward. The storm was enough.

"SAY IT AGAIN!" Brad shouted to Willa through the bad cell phone connection, trying to be heard over the rain and, now, pea-size hail peppering the tour van. The tourists in the back looked out the windows eagerly, trying to pick out features in the storm they were blasting through. It was an almost hopeless task. In the downpour, Brad couldn't see a damn thing.

"I said, they're all severe! They all have warnings on them," his girlfriend said. "At least, that's what it says on the Internet. It's a bunch of storms in Texas. It looks like they're all in the panhandle."

"Well, which one is the best one?" Brad asked, his always-quizzical eyebrows even more peaked than usual.

"How the hell am I supposed to know that? I pour coffee for a living. I'm not the weather girl."

"Sweetie?" Wheedling never hurt. "You're a genius. We both know that. Can you look at the radar?"

"How do I do that?"

"Ummmm." He tried to think of which website to send her to. It was too complicated, what with the shouting and the slippery driving and the blinding rain. He couldn't think. "Just turn on The Weather Channel and see what they say."

"OK." Brad heard Willa put the phone down. There was

some racket from the TV on the other end of the line as he heard the familiar twang of a pudgy talk-show host lecturing one of his guests about the importance of losing weight. Then the babbling changed to something soothing. With birds. The phone clattered as she picked it up.

"They're showing gardening tips," Willa said. "Did you know daisies bloom more if you behead them?"

"Wow," Brad said, with a complete lack of enthusiasm. "OK, if you can just hang in there, call me back when they show Texas."

"I've got to go to work in ten minutes," she said, impatience in her voice. "They have a new Mocha Minty Freezy Froo on the menu, and I have to learn how to make it before I start my shift."

"Willa, I need you," Brad said quietly, trying not to engage the attention of the tourists. He thought he heard Noel snickering.

"If they show it in ten minutes, I'll call you back. I have my own life to lead, you know. You're not making enough off this storm gig to support two of us."

"All right," he snapped, then softened his tone so he wouldn't lose her help altogether. "I love you."

"And a Freezy Froo to you, too." Willa's tone was all ice as she hung up.

Brad put the phone down. He'd had to drive into the line of storms from the west, playing catch-up, and the road he was on took him right into the core. They were getting bashed by rain and hail, which was getting bigger. Golf balls, now. The racket was deafening. He was glad he got the insurance on the rental van. He wondered how long the windshield would hold out.

Many of the tourists were talking excitedly. Pinky had her

video camera smack up against the back window, filming the hail smashing against the road.

Noel looked out the right side, where the fields were obscured by nature's car wash. "I can tell you one thing," he said. "That radar is starting to look pretty red right now."

"I have good news," Brad said, ignoring Noel's remark. "We're on the best storm of the day! We should be coming into the clear any minute."

"Really?" "All right!" "I love this!" "Is there a tornado?" they were saying.

He had no idea what storm they were on. He didn't know if it had turned into a big, messy line or if, from some perspective, it was a grand, rotating cell. He didn't know how fast it was going or if it was strengthening or dying. As a tour guide, he was screwed. All he could do was go forward and trust to luck.

The winds were picking up, lashing sideways from the north against the windows as he drove east, and he slowed down so he wouldn't skid off the road. The hail was thinning out a bit, and he breathed an inward sigh of relief. He might survive the day with all his windows.

Twenty minutes later, he'd had no phone call from Willa, and they were still driving east. In the rain. Heavy rain. Occasional lightning flashed through the drops, giving everyone a momentary thrill.

"Shouldn't we be seeing something, I mean, like, cloud stuff?" asked Juicy. That's what Brad called the skinny guy with the shaved head who drank big bottles of orange, grapefruit, pineapple, grape or apple juice with his breakfast, lunch and dinner.

"We're seeing the grand violence of nature," Brad replied.

"And we'll be out of this rain any minute now." Even he didn't think he sounded convincing.

❧

JACK WAS KEYED UP, a little buzzed from the nicotine, a lot buzzed from the storm. He ran a hand through his short hair, almost feeling it stand on end. This was a beauty. Even Giselle looked interested as she drove forward. They were heading west again, toward a violently growing supercell that had become a spinning top. The winds were picking up. In the caravan of instrument-topped white cars, everyone's anemometers were twirling like crazy, and not just from the vehicles' motion.

Professor Malik started to give orders over the radio. The cars were dispatched, one by one, with orders to seek out certain sectors of the storm. Marcus, with his hail-catcher van and two passengers, would, of course, be sent into the core. They were already reading potentially huge hail via radar, icy baseballs, the kind that smashes crops and car windows without compunction. Marcus, whose windshield was protected by a metal grate that extended horizontally from the roof out over the glass, would probably have a good day. Whether he broke his tornado-less record remained to be seen. He would have a hard time seeing any structure once he was in the core.

Jack already knew what his role was. They didn't even have to say it. As always, he had to get as close as possible, to dance with the tornado and sample the environment at the heart of the mesocyclone. This was the one thing in life that he could say, without question, he loved. Then came the order.

"FC to Probe 3," Malik said over the radio. "Jack, do I even need to say it?"

"FC, I know exactly where I'm going."

There wasn't a tornado yet, but oh, there were signs. The cell had grown significantly in strength. It had the black, tumultuous look of an atmospheric eruption. Brilliant strokes of lightning spiked out from under the base, which was broad and flat except for the raggedy wall cloud protruding beneath it. This was where he focused his attention as he looked at their gazetteer and the GPS software on the laptop and directed Giselle south on a gravel road. He didn't want to get cut off by the east-moving storm.

He could easily see movement in the wall cloud, as wispy tendrils moved slowly counterclockwise around the edge of the blocky lowering. They were within a few miles now.

"Jack." It was the first time he'd heard nervousness in Giselle's voice.

"You're doing great," he said, almost unconsciously, as he double-checked the tape in his video camera and made sure his Nikon was loaded for bear. The laptop mounted on the passenger-side dashboard was recording temperature, humidity, pressure and wind from the instruments on top of the car, and once in a while, he voiced an observation that was recorded, along with their position, into the computer.

"Jack, are we getting a little too close?"

He looked at her in disbelief. Too close? For him, there was no such thing. "This is what you signed up for, isn't it? Don't worry. This is going to be the best time you ever had."

She didn't respond, but her jawline showed how tense she was. She wasn't singing French folk songs anymore.

"Turn left here," he said. As they turned south, another car from the mesonet shot west. It would be turning north shortly. Jack and Giselle had left another car farther east, and some members of the caravan were already headed south, farther from the heart of the storm but in good intercept position. They chattered occasionally on the radio, noting their positions and observations, but mostly they kept radio communications down so they wouldn't interfere with readings. Jack's scanner was tuned to weather radio. There were severe-storm warnings up and down the panhandle.

Now they were on a nominally paved road, pretty bumpy, but it slowly curved west and should take them right to the wall cloud. High above them and extending east was the storm's anvil, already pouchy with the low curves of mammatus clouds. Lightning arced across this scalloped ceiling in bright and energetic zits of electricity. Soon, they would be under the base, and that would be all they saw when they looked up — cloud, inky and ominous.

It was here, as they dipped and rose on the small hills that led them to the meso, that they could really see the storm spin. The enormous cell was doing a slow turn, like an ice skater in zero gravity, floating and twirling. Make that a fat, angry ice skater.

They were getting some rain, but not too bad. They weren't in the worst of the precip. Then the air cleared and the car trembled a bit as they drove into a strong stream of warm, moist air. Tumbleweeds and dirt and bits and pieces of Texas prairie blew past them, caught up in the colossal inhalation of the supercell.

"Let's pull off here for a minute," Jack said. It was the top of a gentle slope with an excellent view of the base of the storm. They were so close now. He popped the video camera into the dash mount, zoomed a little and pressed the record button. He opened his door to get out, first telling Giselle:

"Stay here. Listen to the radios. Call 9-1-1 if lightning hits me."

He closed the door on the sounds of the radios and the stimuli of the electronics, took a breath, and listened. Thunder bashed and clattered loudly, the sound waves rumbling past him, close on the heels of a nearby lightning strike. His white T-shirt fluttered in the wind. A few drops of rain struck his face and arms. It wasn't too smart, standing out here, but for just a minute, he needed to feel alone, alone with the storm.

The yearning he felt inside him at this instant was almost unmatched. Here is where he made his connection. Storms made the only electricity that reached the socket in his heart. He knew them so well, yet they always surprised him with their enchanting variations in color, movement and structure. These were personalities he could love, could understand. In an instant, a hundred other storms flashed through his memory — summer gust fronts at his aunt's place in Florida when he was a youth, after his mother died; a North Carolina hurricane on a strained vacation with his father; a mountaintop storm he'd experienced once in West Virginia, after a long hike, during his personal look-for-America tour after high school — the exhilaration of the lightning, roaring thunder and rain as they whipped around the tiny, stone hiker's shelter on the precipice.

There. Dust kicking up beyond the mesocyclone. In short order, it was a plume of reddish dirt spiking high in the air, the kind of feature local law enforcement sometimes called in warnings for. But this was no "sheriffnado." It was the hallmark of a rear-flank downdraft. The first tumbler rolled in the complicated lock, a turn of the tornado key.

The downdraft cut magnificently into the storm, sculpting the wall cloud with a deliberate elegance that disguised the cell's barely contained violence. Now the rounded lowering began to extend, ragged at first, but smoothing, spinning, reaching toward the ground.

"Jack!" Giselle had rolled down her window and was shouting at him. "Jack, there's a tornado warning!"

"No shit." He grinned with delight at the elongating funnel. Then he remembered himself, his job, what lay ahead. He opened the car door and jumped in, grabbing the radio. "FC, this is Probe 3. Dust under the funnel. We have a tornado."

"What do we do?" Giselle was a little out of breath.

"Forward, my dear," he told her. "Time to earn that student stipend."

ON A ONE-AND-A-HALF LANE, potholed road that had probably seen five cars pass in a year, approximately three dozen now were vying for position under the spinning supercell Judy and her friends had thought was theirs alone. They hadn't seen any other chasers for hundreds of miles. Then they'd gone south, and west, and taken a gravel-road shortcut north to another east-west road. There, within a few miles of the storm's heart, chase vehicles were crawling around like insects, pulling out in front of one another, trying to get the best view. Anyone driving forward had to creep around all the cars parked on the shoulder.

"This is not good," Whit said over the radio.

Judy just shook her head. It was getting like this every time there was a big storm. Given there were so many cells to choose from today, she thought there wouldn't be as many people, but maybe this one was more accessible from Amarillo or had shown first on radar or something. There were a couple of the more reputable tour groups, plus one of the smaller university Doppler radar trucks, its dish swinging back and forth, profiling the rotation in the storm. And there were miscellaneous chasers, along with a couple of locals who were following the chase cars to see if they could see a tornado up close. While the locals had probably experienced more of the trauma of severe weather over the years, they had almost no idea what they were doing out here. They were prime candidates to get killed.

Complicating matters, a large, green farm tractor was trying to thread its way among the cars stopped along the road.

"Crap," Robinson said on the radio. "We've got to get ahead of this thing. I don't want to get behind it *and* all these cars. We could be caught seriously out of position."

"If I'm right," Whit said, "it's also starting to take a southward turn. If we stay on this east road, we could get caught in the core."

Their storm had already cycled through two wall clouds, but something wasn't quite right. It hadn't produced a tornado. With each cycle, it had become loose-looking and disorganized, then tightened up its circulation to try again. It wasn't raining much. Yet the cell was beginning to acquire a most extraordinary appearance, Judy thought. It was as if it had reached a kind of balance, unwilling to cycle again, and distinct layers began to appear as it spun. It wasn't chewing into the earth; it was spiraling up to the sky.

"My GPS shows a south-southeast gravel road," Bruce said from the lead vehicle. His black car was so big, its shoulders and antennas seemed to rise above the crowd around them.

"It might be dodgy, but it should put us out on a real highway in about six miles."

"And we might get some good pictures along the way, away from this crowd," Robinson said.

"I'm all for good pictures," Judy said. "I think my car can handle it. I don't think it's rained enough to make it too muddy."

"Can we avoid Lake Meredith?" Whit said.

"We'll sneak over the north end of it," said Bruce.

He shot ahead of another group of slow cars that had just pulled off on the shoulder, and Whit, Robinson and Judy followed. Red inflow dust started to blow across the road, sucked into the storm. The few trees along the shoulder bent with the gusts. "Wow," Judy whispered to herself. It was *breathing*.

Bruce flicked on his turn signal, and they followed tight behind as he veered right. The cars in front and behind them kept going east, to Judy's relief. She didn't mind playing tag with a few chasers, but this mess was ridiculous.

After a couple of miles of blessedly deserted road, they stopped atop a slow rise, pulling into a narrow gravel lane so they wouldn't block traffic. They got out, setting up tripods to videotape the storm. Judy zoomed all the way out, wide-angle, so she could do a time-lapse later, then pulled out her Nikon.

The shape of this storm was unlike any supercell she had seen, and yet it was familiar. It reminded her of something. Yes! A wedding cake! So she was videotaping a wedding cake today, after all.

It was frothy with vaporous icing, daubed onto circular tiers, layers of rotating cloud. The storm was evolving from a flying saucer to a multi-storied cylinder hovering above the earth. A few layers up, the cloud swept inward and then out again, like a wave, with an ocean of dark cloud above. Yet the sky was clear under this bank of cloud on the south side of the layer cake. Rain fell north of it, and from the cylinder's center. That rain shaft was the pedestal upon which the cake sat. And as the now southeast-moving storm crept closer to them, the late-day sun began to shine through the curtains of rain flanking the cake, turning everything an almost vibrating color of orange.

Judy filled the first memory card in five minutes, then started on another one. They were getting a little rain now, so she put a vinyl cover over her video camera and slipped on her yellow jacket, tucking her braids back under the hood. With her still camera, she composed dozens of images — some wide-angle shots, some zoomed in, trying to capture every magnificent detail. Then she tucked the camera under her jacket so it wouldn't get wet and just watched. This was beautiful by any definition. It was exquisite, unusual, a top-ten storm. It was a piece of the puzzle, the mystery she wanted to solve. Still, she had a little empty place in her heart. She knew that today she wouldn't find the image, the experience she sought. She relaxed and let the desire pass.

Robinson, now wearing a cap over his wavy hair, came over to her. "I can't even believe my eyes," he said. "That's the most amazing structure I've ever seen."

"Tremendous," Judy agreed. "Almost architectural." Her eyes never left the storm, which shot occasional licks of lightning from its curvy sides and base.

"This is what I come out here for," Robinson said. "This makes it all worth it. Three or four weeks of driving, pricey gas, bad hotels. No traffic except tractors, no noise except thunder, no TV, just the Mother Nature channel."

Judy chuckled. "Unless you go into Bruce's truck. I think he has two TVs."

"Well, he's an exception."

Whit sidled over, scratching his red beard. "I got a call from my office. They say this thing has softball-size hail in it."

"Really?" Judy replied. "From here, it looks almost peaceful."

They all felt more peaceful now. They had found their storm. They had seen its amazing evolution and had a beautiful view of it as the day grew long. Their thirst was nearly quenched.

The cell was getting closer. They would have to move soon to stay ahead of it, as it seemed to be passing just to their west. And the lightning was getting more dangerous.

Flash-crack-bang! A brilliant bolt struck the ground less than a mile away. Judy felt her heart beat faster and knew they needed to return to the relative safety of their cars. She instinctively started packing up for a quick departure.

Bruce came over to the rest of the group, holding a road atlas. His goatee gave him a devilish appearance in the scarlet light. "If we go on to Borger, we'll have some road options," he said as the wind picked up. "It'll start to get dark soon. That way will bring us closer to the Interstate. It looks like tomorrow's show will be farther southeast, so we can start thinking about where we want to stay. Or I should say, you can start thinking about where you want to stay, since I have to drive home tonight." His brow wrinkled with the thought.

"I'll look at our options," Whit said, his red hair glowing even more orange with the tilting rays of the sun. "Let's get going. We might be able to get a great sunset shot."

"Sounds good," Judy and Robinson said simultaneously. They looked at each other and smiled as they resumed packing up their cameras. Robinson's face was in shadow under the visor of his cap, but she saw his brown eyes sparkle, touched with the magical light of the storm. Another crash of branched lightning and thunder hit close by, hastening their exit as they loaded up their cars and started their engines, ready to move on.

THOR'S TOURS had been driving east in the rain for nearly an hour, a gray, shapeless rain punctuated by watery lightning and not much else. Brad's weather radio was working only intermittently, but he got enough to know that his storm was still labeled severe — and storms to his south and north were producing tornadoes, or at least radar-warned ones. He had a sick feeling in his gut. There was grumbling in the back. If he didn't produce something photographable, there would be a revolt.

It was getting lighter ahead. "I think we're coming out of it," he said, for the third time in fifteen minutes.

"I don't see any tornadoes," said Pinky, half-sarcastic, half-sad, her pink tufts of hair looking limp. Her brunette, nose-ringed roommate was despondent next to her, not even looking out the window anymore, just playing with her phone.

"It is getting a little brighter," Juicy responded. "Maybe we really are coming out of it."

"Despite our worst efforts, we have to come out of it sometime," Noel said from under the brim of that damn Braves baseball cap.

Brad, annoyed, pressed the accelerator. He was tired of driving in the rain, and the van was beginning to smell of sweat and frustration. It *was* getting lighter, damn it. They were going to see *something*.

As the rain slackened, above and ahead of them he saw subtle layers in the edge of the cloud, where the light changed in steps. This wasn't a rotating storm anymore. It was a line, and it looked as if it was gusting out.

That's OK, Brad thought. Gust-outs mean wind. They were going to see a real storm, even in its dying breaths.

The wind was almost pushing them now as they headed east, out from under what looked to be a fairly decent shelf cloud. Pretty layers were developing. Dust kicked up under the edge as the collapsing storm spewed all its energy outward in a cold blast. Some of the dust formed little spirals, some bigger ones, impressive swirls that tossed branches and leaves into the air.

"Is that a tornado?" Pinky practically screamed.

"You could call it that," Brad said, not sure what the answer was.

"It's a gustnado," Noel said. "It's just a quick spin-up, kind of a cross between a dust devil and a tornado."

"I'm going to get ahead of this so we can film it, OK?" Brad said to the tourists.

There were murmurs of assent and the rustle of camera bags as their flagging hopes were renewed. Brad sped up, trying to beat the outflow and find a place to pull off that didn't have trees or other obstructions to their view. He saw a farm and garden supply store with a big, open parking lot just to its east. That should be perfect. They could stop far enough away from the building to get a broad look at the storm.

He spun into the gravel parking lot, past the combines and tractors and birdbaths and gnomes and jockeys and miniature windmills, and wheeled around so the van faced the gust front. He had to admit, it looked impressive. A few scalloped layers, glowing almost green, drooped over the landscape. Dust blew up under it. The whole roiling line was headed for them.

"You can get out and take pictures, but be prepared to get inside fast," he said.

All seven tourists, sick of being trapped inside the van, started tumbling out the side door immediately, clutching cameras. Brad put his head down on the steering wheel and breathed a sigh of relief. At least they were seeing something. Maybe on the Thor's Tours website he would say they saw a tornado. There was that gustnado, after all. Photoshop could fill in the rest.

He lifted his head and was shocked to see another gustnado about a half mile to their southwest, churning through an open field. It held together for a good minute before dissipating. The tourists were practically jumping up and down, except for Noel, who was calmly but apparently happily snapping photos with his digital camera.

Pieces of straw started to smack the van. Hapless bugs, caught in the outflow, left large splats on the windshield. Little bits of gravel began to fly up and hit it, too. He heard an abrupt chorus of ouches from the tourists, who quickly clambered back inside the van, breathless and windblown.

"That stung! It's really starting to blow out there," said Old Blue Eyes, another tourist — at fifty, old by Brad's standards — whom Brad had nicknamed for his blue-toned sunglasses.

"I'd guess those are sixty-mile-per-hour winds," Noel said. The van was being buffeted now, too.

Another gustnado formed almost due west of them, just beyond the garden supply store. It was headed their way. It looked like a real tornado. Brad didn't think it was, but it was probably going to pelt them with little rocks and such. He was thrilled. He could finally give the tourists some excitement.

"It's coming right for us!" he said. There were cries of enthusiasm and some dismay from the back of the van. "We should be fine here. Just hang on and enjoy!"

The gustnado began to cross the store's display yard. To Brad's surprise, it jostled one of the big tractors, and then it started knocking over birdbaths. A large garden gnome wobbled drunkenly as the angry whirl of dust briefly caught and spun it. A line of wind chimes hanging from the store's eves began to swing and ring wildly, a banging tangle of bangles.

"What the —?" was all he got out before the tiny twister picked up one of the green-and-yellow miniature windmills, dangled it in midair for a split-second and then hurled it right at them. The blades spun like a propeller.

"Shit!" Brad screamed, along with everyone in the van, as he ducked and it slammed into the glass with a tremendous noise. The four-foot-tall metal ornament smashed a spider web of spectacular veins in the windshield but didn't quite shatter it. A small shower of glass pieces fell on Brad and Noel in the front. Two of the previously spinning blades stuck through what was left of the window, and the whole thing trembled as the gustnado rocked the van violently and then moved past, dissipating just beyond the parking lot.

They all sat, stunned and silent, for a long moment.

Brad's cell phone rang.

He held it up to his ear and pressed the answer button, but he couldn't bring himself to say anything.

"Brad? Brad, are you there?" It was Willa.

"Yes, I'm here," he answered slowly.

"I'm at the coffee shop, and they're showing some radar on TV from around Silverton. They say it's a big tornado. Are you in Silverton, Brad?"

"Thank you so much for calling," Brad said and hung up.

As he drove, Marcus heard Jack and the others in the research caravan chattering over the ham radio. "Confirmed — tornado on the ground," Jack was saying.

"Damn it," Marcus said, pushing his glasses up on his nose. "Second one today."

"What's the problem?" asked Dennis, who was amply filling the passenger seat of the hail-catcher van. Some days, Marcus sat there, checking data, but he'd wanted to drive today and give Dennis the chance to monitor the laptop.

"Another tornado, and I'm stuck in the core where I can't see it!" Marcus said.

"Yeah," said Dennis, practically shouting over the din, "but we're going to see the bitchin'est hail ever."

Golf balls of ice slammed into the van. Some broke apart on the metal cage that extended out from the roof, above and over the windshield.

"That's true," Marcus said. "I have a good feeling about this one. You are witnessing the birth of bouncing, baby, frozen drop embryos!"

The hailstones falling outside the van were indeed bouncing in the scrubby vegetation on either side of the road. A few of the harder ones boinged off the pavement, but most just smashed. A fair number fell into their hail collection system.

Sitting on a bolted-down stool behind the driver's seat

was the frequently dozing, freckled freshman Frank, an Opie type with a flat farm-boy face. The noise right now was too loud even for Frank to sleep. He stared at the rumbling contraption in the center of the van. Every few seconds, the circular net that protruded from the roof funneled hail through a separation tube. Inside the metal tube was a screen that let rain fall through and diverted the ice balls through a soft-sided, clear plastic tube and into a jar of cold hexane that was surrounded by dry ice in a cooler. As if he were removing french fries from the McDonald's deep fryer — a task Marcus was sure Frank had done often — Frank periodically lifted out the jar, stowed it in one of the dry-ice-lined coolers near him and inserted another jar. Later, they would dump the chilled hailstones into bags, freeze them and slice them up for evaluation.

In the very back, another laptop computer strapped to a plywood desk took continual readings from the rain gauge, anemometer and other sensors, which were pole-mounted on the roof. On the floor were their bags, topped by Marcus' pith helmet. He carried it just in case.

"We're getting into bigger stuff now," Marcus said, looking quickly from side to side, causing his unkempt, dark locks to swing back and forth and his glasses to shake down his nose again. "I want to be sure we're in the sweet spot, and then I'll stop."

"A two-incher!" Frank said in his permanently raspy voice, as he bagged some more hailstones. Marcus had a chill. He wasn't sure if it was really colder as nature dumped her ice machine into the vehicle or if he just had a rush of nervous woozies.

Wham! Wham! Baseballs were starting to hit the van. He couldn't see all that well through the rain and the shattering orbs, but he thought he caught the glint of new dents in the hood's white paint.

"Weird!" Frank said from the back.

"What is it?" Marcus asked.

"Look!"

Marcus snuck a look over his shoulder and saw Frank, who wore thick gloves, holding up a glistening, white object that resembled a chunky sea anemone.

"Cool, spiky hail!" Marcus said, turning back to the road. "I've only seen that twice before. Be careful with those. Try not to snap off the spikes."

When people thought of weather on the Plains, they mostly thought of the destruction wrought by tornadoes. But these little bombs could do as much or more damage to crops and property. Marcus grew up in Massachusetts, but his grandparents were farmers in Nebraska, and they had struggled for decades with the trials of nature. If it wasn't hail from severe storms, it was drought. Marcus had fantasies of diverting or weakening such storms, ideas about weather control that were probably inspired by too much science fiction and the hopeful theories of cloud-seeders. Even if his ideas were a little crazy, he knew that he was on the right track with his hail research. The more they understood about how the stones formed and fell in these storms, the better chance they might have someday to alter or at least predict barrages like this one.

He wanted so badly to be as good as Jack, whose focus blew his mind. Jack seemed to live from moment to moment when he was off duty, and he had an ease with women and drink and other people that Marcus envied. But what Marcus really admired was the laser-sharp way Jack could cut through a meteorological problem or, more to the point, look at a storm and read almost exactly how it would behave. It seemed like all Jack really cared about. Marcus's brain was full of distractions: trying to scrape together enough money to get through grad school; dealing with two parents, both demanding professor types, who had continual health problems; playing guitar with his indie rock band on weekends; and pursuing that cute girl who ran the Posh Wash, the petite brunette who tortured him occasionally by agreeing to go to a movie and not much else. Not like Jack. The storm was first. Marcus didn't understand how life never got in Jack's way. The storms *were* Jack's life.

They heard Jack occasionally over the radio, describing the latest tornado. It sure sounded pretty. Maybe, someday, Marcus would see one.

The wind blew the smaller hailstones horizontally now. The big ones still fell almost straight down. Sticks and tumbleweeds and rain blew across the road, too, and the van rocked a bit as it pressed forward. "OK, I'm going to pull off," Marcus said.

Just then, there was an awful clanking sound on the roof, then a recurring *flap-flap-flap*.

"Uh-oh," he said.

"What was that?" Dennis looked up at the van's ceiling, as if he could see through it. "Did we drive under a tree branch and whack an antenna?"

"This is the Texas panhandle. Do you *see* any trees?" Marcus asked.

"Sometimes there are trees," Dennis said, a little abashed.

"Frank!" Marcus said. "Look through the periscope."

The periscope was the invention of another grad student who liked to tinker, had access to marine surplus and had way too much time on his hands. Usually, they couldn't see much out of it, but Frank scooted to the back of the van to try. He pulled the lens to his eye.

"Shit," he said, raspier than usual.

"Is it the basket?" Marcus had a feeling. The hail catcher had gone quiet.

"Yeah, ripped right off. We're not catching anything else unless we can fix it. It's just dangling."

"We don't have the tools," Dennis said.

Marcus slammed his hands on the steering wheel. "Damn it! Now, no tornado *and* no more hail!"

"But we have each other," said Dennis, always the smart-ass.

Marcus allowed himself a small guffaw. They would need to look at it and see if there was anything they could do. They had the same instrumentation the other cars had, but the spinning plastic cups on the anemometer wouldn't last long in this kind of hail. "FC, this is Probe 6," Marcus said over the radio. "Our hail-catcher is toast. We're going to stop and check it out, but I think all we can offer you now is another instrument pack."

"Probe 6, this is FC," Malik's voice came back. "Sample the atmosphere, and we'll worry about the hail later. Just wear that stupid pith helmet if you go outside, OK, Marcus?"

THERE USED to be a time when tornadoes were legends. They weren't captured on video and rerun in dozens of pseudo-science TV shows. They were rarely seen in photos. When they appeared and scoured the earth and vanished, the only snapshot small-town newspapers and scientists had was the account of each farmer and railroad man who had seen it, as he described a few minutes in the twister's life. Yet, in the old days, tornadoes had wild reputations. They made chickens' feathers explode. They sucked up whole lakes and dropped biblical plagues of trout and frogs on guilty little towns. They dug a furrow through three states without ever letting up.

The truth was that, although a few tornadoes have rained fish, most twisters lasted about ten minutes. The largest, perhaps an hour, with incredibly rare exceptions. The storms that spawned them, however, could endure for much longer, and they often cycled through tornadoes, putting down one after another, or two or more at once. Often, the funnels became larger and more violent, until the supercells seemed to exhaust themselves in the cooling dark of night.

Jack believed that this was the tornado forming now, as the sun began to set, a powerful culmination of all that had gone before. Even if it dropped more tornadoes, they wouldn't chase them after dark. This was the day's finale.

The storm had been a twister machine, producing the first slender funnel he and Giselle had seen, then the short-lived elephant trunk east of Silverton, then a stovepipe that ripped through a rancher's outbuildings west of Quitaque, and now this. So far, it was just a spinning dust bowl, but Jack knew this storm wasn't about to quit.

Giselle had been cursing a lot. At least, he thought it was cursing, even though it was in French. *Merde* was the only thing he recognized. At least a dozen chasers were on the storm now, and he saw Malik, Rainier and the others wave as the lead research van blew by. Jack and Giselle's car pointed east along the side of the road, parked in the open. Their vantage gave them an enviable view of the rotating dust in the field to their left.

Out of the corner of his eye, Jack saw cows dashing madly away from the tempest. He wondered when the animals would run into some fence and couldn't run any more. "Moo," he said, almost unconsciously.

"What?" Giselle sounded a bit frazzled as she looked out the driver's side window at the growing circulation.

"It's a right-turner. I think it's going to go south of Turkey," Jack said after glancing at the atlas. "We can't stay on this road, or we'll run right into the tornado or the core. Let's get ahead a little bit. Take the right toward Gasoline. That should put us in good position for now. We'll take a dirt road east if we have to."

"All right." Giselle sighed, resigned to her fate. Her usually impeccably made-up face had the faint sheen of nervous sweat, and her reddish-brown hair was mussed from every time they hopped out of the car to shoot video in the wind and rain. They didn't dare get out now. This close, they had to stay mobile.

As Giselle moved the car back onto the road, Jack took the video camera off the dash mount and twisted around so he could aim it out the rear driver's side window. The bowl of ground dust now had a distinct funnel above it, which descended from a huge, perfectly round meso at the storm's base. He didn't want to get too far ahead, but they were getting blasted by inflow here as the tempest sucked in warm wind and dust with it. Just another mile, he thought. The storm was moving slowly southeast, and they would need to stay ahead of it.

As they made the right, he turned forward again to get a breathtaking view out the passenger-side window. The funnel, a softly symmetrical cone, reached into the jaws of swirling dust. The tendrils from the ground and the cone seemed to kiss, then entwine into a continuous, dark funnel from cloud to ground. In this empty moonscape, it looked like a mothership beaming its crew to Earth.

He rolled down his window. "Stop here."

They were close, and as the tornado got closer, putting them under the edge of the circulation, they weren't even getting rain. A blinding lightning bolt hit nearby, coinciding with the snap-bang as the superheated air particles broke the speed of sound. It was a perfect, dangerous spot.

"Listen to it," Jack whispered.

Here, in the bear's cage, the tornado made a rushing sound. It was not like a freight train. Right now, it was not tearing apart anything except the earth. It reminded him of a waterfall he'd heard in the Appalachians, only more eerie. *Shhhhhhhhh*, it said. *Shhhhhhhhhhhhhhhh*.

It was hypnotic.

"It's so quiet," said Giselle, looking out Jack's window but still gripping the steering wheel tightly with both hands, ready to bolt.

"It's only air and water," Jack said. "Air and water and earth. Here, pull up in that side road on the left and turn around, so we're facing it. We'll still be able to get out in a hurry."

"Good," Giselle said. She drove forward and got the car turned around so that it, and she, confronted the full, fearsome tableau. "My god. Shouldn't we get out of here?"

"Wait for it," Jack said, feeling a rush of confidence and satisfaction. He put the video camera back in the dash mount and grabbed his Nikon to snap some stills. The dark cone had expanded into a rotating cylinder, with a fringe of cloud spinning around its crown, just below the round, black storm base from which the tornado hung. Beyond the curve of the mesocyclone was the orange light of the setting sun. Numbers spilled across the screen of the laptop set between them. "We're getting great data," he said.

A few cars whizzed by them, one from the mobile mesonet, and a mobile radar truck, too. Now, no one was as close as they were. Malik's voice came over the radio. "FC for Probe 3. Jack, don't do anything stupid unless you absolutely have to."

Jack grinned. A half mile away, the tornado started to cross the highway they'd abandoned. It ripped a few thin trees along the margin out of the ground, spun them about and tossed them several yards. The rushing sound was more complex, now, as the twister began to chew through vegetation and road signs, but the ceremonial hurling of debris almost seemed to happen in slow motion. At the tornado's base, however, it was clear that its motion was not slow. It sucked in dust at a dizzying rate. Before the densest part of the funnel even reached the trees, winds wrenched them into the air at speeds Jack put near two hundred miles per hour.

"Christ," Jack said. "I didn't even notice that cell tower there before. Move. Move. *Move.*"

His voice hadn't risen much, but Giselle, who needed no encouragement, picked up on his urgency and pressed the gas, hard. The car sputtered, then sputtered again as she muttered more unintelligible curses.

"Easy. Just coax it." Jack didn't feel as calm as he sounded. He looked at the tower, diagonally across the road from them, and thought he heard it creaking as the winds began to stress the steel latticework that rose high above them to the triangle-shaped top, which bristled with metal branches. "I hate government cars," he said.

Just then, the engine roared again, and Giselle spun the car out of the turnoff and swung south.

"Not too far! Stop. Here, on the left, there's a place where we can turn around." It was a wide spot next to a slowly pumping oil well, the metal drinking-birds of the Great Plains. She wheeled across the road in a wide arc so the car faced the oncoming tornado.

It was mean, and it was large. The cell tower, swaying now, blinked innocently and then was consumed by the dust ripping around the funnel. The metal tower twisted, bent, broke off and flew several yards, close to where they'd been parked. There was a faint crunching sound amid the rush of wind.

"I don't like this!" Giselle said.

"I *love* this. Besides, you've been saying that all day."

"Maybe meteorology is not my destiny."

"In France, you probably won't have to worry about this sort of thing," he said dryly. He glanced at the screen on the video camera mounted on the dash. The dark and potent tornado nearly filled the display. He had plenty of tape. The instruments were doing their thing. All they had to do was enjoy the adrenaline and avoid flying objects.

"Uh, Jack?" Giselle's voice was even quieter, brittle with tension.

"What?" It was like she was talking during a movie. He hated that.

"What's that?"

She wasn't looking out the front window at the tornado, as he was. She was looking left, out her window.

"Oh." He tried not to sound too alarmed. "Shit."

"What?" Her voice rose sharply.

"Satellite tornado. This thing's putting down satellite vortices. We're too close."

He didn't need to tell her twice. She was already lurching south, staring down the small vortex crossing the road as she glanced in the rearview mirror at the growing monster behind them. As they paused to let it pass, he peered in the side mirror, where killer tornadoes were closer than they actually appeared, and caught a glimpse of his flushed face, framed by the fat column of violently rotating dirt.

"I thought you said there was no such thing as too close!" She pointed left. "What if we drove into that field?"

"Forget it," he said. "Rain has already turned it to pudding. Do you want to be stuck in the mud while the big one eats you up? Just hang on. Let it pass. Then floor it."

The tiny twister in front of them rapidly traced the curving edge of the meso. Even he felt the prickle of fear as he wondered, briefly, if he'd pushed them too far.

The satellite tornado buzzed across the road almost as fast as it came, dissipating in bushes that it ripped apart in the process. She floored it again, and the engine strained under the pressure.

"We're good, we're good!" Jack said after a mile. "Slow down!"

Now they were back in the company of other chasers, a number of cars and trucks parked along the road. In and out of their vehicles, people filmed the tornado, a wedge hungering across the burnt-umber prairie as darkness fell. Giselle turned the car around in a parking lot next to some abandoned gas tanks and stopped so she and Jack could see it, too. She breathed fast but seemed calmer, now that she was amid people with slightly more circumspect judgment. She rolled down her window and sucked in the fresh air.

Malik called in the teams as the tornado pushed into road-less territory. They were done for the day.

"Nice driving," Jack said, touching Giselle's shoulder. She gave him a weary look that brooked no tenderness, and he withdrew.

The radio crackled, and Jack heard Malik again. "Probe 3, this is FC. Just how crazy are you, Jack?" Jack looked around and saw the lead van a few yards away. He spotted Malik's amused face through the windshield. Jack grabbed the mike.

"It's all in the name of research," Jack responded, grinning back. Malik's colleague Samuel Rainier, his long, white hair blowing in the inflow, was outside the van, taking stills, as students Micki and Travis filmed the tornado.

"Jack," Malik said, "I can't question your priorities, only their execution. But maybe *you* should question your priorities."

Jack felt a little flutter of doubt, then pushed it aside and focused on the massive tornado, trying to see it in the remains of dusk. Lightning occasionally backlit the funnel as it lumbered forward. It was getting too dark to chase it safely now.

They would hear later that it had destroyed two houses, injured a little girl and obliterated some chicken coops.

The cows survived.

❧

JUDY, Robinson, Bruce and Whit pulled their caravan of cars into the parking lot of the Range Restaurant, on Avenue F in Childress. It was about the only thing open this time of night, in a town that served as a crossroads for the outback of Texas.

There were dozens of cars, and with all the antennas, anemometers, sensors, stickers and satellite receivers, it looked like a storm-chaser convention.

It was a logical stop for the night, halfway between the adventures of today and the forecast for tomorrow. Judy breathed a sigh of relief as she turned off her car. She was ready to relax after their long chase, which had continued as they drove south, with a couple of stops after dark for lightning photography. She thought she might have caught a few nice bolts, and she couldn't wait to look at the pictures on her big monitor at home.

She dug a brush out of her purse and ran it through the tassels on the end of her braids, pushed back the strands of hair set free by the wind, then dabbed on a little lipstick. She wasn't much for makeup, but she might was well give it a little effort. Who knew who might be in there.

They gathered and started their walk in from the periphery of the parking lot, which was big enough to hold several tractor-trailers. Now, it was full of chase cars, including what looked like the university's mesonet. Judy goggled at one van that had an ornamental windmill poking through the windshield. The guys were laughing at it.

"I guess they thought it might be too hard to get it out," Robinson remarked.

"At least they have part of a window now," Judy said. "One good yank, and they'd lose the whole thing. I think they're going to need surgery."

"Thor's Tours," Whit said, mulling the decals. The street lamps glinted off his glasses and red hair. "Looks like they had a fun day."

"Ours was pretty darn nice," Bruce said. He carried his

expensive video camera, like the head of some animal he'd just slain, so he could show off his bounty. He had all the swagger of the great hunter, glowing with glory and goatee.

Robinson still wore his black baseball cap, which advertised the Maryland Film Festival, and he looked tired. He sensed Judy's gaze.

"I think all this traveling's catching up with me," he said. "I'm going to get some nachos or something, and then I'm going to bed."

They'd called ahead and grabbed the last few rooms in one of the economy motels on the strip, just down the road. At least they knew they had beds for the night and a meal in the offing.

The inside of the cowboy-meets-chintz restaurant was noisy and, Judy was pleased to note, a geekfest. There were chasers at nearly every table, showing one other video, excitedly jabbering over their steaks, salads and sodas. Steaks. That meant that some of them had seen tornadoes. She was true to the tradition and wouldn't order one, even though her group had seen a beautiful storm. A tall, skinny guy with a Thor's Tours T-shirt and ever-lifting eyebrows was holding forth at the head of a table of tired-looking people who didn't seem quite as enthusiastic as the rest. Must be the tourists. One had shocking pink hair. Judy kind of liked it and wondered how her braids would look in that color.

A weary but quick forty-something waitress with thin, short, wavy hair the color of an orange Creamsicle showed them to a booth, waited impatiently while Robinson and Whit scooted into the padded benches first, then handed the menus to Bruce and Judy while they were still sitting down. Her plastic nametag, pinned on a once-white apron, said "Irma." She took drink orders and dashed off to deal with what was presumably another crisis. The place probably hadn't seen this much business in months.

In a few minutes, Irma was taking food orders and putting coffee down in front of Bruce, who still had a long drive ahead of him; colas in front of Whit and Robinson; and ice water in front of Judy. She sipped it eagerly. She usually ended up dehydrated after days like these, since she didn't want to drink so much that she had to empty her bladder in the middle of some field. Just another example of why it was easier to be a guy.

And boy, were there guys here, the whole gamut, from college kids to graying professors. She was heartened to see a few women, especially on the younger side. Maybe she'd find more friends on the road this year. She didn't have enough pals at home, or anywhere, really, and her sister was sketchy support.

As she scanned the crowd, she caught the eye of a man staring at her and realized, with girlish joy, that it was Jack. It was funny how that brief encounter had made such an impression on her. There was that intensity she'd noticed before. She liked intensity. She liked his short black hair and green eyes, his lean, subtly muscular body. He smiled, and she knew he recognized her. After a moment, he turned back to his burger, beer and friends, but he slid her another glance before she tore her gaze away, feeling a little flush.

"I wish my son could have seen what we saw today," Whit said in that pleasant Texas drawl.

"Why don't you take him?" Judy asked.

"I think he's a little too young yet. He's only ten. I want him to understand the risks, maybe even learn to read a map before he comes along. I told him I'd take him when he was twelve."

"My two girls have no interest at all," Bruce said. "My wife is driving them to the gymnastics studio what seems like twice a day. The first one enters high school next year. Hell, after seeing those pixies in the Olympics, I figured high school was too old for gymnastics."

Judy laughed. "I was always rotten at gymnastics. Give me a team sport any day."

"I'll tell you what I kicked ass at," Robinson said. "Lacrosse."

"Lacrosse?" Bruce exclaimed. "What a wussy sport!"

"You get whacked in the head with a stick and you'll see how wussy it is," Robinson said. "What did you play in high school, mailbox baseball?"

Bruce snorted and almost spit out his soda. "Um, actually, I did whack quite a few mailboxes with my Louisville Slugger," he confessed.

The others laughed.

"To this day," he said, "I always give the neighbors I remember good deals when they buy a car from me. They probably have no idea why, but I know."

"Karma catch-up," Whit said.

"Exactly," Bruce said.

"If I'd tried to whack a mailbox with my lacrosse stick," Robinson said, "the webbing would have caught on one of those little metal flags and yanked me out of the car. I've learned not to tempt karma. I try to do it right the first time."

Judy chuckled. The waitress reappeared shortly and delivered their orders, all sandwiches and fries except for Robinson's nachos. As the guys kept talking sports, Judy snuck a peek at the man in the white T-shirt and green eyes. She caught a few words. He was describing tornadoes, not selling the story too much, just telling it. The people around him had their mouths open. He sometimes gestured to the chestnut-haired girl across from him, and Judy assumed she was involved in the tale. The young woman had a smile on her face as she relived the experience through the filter of his account. Judy wondered what their relationship was.

"Hey, look at this, Judy," said Bruce. She turned back to the table. He held up his video camera with the flip-screen open so she could see the footage. It showed her silhouetted against their orange, layer-cake storm, with the wind blowing her hood back.

"Pretty shot!" It really was. Did she look like that, all wrapped up in the glow of the atmosphere? Sometimes pictures were even better than reality. Almost always, in fact.

"Is that what you saw today?" It was a deep voice, over her shoulder. She looked up into the face of the green-eyed man. "I'm Jack," he said, reaching out for her hand and shaking it, slowly. "I don't think I caught your name last time, if you remember."

"I remember you, Jack. I'm Judy Hale," she responded with a smile, firmly returning his grasp.

"Judy," he said, turning her name over on his tongue as if it were a chocolate dessert. "Judy."

Then he exchanged handshakes and names with everyone.

Bruce turned the video camera so Jack could get a good view. "We caught this storm up near Borger."

"That's amazing structure," Jack said, looking more at Judy than the video screen.

"What did you see today?" she asked.

"We caught a few tornadoes near Silverton."

"Oh," Whit said, "you're with the university, aren't you? I've read a couple of your papers. I work for the Weather Service out of Fort Worth."

"I know your name, too. I've seen it on some dryline research, haven't I?" Jack asked.

"Yeah, I've presented at the severe storms conference and stuff," Whit said modestly. Judy liked that about Whit. And she liked Jack's interest in all of them, and in her.

"What were the tornadoes like?" Robinson asked. "We heard something about them on the radio."

"It was like a meteorology class. We saw just about every kind of tube you can name. Let's just say we felt the breath of the beast."

"I can't wait to see the pictures," Judy said.

"We'll have some on the website by the end of the season, but I can email you some. Would you give me your email address?"

There. It was that easy, she thought. "I have some cards." She dug around in her bag and pulled one out. It wasn't your typical business card. The front was a slick, color photo, showing a happy, clingy couple in formal wear in the foreground and a supercell against a spectacular Kansas sky in the background. "Some Photoshopping was involved," she admitted. "My contact info is on the other side."

"A wedding photographer?" He laughed. "That explains those matches you gave me. If I ever got married, and there was a storm like that in the distance, the ceremony would be extremely short, and the honeymoon would start with a hell of a chase."

"Most good relationships do," Robinson said. "I mean, start with a hell of a chase."

Whit and Bruce nodded, smiling.

"I guess that's my cue," Bruce said, putting down cash to cover his dinner. "I've got to drive to the metroplex and get home to my wife and her picnic planning before I fall over unconscious."

"You'd better be careful," Whit said.

"Oh, I didn't buy that fifteen-hundred-dollar car stereo for nothing," Bruce said. "I can crank that thing so loud it'll keep me awake into next week."

"It was nice to meet you, Bruce," Judy said, and there were more handshakes all around before he took his video camera and was gone.

Jack looked over at his friends getting up from their tables. "It looks like we're heading back to the hotel." He looked right at Judy. "We'll talk soon."

She offered her hand again, just to feel him clasp it, and knew that he was right.

WHAT SHE DIDN'T EXPECT WAS to find him waiting in the parking lot when they emerged. He was leaning against a crazy-looking research van topped with instruments as he smoked a cigarette, and he watched as she said good night to her friends. It was the kind of scene in a thriller where the girl realizes she's in terrible danger and runs. But she felt nothing but a calm, cool vibe, pure pleasure at the chance to see him again so soon. He caught her eye and smiled. "Judy," he called softly. It was all she needed, an excuse to talk to him, and as the guys headed to her cars, she strolled to where he stood.

"I thought you all had left," she said.

"Most of them did. I wanted to walk. I'm too keyed up after today."

"That's not your van?"

"No, it's the hail-catcher. Somebody left the electronics running, and the battery's dead. They'll jump it in the morning."

"Fun," Judy said, looking at the top, where a tangle of metal and gear seemed to be held on with bungee cords. "Do you deploy it like that?"

"Ah, no. Marcus had a bit of trouble on the road." Jack chuckled.

"It's not a chase trip without some sort of trouble on the road."

"You guys have an incident?"

"No, we were lucky today, just some data holes and a traffic jam around our storm," she said.

"I know, it's getting ridiculous, isn't it?"

"It's still worth it," Judy said. "But I don't know for how long. I want to chase in a helicopter next year."

"Save me a seat!" Jack said, then furrowed his brow. "Can you afford a helicopter?"

"Oh, hell, no."

"That's good. As much as I'd like to chase in a helicopter, I don't think I can afford to hang out with a woman who owns one."

"What, you don't want to be a kept man?"

"The question is, how long can they keep me?" He grinned.

"I suspect not long," Judy said with a touch of sarcasm.

"Oh, you never know," Jack said. "Want to walk with me?"

"I do, but my car's here, and I've got to get all my gear to the hotel."

"Well, why don't we just walk around, and then you can give me a ride? I mean, if it's not too much trouble."

"Not at all." Judy smiled, then joined him in wandering

toward the road. "Not the most scenic walking route." This part of Childress was a maze of adjoining parking lots and scattered retail.

He flicked his cigarette into a nearby trash can. "One thing I regret about chasing where we chase is I'm in the car all the time. We pass through some beautiful country, but I don't get to experience much of it foot-to-ground. Breathe the air."

"Smell the cows," Judy said, and he laughed.

"Oh, I can pretty much smell the cows whether I'm in a car or not."

"Sniff the dirt."

"Yeah, me and Bill Paxton." He smiled at the *Twister* reference. It was one movie pretty much every storm chaser had seen, often many times over.

"How long is your research project going on?" she asked.

"We've got a month. We've really just started. I hope we have more good days like today. We need several to get a good data set."

"Wish I could chase for a month straight, but I have to work sometime to pay the bills."

"It's awesome but exhausting," Jack admitted. "Today was ... almost transcendent."

"How so?"

"We were so close. So close even I was worried for, you know, a nanosecond or two." He looked wistful. "To come so close to touching nature's violence, to see this chaotic force that nonetheless comes from an intrinsic order of things, something we can actually study — well, you know."

"It's incredible," she said.

"Yeah. Words can't describe. But we still try."

"I visualize more than describe. Photograph or paint. I'm a

visual thinker. But a two-dimensional image seems inadequate, somehow."

"Ah, yes, the wedding photographer. What's it like in Pancake?"

"Flat," she said at the same time he did. They both laughed.

"It's a sweet town," she continued. "Small to medium, but you know, it means you get to know everybody. On the down side, you get to know everybody."

"I haven't ever really lived anywhere long enough to get to know everybody," Jack said. "Hey, look, you can see a few stars now. That's ... Virgo, I think. Yes, there's Spica. That's the star to look for."

"Where?" She felt him move behind her and gently hold up her right arm so it was pointing where his was.

"It's that bright star."

He felt warm next to her and strangely magnetic, his body somehow pulling her closer without her conscious compliance. It was like falling. She liked the feeling more than she wanted to admit. "Oh, I see it," she said softly. It took a moment before she recovered herself, straightening, subtly shrugging off his closeness. "Seriously, I'm much better at the constellations that are more square."

"There's nothing more square than a virgin," he said as they continued walking.

"Don't knock her," Judy said. "She's the only girl in the Zodiac."

"I admire her individuality," Jack said. "I love a challenge."

There was a moment, looking into the mischief of his gaze, when Judy felt the breeze intensely, and she wondered how much she wanted to resist him, this nearly irresistible force on this magical day. She broke the spell and looked up again.

"Oh, more clouds. I wonder if we're going to get another round."

He looked west. "I wouldn't be surprised. I suppose you'd better take me home."

"Home?"

"Oh, Wishwell is home, for now. I mean the hotel. It's all home when you're on the road."

"True," she said, and they walked back to her car, chatting about the weather.

Somehow, they couldn't stop talking, even when she'd driven the few minutes to the hotel — the same as hers, as fortune had it. It was strange and nice to have someone in the passenger seat, this man with his resonant voice. They talked about roadside attractions, about music — his tastes ran to jazz and hard rock, hers to musicals and alternative — and about chasing. Of course.

"Were you always into storms?" she asked.

"My mother used to sit up with me at night when there were lightning storms back home in Virginia, when I was a little kid," he said. "We'd sit on the wood floor, by the sliding screen door that led out to our deck, and watch the weather roll in over the trees. I guess she didn't want me to be scared of it. She probably didn't know she was creating a monster."

"I'm sure she's proud of you."

"If she were still around, maybe." His expression was dark.

"We never sat around and watched storms come in," she said, her voice softer. "We generally hid in the cellar. Post-tornado stress syndrome."

"You went through a tornado?" he asked.

She gave a dry little laugh. "You might say a tornado went through me. Through our whole town. It killed my aunt and other people I knew. It changed everything." She paused. She didn't want to get into the details.

"I'm sorry. I remember now. The Pancake tornado. It's pretty famous, as tornadoes go."

"Well, Kansas has to be known for something, I guess."

Jack smiled. "Why do you stay?"

"I've asked myself the same question sometimes, but I can't help myself. I've visited a few places, New York, New England, all over the West and Midwest, London once. But Kansas is part of me. I'm just corny, I guess."

He chuckled. "Yellow-corn hair, cornflower-blue eyes. But not so corny. Pretty, yes." There was more unsaid than said in his expression, and she held her breath. "I suppose I should go. We'll get up early and do a forecast. Will I see you again, Judy Hale?"

"If our luck holds," she said lightly, offering him her hand to shake. He took it, squeezing it, then slowly lifted it to his lips, impressing upon her skin a tender and lingering kiss that electrified the tiny hairs on her arm and threatened to transform her into a pool of lava.

"Good night," he said, releasing her, then got out of the car and headed to his room.

❜

JUDY FLIPPED ON THE LIGHT, pushed her motel room door shut and leaned against it for a heartbeat. She'd gone through a laborious check-in process typical of these motels, which seemed to want every bit of personal information short of DNA code, even when she was the only one checking in at eleven at night. She'd struggled up the outdoor staircase with her luggage, and all her cameras, laptop and overnight bag were in. Now, finally, she could decompress — and think about Jack. She had the feeling neither of them wanted to say goodbye.

The room smelled a little weird, and it had the hallmark of a cheap hotel — matching bad art on the walls: two identical prints of a painfully inoffensive painting of a Mediterranean seaside scene, about as far from Childress, Texas, as it was possible to get. The bedspread was printed with a pseudo-Native American design in burgundy and blue, and the carpet was a dull, stained jade green. The wallpaper had tiny dots and vertical lines in a shade of red that wasn't close to matching anything else in the room. The color scheme inspired an immediate, dull headache. Judy blamed her artistic sensibilities.

She picked up the remote from the top of the TV, a pre-stereo tube model, and switched on the box. She sat on the edge of the bed, not even taking off her jacket, and flipped through channels till she found the weather.

"No way," she said when the radar loop came on.

Although the cells they had all chased earlier had weakened and, in some cases, joined forces in a line that already was east of them, it appeared another line was forming to the west. It happened, sometimes. These weren't big, vicious, independent supercells, but there was some good intensity in the line. There would be lightning.

"Damn," she said. Compulsion was a terrible thing. She was exhausted. She was ready to sleep. There were storms. She had to go.

She used the bathroom, then grabbed one video camera and her Nikon with just one lens, a small zoom that should give her the range she needed, and stuffed them into her backpack with extra memory cards and her wallet, not that anyone would stop to check her ID in the middle of nowhere. Her tripods were still in the car. Briefly, she thought about calling Robinson, but she knew how tired he was. She decided to go for it alone.

Out on the empty second-floor balcony that served as a hallway for the rooms, she paused with her bag and looked to the west. The night was quiet and breezy. She could see the distant flashes but not too many distinct cloud-to-ground strikes yet. Still, there was a cool stirring in the air, and she knew this squall line would be upon the town within an hour or so. At least she wouldn't be out long.

She heard a door open and close and looked to her right. Maybe eight doors down was Jack. He gazed intently west, too, his hands on the railing, the wind flapping his T-shirt. His hair was inky black in the yellow lights of the parking lot, and his face was nearly in shadow.

He turned and saw her.

Part of her wanted to run in that millisecond, to sidestep the possibilities, the risks, the complications of what he might offer. But she was transfixed, and he was already smiling as he strode toward her, spreading a light that washed away some, if not all, of her instinctive fear of what might or — perhaps worse — might not happen.

"Judy," he said. "You look like you're going on a chase."

"That's what I do." She smiled.

"Is that all you do? I mean, chase and take wedding videos." He laughed, as he had in the restaurant, implying again that wedding photography was hysterically funny.

"It's a living. It's kind of fun. Besides, those who can't 'I do' take pictures of those who can."

"Why can't you?" Jack said. "Surely some man must have tried over the years."

"Not without the influence of alcohol."

"That's just the kind of influence I like."

She looked out toward the squall line in the darkness. The occasional flashes of lightning seemed more frequent. There was electricity in the air.

"Want company?" Jack asked.

She looked back at him, at his green eyes, and felt inclined to suspend the proprieties. There were different rules on the road, sometimes. She wanted to chase the tornadoes. She wanted to run with the wind. She wanted to play with lightning. And she didn't want to be alone.

"Yes."

"I'll be right back."

He walked briskly down the balcony and vanished into his room. A minute later, he was back with a soft camera case slung over his shoulder, a small tripod and a paper bag shaped strangely like a bottle. He caught her staring.

"It's wine," he said. "Lightning and wine go together very well, I find."

She couldn't help but laugh. "You sure know how to pack."

"Come on. Sometimes the only thing you can do in west Texas is drink."

She was still chuckling as they walked to the other end of the balcony and trotted down the stairs to her SUV.

THEY WEREN'T USING GPS, and the radio wasn't on. Jack occasionally referred to the gazetteer to make sure they were on the best road, but other than the map light, they were electronics-free, enjoying the sound of thunder and the wind from the open windows.

Jack put his SLR on the dash mount and took long exposures as she drove, capturing streaks of yellow and red light from the occasional passing car and bolts of lightning in a blurred purple sky. The images flashed onto the camera's screen as he released the shutter with a remote.

"Amazing color," Judy said.

"I love that purple shift. But I'm more of a blue guy."

"I just love color, all colors, in combination and contrast. The colors of nature, I guess."

"Pick one," he said.

"All right. Today, it's green."

"Why today?"

She blushed and looked straight ahead at the road. "Look in the mirror."

He flipped down the sun visor and looked at the mirror there. "What am I looking for? It's too dark to see anything."

"Well, if your eyes don't glow in the dark, I guess that's a good thing."

"Ah, my eyes. Not nearly as pretty as your baby blues."

She let out a small laugh of delight, at the absurdity of these compliments and the beauty of the night.

"I think we're close enough now," she said. "Oh, look, a windmill. That will be the perfect foreground if the CGs cooperate."

There were some CGs now — cloud-to-ground lightning, dazzling stuff, forked fireworks. Their timing was nearly perfect. At least she hoped so, as she pulled the car into a half-overgrown gravel road and shut off the motor and the lights.

The night was as alive as a rushing stream, swirling with cool eddies of air and the sparkling lightning. The wind and thunder filled their ears, punctuated by the lonely creaks of the windmill several yards away. Judy and Jack each set up tripods on the dark road. He put a video camera atop his; she set up her Nikon and put it in bulb mode so she could do the long exposures necessary to capture nature's fire. He hit the button so his could record without his attention, then opened the car to get out the wine, a corkscrew and one clear plastic cup.

Judy laughed. "At least you have your priorities straight."

"Be prepared. They taught me that in my two months of Boy Scouts," he said, working out the cork, filling the cup and setting the bottle on the hood.

"What kind of wine is it?" she asked.

"Oh, it's nice, if sweet. Blackberry. It's from this winery in northeast Oklahoma." He moved closer to her, offering her the cup first.

She looked into his eyes and took a deep drink, sensing him so strongly next to her that she could barely process the bittersweet potion swirling around her tongue. Had it been that long since she'd been drawn to someone? And why now, why him? She hardly knew him. Perhaps that was part of the charm. Perhaps it was the storm.

"Not bad, eh?" He took the cup from her and took a healthy quaff. "I mean, it's not a California cab, but for the prairie ..."

"Our standards aren't high for wine, true," she said, "but we have other attractions. Look at this." She nodded at the night and the encroaching storm. "It's gorgeous." Just then another brilliant lightning bolt ripped through the darkness, illuminating the scudding clouds. "See! This storm won't last long, but then there will be another one, and maybe this time, I'll be in that perfect place to see it, to feel it."

Jack leaned in and whispered in her ear. "This seems like a pretty good place to me."

She felt the charge between them. "Yes, it does," she murmured. She found it difficult to pull away, but adjusting her camera gave her an excuse to catch her breath for a moment.

"All that really interests me about the Plains is the sky, but it's enough," Jack said. "I can't leave it for long. If I miss a storm, I get crazy. Every time it's different. Every time it's amazing. There's nothing like this back East. I never go back there anymore."

He didn't have to continue. Memories flitted across his face, old ones, sad ones. She reached for his hand, and he covered hers with his.

JACK FOUND himself surprised by Judy, by her intense connection with the storms. He almost never met women who felt that way. It was rare to have a day like this, with such tremendous tornadoes, and then to run into her again — and again — seemed uncanny, lucky. There was something going on in there, behind her blue eyes and that girl-next-door beauty. He could sense it. He wanted to find out what, unlock her puzzle. And, more simply, he wanted her.

He closed his hand over hers, then linked his arm with hers, and they leaned against the car, side by side, body against body, facing the lightning. He let the storm do the talking, the storm and the heat of their nearness. He thought it funny that she still set off the camera remote now and then, so the shutter opened. Several seconds of quiet passed, with a few flashes from the sky, and then came the release and satisfying click, a mechanical metronome to accompany his elevated pulse as he waited for the right moment.

They had mutual attraction, but also, he saw, mutual obsession. Jack could appreciate that. It was almost too easy, he thought, though he sensed she didn't choose to be here lightly. He could adjust to that, give her what she wanted so he got what he needed.

The strikes got closer, and the windmill spun faster, twisting on its pole to face the strengthening west wind. He slipped an arm around her shoulders and, with his other hand, played with her fingers. The stuttering lightning caught a few faded spots of color on the tips of her fingers.

"What's this?"

"Oh." She seemed self-conscious for a moment. "I paint."

"Walls?"

"One wall. I have this painting in my living room, all over one wall. It's a mural."

"Of what?"

"It's hard to explain. It's Kansas and the sky and the world. It's sunflowers and windmills and lightning and tornadoes. It's death and darkness and light. And I can't finish it."

"So it's art?"

"Depends on your definition. I just can't get it right. And then reality intrudes; I have to work, of course. I have to deal with the everyday. But that mural is always there, behind my back when I'm watching TV or napping on the couch. It's my memory, I guess, or a dream that makes no sense."

Lightning flashed brightly beyond the windmill, strobing, freezing the yellow blades multiple times with successive, split-second slaps of white light. A crack of rip-roaring thunder followed.

"Wow!" Judy hit the button on the remote and leaned forward, away from his grasp, to look at the camera screen as it flashed an image of her shot. "Oh, that was framed perfectly!"

He went over to his video camera and turned it off.

"What are you doing?" she asked.

"I can't top that. Besides, it's starting to rain."

It was, just a few drops. That was always the way. Just when the show was getting good.

"Damn," Judy muttered.

"We can still watch it. We can get a little wet, even if our cameras can't."

They put their gear and the wine in the car, then leaned against the closed metal doors, against each other. She nestled easily into the curve of his left arm again, and as scattered drops fell, he felt her shiver slightly — not, he thought, from any chill.

He couldn't help himself. That straw-gold hair was too tempting. It shone in the darkness, especially when the lightning flashed. He pulled at the elastic ties that held the ends of her braids. He freed one loop, then pulled the circlet away and pocketed it. The thick braid loosened ever so slightly. He began running his fingers through each plait, pulling the strands loose so they lofted on the breeze, a tangle of smooth, soft light. With his other hand, he deftly loosened the other braid, looking at her face as he did so. She was leaning against his shoulder, and her eyes were closed. The lightning, more frequent now and softened by the rain, revealed drops glistening on her smooth cheeks.

He turned to face her, running both hands through her hair, which tumbled thick and wavy to her shoulders. She opened her eyes, and they simply looked at each other for a long second.

It was Judy who reached up, held his face with both hands

and pulled him toward her. The kiss that followed was as deep as any he'd had, as sensuous and thrilling. Part of it was the storm. Part of it was her need, which he sensed and drank in like wine. Ah, the wine.

"Let's get inside," Jack murmured into her ear, "or we'll be swimming soon."

He popped open the back door as the raindrops got bigger. She got in, shrugging off her jacket, and he followed her into the back seat. He shut the door behind them, then found the cup and filled it with wine. The rain intensified against the windows. He could smell her hair, loose now and lovely. Honeysuckle and heartland. He took a drink, then handed the cup to her, watching her lips, full and pink, become moist with the glittering dark wine as she drank.

"I want a taste," he said, taking the cup away, dropping it in a cupholder and pulling her close in one elegant motion. He pressed his mouth on hers, drank her in, drenched in the sensation.

Judy had a dreamy expression when he let go. "Are you always this charming?" she asked, drawing even closer, their legs and hips and arms touching. Lightning and thunder clattered outside as the tempest, now upon them, lashed against the car.

"It's seasonal."

"Oh, really?" There was that sarcasm again, but a smile played about her lips as she leaned back against the seat, watching him, her eyes an invitation. He reached for her, and they slipped their arms around each other, kissing gently, then with more urgency, entwining limbs, their tongues exploring the other's flavor, their hands caressing whatever skin they could find. He pushed her back, cornering her where the seat met the door, and pressed a knee between her legs, feeling her respond, rising. He let his hands roam up under her T-shirt, light blue like her eyes, as he moved his mouth down to her neck and the curve of her breasts.

Her hands were roving, too, and he felt her fingers sneaking under the waist of his shorts and briefs and down, first a hesitant touch, then stroking and squeezing his hardened cock till he had to stop kissing her just to abandon himself to the sensation. He unbuttoned the shorts and lay back, watching her, letting her play with him, squeeze him, letting her pull off his shirt and kiss his belly and neck and chest as she stroked him. He closed his eyes and expanded inside like a prairie fire.

He came under her hand, desire unbound, and slowly opened his eyes. She lay quietly, breathing softly, eyes closed, her arms around him now, her hair spilling across his chest, and he wanted to kiss her again, to make her feel as he did, to possess her in the same way. He pulled her up, pressed his lips on hers, then reached under her soft, cotton shirt and bra and cupped each breast, one at a time, pinching her nipples till she moaned softly. Then, still kissing her neck and ears and mouth, entangling tongues, he reached into her loose clothing, between her legs. He touched her with the knowledge of someone who had seen and tasted that place many times before, toying with her, rubbing her harder and then penetrating her with his fingers. She came with shudders of ecstasy and a long sigh, in a familiar, almost melancholy release of pain and pleasure amid the now slackening rain and enveloping darkness.

They lay there for a while, curled up together on the somewhat uncomfortable seat. Jack refilled the cup, and they drank the last of the wine and each other's warmth. Rare flashes of lightning lit the landscape as the storm passed; otherwise, there was only the dimmest glow of night, of the suggestion of distant lights, of obligations that awaited them. Soft rain lingered. Jack's mind was a blank. He liked it that way, in this moment. There was nothing else he needed.

"This isn't what I expected to be doing tonight," Judy whispered into his shoulder.

"Isn't this better than a sunny day? Anyway, tomorrow's shot with this line going through. It's going to scour everything."

"It's always about the storms, isn't it." Her voice was matter-of-fact, tinged with the understanding of someone who knew.

"Yes, it is."

"And I won't see you again," Judy said. He thought he heard ambivalence in her voice. He couldn't say why, but he wanted to see her again, to take her beyond where they'd been.

"We'll probably have to chase this crap tomorrow, since we've got the mesonet out," he said, "but after that, while the atmosphere recharges, I'm going to have a few days off. I've always wanted to spend some quality time in Pancake, Kansas."

The look of restrained joy that filled her eyes as she looked up made him wonder if he could meet her hopes halfway.

"I have a couch," she said, "under the scariest mural you've ever seen."

"Hmmm, the couch. I hope it's wide enough for two."

JACK WAS right about the weather. Judy awoke in a faded T-shirt, alone in her room — they'd separated with one more lingering kiss in the rain upon their return to the motel — and sleepily wandered to the window to peek out the blinds. It was cloudy, apparently cool. People in the parking lot wore sweatshirts. A look at data online confirmed her suspicions. The second line of storms had finished the job the first line started, and the dynamics weren't nearly as good today. She could chase a low potential for a boring squall line, or she could go home.

She showered and dressed, braided her hair, then tracked down Robinson outside in the gray light of day and talked him into breakfast at the same restaurant where they'd eaten dinner. Whit had already started his drive back to Fort Worth.

"You look tired," Robinson said amid the clatter of plates and country music.

"You have no idea." Judy's brain felt rumpled.

"When did you go to bed?"

"Late. I ... I chased that lightning last night."

"Oh, you should have woken me up. Or maybe not." Robinson sipped his coffee and cast a dubious eye on Judy as the waitress delivered their breakfast. "What is it?"

Judy poured the syrup. "French toast, silly," she said, taking a big mouthful so she wouldn't have to say anything else.

Robinson shrugged, smiling a little, good-natured as always. He started talking about a script he'd been working on in his spare time, when he wasn't designing websites or writing articles, and it sounded pretty funny, all about a couple of old private pilots who decide to have a cross-country air race with their cranky wives in tow. In her mind, though, dwelled distraction, half-real sensations, sweet rumors of the night before. The university chasers were already on the road, and so was Jack, but she would see him again. She would see him again? It seemed almost impossible.

She and Robinson parted with a promise to chase again that spring. He had nothing to do but chase, since this was his vacation, and he was off to see what kind of storms he could find in Oklahoma. She started north up Route 83, alone, on her way home to Kansas. The drive gave her too much time to think. Sometimes she felt a thrill as she accelerated, thinking of the romantic possibilities that might unfold. Then she sank into a morose kind of fear of the unknown, fear of the unknown relationship. They'd failed so often in the past, and she barely knew this guy. Her surrender had surprised her, yet she enjoyed the guilty sensation of being ever so slightly out of control.

She stepped outside herself by stopping to shoot photos of anything that struck her fancy — horses, a dilapidated gas station, a town full of painted cow statues. It was after dark when she pulled into Pancake and into her driveway. She parked outside the detached garage, weary from reflection and travel, the former more than the latter.

As she extracted her bags, she spotted the empty bottle of blackberry wine on the floor of the car and allowed herself a small smile. She left it there and lugged her stuff up the sidewalk, past her flowers, up the porch steps, wondering why she hadn't left the light on.

The main door was open, she saw, with a rapid rush of fear and confusion. Through the screen door, a shadow moved. For a second, Judy thought she was looking at herself in a mirror.

"Sis," came the voice.

"Shannon?"

Her sister flipped on the porch lantern's yellow bug-bulb and stepped outside. She looked a lot like Judy, only more graceful, somehow more symmetrical, with finer features, expressive eyebrows, gray-blue eyes and a rosebud of a mouth. Her hair was more corn silk than Judy's straw, a cropped cloud of wavy, light-gold glory. Annoyingly pretty, as Judy often described her.

"You scared me," Judy said.

"Well, that's my job. About the only one I have right now. Do you mind if I stay with you for a few days?"

"The spare bedroom is ready to go."

"Oh," Shannon said, "I've always preferred the couch."

2

WHIRLWIND

W hen Judy went downstairs to the kitchen the next morning, she was a little startled to see Shannon there, sipping orange juice and reading the *Pancake Pioneer*. As a rule, Judy wasn't used to seeing Shannon.

The younger sister's medium-cut, blond hair was pinned back in crazy places, and she'd thrown on a light green tank top and jeans. Though casual, and maybe a little tired, she still looked beautiful. Judy, in shorts and a T-shirt, knew from her half-conscious tooth-brushing experience in the mirror this morning that she simply looked tired.

"Shannon, I have a question for you," Judy asked after popping two slices of white bread in the toaster. "Where's your car?"

"I had to sell it. I needed some money."

"What did you drive to get here?" Judy asked, pouring herself some juice.

"I didn't drive. My buddy Raoul was passing this way in his eighteen-wheeler, and he gave me a ride."

"Sooo," Judy said, sitting down, trying to figure it out, "you're staying for a while, huh?"

"Not necessarily," her sister said. "Remember Jenny Wiggins from high school? Her brother Oscar is selling his motorcycle. I thought I'd check that out, you know, and get in a little vacation in the meantime."

Judy was almost too overwhelmed by these details to investigate further, but she had to ask: "Have you been working a lot, then?"

"No, I quit my job. Well, I sort of was laid off."

"Which job was that?"

"I was managing a cute little clothes shop in the Sooner Mall," Shannon said. "I got a great discount."

Judy took a sip of juice. "How have you been getting by?"

"I always manage to find something. Besides, I've been living with Isaac, and he didn't care much about the rent."

"Who's Isaac?"

"Kind of a friend," Shannon said. "Cute as hell. Teaches philosophy. I love a funny Jewish atheist, don't you? And he was sweet, too."

"So are you still living with him? Is he your boyfriend?"

"I try not to have boyfriends anymore. He's more of a friend with benefits, if you know what I mean, but I got tired of the benefits package, even if it did include the rent. It just seemed like a good time to take a break." She turned back to the paper. "Hey, look! Mr. Beasley is dead! Remember him? The band teacher? He always told me I wasn't throwing my baton high enough during the football games. Not that anyone watching cared, my skirt was so short." She giggled.

The toaster dinged, and Judy got up, extracted and buttered the slices and sprinkled cinnamon and sugar on them. She wasn't sure what to make of her sister's latest adventures. Shannon had always — flitted, that was the word, flitted from one thing to the next. Judy thought it started with the tornado, but at the time, she was going through so much doubt and dejection of her own that it took her a while to realize how much she and Shannon had grown apart.

"Hey, sis," Shannon said. She almost never used Judy's name. "What the hell is that thing on the living room wall?"

Judy sat again at the round oak table, trying to figure out how to reply. She took another sip of juice and a bite of toast. The sun was streaming in through the breakfast nook window, lighting up the yellow walls and the contents of the table — the funky corncob salt and pepper shakers, the clear plastic pepper grinder, the little struggling and definitely not blooming paphiopedilum orchid, and the old wooden stirrup she used as a napkin holder.

"It's like I'm trying to take all this sunlight," she said by way of explanation. "and pour it right into my head. Then my eyes become a projector, putting the contents of my brain on the wall, beaming out everything, like all this light. I try to use paint to fill in the picture, save it, like paint by numbers, only sometimes the picture changes, and I have to repaint it. Start over."

"Geez, you're weird," Shannon said. "I'm unusual, but you're just plain weird."

Judy knew Shannon was trying to irk her, but compared with her sister, Judy was a rock, and Shannon brought out the granite in her. She smiled.

"Bothers you, doesn't it," Judy said.

"I wouldn't say that. I just think if you're going to have a tornado in it, you should make it bigger. Don't fuck around. Really make it *big*."

"It's not all about the tornado," Judy said.

Shannon shrugged, then got up and put her juice glass in the sink. "I'm going to go see Greg. Is he still working at the store?"

"Pretty much every day," Judy said. "Hey, Shannon, just FYI, I'm going to be having another visitor the day after tomorrow. So there might be a, you know, man around."

"I love having men around," Shannon said, grinning, sensing Judy's hesitation.

"Oh, boy," Judy said, not wanting to get into a whole thing about it. She was nervous enough as it was.

"Don't worry," Shannon said. "I'll make myself scarce as I can, though I'll probably have to come back here at some point. What is this guy, your boyfriend?"

"Um, he's a storm chaser, too," Judy said.

"Oooo, geek boy," Shannon said, waiting for a rise out of Judy that did not come. "OK, that's all you want to tell me, I'll just have to find out for myself."

"I guess you will."

"Are the bikes still in the garage?"

Judy nodded.

"Great," Shannon said. "I'll go check out the old Hale Hardware, then, and maybe get over to Jenny's brother's and see that motorcycle." She twinkled out of the room, and Judy heard the front door slam.

She let out an incredibly long sigh, like a soft Plains breeze on a spring afternoon, when storms were promised but nowhere yet in sight.

Within a couple of hours, she was in emergency cleaning mode, trying to eliminate clutter and laundry and half-finished projects around the house before Jack arrived. She'd had an email from him, confirming he'd get there Wednesday, and she spent half an hour trying to read into it some tone that just wasn't there. You can't get much out of: "We're on for Wednesday afternoon. Let's go see the sights. Pancake has clouds, doesn't it? Jack." Noncommittal. Not that there was anything to commit to, exactly.

She got a call from Mrs. Grenoble, who insisted on having a portrait shot with her new grandbaby on Thursday morning. Her daughter and the baby were only in town for a couple of days, she told Judy, and it had to be Thursday. Judy wanted to keep her schedule clear, especially with Jack in town, but she needed the money, and there was no wedding to film until later in the month. Besides, it was good to stay on Mrs. Grenoble's good side, as she had at least fifteen grandchildren and wanted custom portraits of all of them. They'd be coming over at 10 a.m., so to keep the appointment as short as possible, Judy straightened up her studio and configured the lights and backdrop so they'd be ready.

The studio, at the back of the house, was a converted porch with large glass windows that she could cover with heavy shades if necessary, or use for their wonderful late morning and afternoon sunlight. Beyond those windows was her garden, and by Tuesday afternoon, with all her tasks done and Shannon still test-driving Oscar Wiggins's motorcycle, and possibly Oscar Wiggins, Judy found herself alone under the grand old white oak tree, among the soothing clusters of flowers, foliage and the practical patch of just-planted tomatoes, parsley, basil and chives. There were peonies, colorful coleus, impatiens, marigolds, sunflower stalks that were not yet blooming in a sunny stretch against the privacy fence, and the first, fresh roses — red, pink and yellow — whose scent hung in the air with romantic anticipation. Filling in around the flowerbeds was a profusion of English ivy, punctuated by wild pink morning glory; many gardeners hated its persistence, but Judy loved the way it crept into every opening. Purple cascades of million bells and sweet potato vine spilled over the sides of a couple of baskets hanging on either side of a wrought-iron pole, stuck next to the brick path that wound among the clusters of plantings.

In the corner was a small, white fountain that ran when she remembered to turn it on. Atop a birdbath-style basin, a little sun-worshipping, Pan-like creature turned his mischievous face skyward and stretched out his arms, palms up, seemingly tossing an arc of water from one hand to the other, where the clear droplets splashed with kinetic glee.

A weathered wooden swing hung from the oak that partially shaded her half acre, and after a muscle-crunching afternoon of weeding, planting and puttering, she sat and swung, feeling the breeze and hearing the birds twitter and squirrels chatter. She could almost see the plants growing around her. Mid-May. This was when life unfolded from the ground, waking up from its dream of snow and poking its shaggy green head defiantly into the stormy winds of springtime. She felt strangely free, her mind clear, more than it usually was. She remembered the weeks after the tornado had come through, when so many houses were splintered and trees snapped that the air smelled like a lumber mill. Her family tried to re-create a memory of routine and found a new place to live — this house, which she later transformed. She remembered the stripped leaves returning, bursts of bright young green on the branches that remained; the crushed little daisies popping up again; and broken things swept up and carted away as the life of the town returned through the avenues of plants. That spring, she could smell them everywhere, smell the essence of green. She wondered if she'd ever experience green in that way again.

She looked down her pathways, through the dappled sunlight at the fountain, where that joyous boy awaited his chance to grab a piece of sky, his eyes never dimmed by that glorious light. Then she thought about Jack, the way he'd walked toward her down the balcony of the motel, his smile gleaming.

This boy and that man had little in common, except that both were in her thoughts. He carried more with him than the sparkle of water, Jack did, only she didn't know what. Not yet. Perhaps something as dark as blackberry wine, or as sweet. She closed her eyes and let the scent of the roses embrace her. She needn't think beyond tomorrow. For once, she willed herself, don't think beyond tomorrow, or yesterday. She heard the bubbling as the sunlight turned the back of her closed eyelids blood red, so bright in the dark.

❧

JACK DROVE the car of an advanced graduate student. It was Japanese, used, and fuel-efficient. When he'd bought the sedan, it was a shade of tomato red that was a little too obnoxious for him, so he'd spent two hundred bucks and had a quickie paint job. Now it was a light gold color, subtly sparkling, almost tasteful. It blended in. He liked that. It didn't show him off, and it didn't show him up. He didn't need any personality help from a car. It was just transportation. It wasn't large. He'd installed a dashboard mount for his video camera because a tripod couldn't fit in between the front seats.

As he drove toward Pancake, west through the quiet, pretty roads of southern Kansas, he chain-smoked and wondered how much of this trip was about putting off work on his dissertation. Sure, Judy was a pretty girl, and an intriguing one, and he hadn't had both in one package for a long time. He could at least make a midweek weekend of it. But the work was waiting, an analysis of how Oklahoma's geographical features and short-term changes in the environment, like wet fields after a good rain and boundaries left over from old storms, influenced supercell and tornado development. He wasn't as excited about it as he should be, because he'd already switched topics a couple of times based on Malik's recommendations. It was time to get it done and move on to better things, like a real job with the storm lab. One more year was all he needed.

He passed a complex of grain silos, crossed the railroad tracks and got into town. Pancake was aligned along one long main street. On either side — after a few blocks of houses and garages, fast-food joints and small offices, antique shops and junk shops — the town faded away to warehouses and then fields. He stayed on the main drag, and after he passed the town square and the high school, he began to notice a stretch of newer construction — at least, newer than the houses from the '20s and '30s he had seen till now. The old trees here were misshapen, more gnarled and asymmetrical. Despite their fresh leaves, it was clear that this was where the tornado had passed through fifteen years before. He'd read about it, of course, as he'd read about all of the big ones. Several died in the Pancake twister. He'd still been with his father in Virginia back then. He did the math; his mother had died the year before. So, at that time, he'd been unaware of the tragedy of Pancake. Kansas had seemed a dim and unreal place, something out of a picture book, and not relevant to his daily concerns. In some ways, that was still true. It was just a place where things happened, and none of them were that interesting to him. Except the tornado. He'd have to ask Judy about it.

This town was sort of nice, in better shape than many of the villages of the Plains. So many had lost youth and vitality to time. He saw a sign for a *Wizard of Oz* house and chuckled to himself. This was all Kansas had to hold on to — a story about a tornado. Didn't they know that tornadoes weren't generally considered chamber-of-commerce attractions?

Well, some people liked it. Judy obviously did. The street numbers showed he was getting near her place, and he started looking for it on the left, where the odd numbers were. He double-checked the printout of the email she'd written him: "1301," it said. "Look for the big flowers."

How big could the flowers be? he thought to himself. Everybody in Kansas had sunflowers. They didn't get much bigger than that.

As he emerged from the 1200 block, he saw what she meant.

Overshadowing her green mailbox were three enormous wooden flowers, from five to eight feet tall, painted in vivid, crazy colors and shaped like no flowers he'd ever seen. "Wow," he said, despite himself. A small, square white sign hung from one of the stylized leaves on the flowers' stems, simple, with words in dark green: "JUDY HALE" on one line, in classic capitals; "*photographer*" in italics on the next.

He pulled into the driveway and parked a few feet away from the whitewashed garage, which was separated from the house by a brick walkway. In the open garage, he could see the small SUV he remembered as Judy's and a couple of bicycles. There was a long table and a pegboard in the back overflowing with tools and hardware, fishing poles and gear, and odd items, including a decaying old accordion, a marginally hideous lamp in the shape of a dancing eighteenth-century couple, a retro electric fan, and a pile of ancient hubcaps.

The house was a two-story, pre-Depression number, painted pale green, yellow and white, with pink accents and a long front porch. Judy was doing all right, he thought, as he put out his cigarette and got out of the car, smoothing his T-shirt and long shorts and running a hand through his dark hair.

He started up the sidewalk that led from the driveway to the front door, then thought better of it. He wanted to see what was down the brick path that led to the backyard. He wanted more hints of what he was in for.

The path was in shade and lined with small purple flowers. A trellis on the side of the house sported morning glories. Then the walkway opened up to a friendly little maze that wound through a sunlit garden of inviting variety and color. It wasn't really his kind of thing, but he recognized the work that went into it. And, he had to admit, it smelled wonderful, fresh and green and floral. Then he caught the hint of sunlight on straw-colored braids, and he saw her, facing away from him, crouched over a rose bush along the fence, where she was cutting a few yellow blooms. He quietly walked up behind her, wanting to touch her before she saw him, but she stood up and wheeled around.

"I thought I heard something!" Judy said, her cheeks flushed. She wore denim shorts on this warm May day, and a red sleeveless top that revealed the smooth curve of her shoulders and slender arms, her well-rounded breasts. She looked lovely with the sun washing over her hair and skin like water and lighting up her baby blues. The last time he'd seen her, it had been raining, and night.

"I guess I should have brought *you* flowers," Jack told her, nodding at the yellow roses.

"Oh, not at all, and have them wilt on the drive? Here, let me put these in some water, and then I can give you the tour," she said.

She led him past a white, slanted cellar door to a side door he hadn't noticed earlier. It also was white and painted with the words "photo studio" in dark green. He followed her in, quickly glancing around at the lights and backdrops and cables and a chair or two before following her through another door, this time into what appeared to be the house proper, with warmer colors and much more for the eye to take in. She walked briskly through the living room, but he had to stop there and stare at the wall. This was the mural she'd told him about. Some of it was recognizable — there was a tornado, or maybe tornadoes, and clouds and trees and houses and land, and some of it was more diffuse, like a waterfall seen through a fogged-up lens, colors in motion. And there were white patches that appeared to be awaiting images, or perhaps they were merely erased ones.

"Oh, no," she said from the doorway to the next room. She had an old green canning jar in her hand and was looking back at him. "You've seen the mural."

"I was looking at the couch," he joked. "I needed to assess my sleeping arrangements."

"Well, my sister's sleeping on the couch for a few days," Judy said. "There's always, I mean, I'm sure we can figure out a place for you to sleep." She seemed embarrassed then and vanished back through the doorway. Jack followed her past some overstuffed bookcases and the TV, beyond the hallway and staircase and into the kitchen, where Judy filled the jar with water from the sink and popped the three roses into it.

She put it on the round, wooden table. The walls in here were yellow, and there were little eye-catching gewgaws everywhere on the shelves above the sink and the cookbook-filled bookcase against the wall — funky art pieces, a New York snow globe, a shiny chrome ice crusher, a '50s-style milkshake blender, a whole shelf of small fossils. He found the stimuli a bit overwhelming. He had not yet mastered the art of the knickknack. He had no need for them. He had very little he wished to remember for that long, so souvenirs were pointless. He meticulously kept photos from old relationships and places he'd been, but he rarely looked at them. He was glad they were there, like the National Archives, a record and a validation that had no immediate bearing on his life.

He followed her as she led him from room to room, quickly enough that he barely had time to take them in — a laundry room whose walls were painted in multicolored squares; an office or catch-all room with a beat-up rolltop desk, a computer on a separate table, piles of papers and books, and white walls hung with big black-and-white photos of cemetery monuments; a stairway punctuated by niches that each held an organic-looking sculpture he could only describe as peculiar; a bedroom with weird silver and white wallpaper that had become a workroom for Judy's photography and other creative endeavors; and a neat, relatively normal guest room done all in red, with cherry-finish furniture and floral paintings on the walls. The quilt on the bed was a patchwork in shades of red and pink. On top of it was a half-open black bag, lacy underwear and socks spilling out, that Jack suspected was her sister's. He took special note of the underwear.

The master bedroom, Judy's, wasn't all that much bigger than the others. It had two windows, and a bathroom and closet attached. In the main room, there were a couple of antique wooden dressers, sparsely adorned, and no mirrors. The floors were seasoned wood, and the walls were sky-blue. In clusters of four and five on those bright blue walls were photographs of mostly white clouds of wonderful variety, in sleek silver frames — cumulus, stratus, pileus, mammatus, cirrus and everything in between. The sleigh bed, in dark-colored wood, had a fluffy white comforter and puffy white pillows that underscored the impression of a cloud floating in a blue sky. Compared with the rest of the house, this room was simple and, with its cloud theme, immediately relaxing.

"I took all these on chases, of course, or nice days, which are also chases, I guess," Judy was saying, pointing around the room at the photos. She seemed nervous. One way to stop that. He grabbed her by the waist and swept her toward the bed so they both fell on the pillowy bedding and bounced. He pushed her back and kissed her before she could resist, deeply, slowly.

"I think I *am* floating on a cloud," she breathed as he pulled away. "Look, I'm not done the tour. We have the entire town to do next."

He didn't say anything. He had his own tour in mind. He kissed her neck, felt her yielding as he found her lips again. Then she pushed on his chest, a little harder, making him disengage.

"I told you I wanted to see clouds," Jack said. "We're surrounded by them. Now let me kiss you again."

"I can't," Judy said. "I have to have *some* standards." But she was giggling, and her legs were wrapped loosely around his. He started to kiss her again, but she pushed him off. "Really," she said. "We're going to have a proper date this time, even if I have to drag you all over Pancake."

"Fair enough," Jack said, sitting up. "But I can't promise that I won't be thinking about clouds."

"I'd expect nothing less."

❦

"THIS IS MY FAVORITE PLACE," Judy said. She'd just driven him around town, pointing out historic houses and a couple of good restaurants and her old high school and similarly thrilling sites. She didn't think he was that interested, as he hadn't said much, but he'd leaned his arm on the back of her seat and stroked her neck the entire time. It was very distracting. She liked it.

Now, she brought him to the place where she always went when nothing else was working for her. "I like to think here."

It was the windmill park on the edge of town, away from prying eyes and most traffic. On a couple of acres were a few dozen windmills of fascinating variety: the Monitor L, the Baker, the Currie, the Andrew, the Freeman Special, the Imperial, the Althouse Wheeler-Giant, the Challenge Steel, the Aermotor, the Duplex Vaneless, the Eureka Steel, the Appleton-Goodhue, the Railroad Eclipse. The latter was large and yellow, and it gleamed like a sun rising inside the park.

"Cool," Jack said.

Well, it was the most she'd gotten out of him. It wasn't like Texas. He seemed quieter, preoccupied. She took his hand and led him through the gate to one of the benches in the middle, under a big, old river birch, the park's lone tree, with its strange peeling bark that made Judy think of ancient scrolls.

"Now," Judy said, "just listen."

It was a breezy day, and after a moment of focus, filtering

out the whisper of leaves and the occasional, distant sound of car motors, the park came alive. Everywhere, all around them, it was creaking, flexing, rhythmically clicking and clacking and spinning, voicing the energy of wind.

Jack put his arm around her, and together, they listened to the sounds for a few minutes.

"Not much for television, are you?" he quipped.

Judy smiled. "I come here when I'm sick of television, of people, of the world going to hell. When I want to think, like I said."

"What do you think about?"

"Oh, stuff," Judy said, butting her head against the blunt question.

"The tornado?"

"Sometimes," she said, running her fingers along the rusting metal arm of the bench. "I told you my aunt died in it. Other people I know did, too, including a friend from school. But it was more like, after that, we just didn't feel safe. My parents got weird. They were annoyed that I became even more interested in storms. They fought more. I used to come here to get away, even if I was just doing homework or something like that."

"Where are your parents now?"

"Arizona. They're happier now that their lives are filled by golf and tole painting. We talk by phone sometimes, get together maybe once or twice a year, for a painful holiday or two, either here or there. My sister somehow avoids even that, though she seems to get checks from them regularly." Judy took a deep breath of the warm spring air. "What about your dad?"

He didn't say anything for a minute, just dug around in one of the many pockets in his shorts until he pulled out a cigarette and matches. He lit the cig, took a drag, then spoke.

"We don't talk unless we have to, like if he wants to know where to forward a piece of mail. Sometimes he types up these little postcards, discussing some new scientific discovery or something, news he thinks I might be interested in."

"What does he do?"

"I guess you'd call him a rocket scientist. He's an engineer. Helps design space missions at Goddard."

"That sounds cool."

"If he cared about anything else, it might be. He has about as much perspective as a pre-Columbian map." Judy didn't say anything, at first, as Jack stood, looking up at the grove of spinning windmills, their blades, some thin, some wide, flashing against the sky. He stared and smoked for another minute, then dropped his cigarette and ground it out with a high-top sneaker. He reached back toward her, and she got up and took his hand. They walked slowly through the metal and wooden towers.

"He must care about you," Judy said, hesitant, sensing this was a touchy subject.

"This is how it was." Jack's deep voice was curt. "He worked. Sometimes he stayed out late. He worked, or he drank. Mostly, he ignored me or found interesting ways to make my life more miserable if I wasn't performing up to standard. Sometimes, he gave my mother the time of day, and most of the time, he didn't. Sometimes, they went out. One time they went out, and she didn't come back. Car wreck. I don't know if he was drinking, but he was definitely driving."

"God, I'm sorry," Judy said.

"God didn't have much to do with it. Anyway, it was never

good between us after that, but it certainly wasn't before, either."

"I don't know the situation." Judy gave his hand a squeeze. "But maybe, if he still sends you postcards, he's trying."

"Maybe he's just wasting stamps." Jack stopped, faced her squarely, grabbed both of her hands. His green eyes were hard. "You're sweet to ask about it. But don't." His voice softened. "Look, I'm hungry. Let's go back to one of those restaurants. You did say there was a good one, right?"

"Two." Judy smiled a little, relieved to change the subject. "One's Italian; one's sort of, um, interesting."

"I like interesting," Jack said, back in charmer mode, his arm around her again as they walked toward the gate. "I know we have a nice evening ahead of us, and I want to get on with it." He surprised her by leaning over her quickly and kissing her, swift and pointed, like the period at the end of a sentence, before opening the gate and letting her back into the everyday world.

❡

THE MEAL WAS, as she said, interesting, in a Main Street restaurant that had been decorated with old toys and fairy lights. The menu had a lot of what he liked to call Fun With Sauces, a little strange but really not bad. He had a beef thing with Interesting mashed potatoes, and she had a chicken thing with Interesting pasta. The wine, an Australian shiraz, was nice, too.

There was something still a little nervous and rough between them, and he wasn't sure why he'd told her about his father, only that his well-developed sense of what a woman wants suggested that she seemed to respond more to the subterranean than the superficial. He brought her out, her interest in art, her travels, her garden, and though his eyes lingered over her figure as much as his ears listened to her voice, he enjoyed what she had to say. When they got around to talking about storms, which was soon and often, Jack had that flash of recognition as she voiced her need to find the perfect shot of the perfect second of the perfect day, that moment in which all her understanding would crystallize. It wasn't so abstract for him, but he also sought and found a symmetry in nature, in the ways its elements danced together. Only they, people with their obsession, would recognize perfection in the balance of ingredients that created a tornado, a magnificent matrix, a feast for their storm-starved eyes.

Like Judy, he was always storm-starved. He could see a spectacular supercell and multiple tornadoes and feel his hair stand on end when a lightning bolt hit too close, and he still wanted to go back at it. It was exactly the way he felt about sex, only perhaps the storms were more sublime. Maybe that was why he was drawn to her. The storms were as much a part of her as they were of him.

Back at her house, Judy told him she wanted to take a shower after their long day, and she pointed him to a downstairs bathroom in case he wanted to freshen up. That wasn't an invitation, he presumed, as he heard her trotting up the squeaky staircase. He was done first and sat in his usual uniform at the kitchen table, shorts and a T-shirt, his feet bare on the linoleum floor, and leafed through an old pie cookbook he'd found on her shelves, its margins filled with little notes from generations past. He breathed in the scent of the yellow roses in the jar and marveled at the various ways people could assemble fruits between two pieces of pastry.

"I like just about everything in there except rhubarb," she

said as she came through the doorway, wearing a little cotton knit dress, light blue, casual, almost as casual as his shorts, but clinging to her curves. "Who decided it would be a good idea to eat rhubarb, anyway?"

"Good question," he said, letting his eyes roam over her body. Her straw-colored hair was spilling about her shoulders, out of its braids, still damp but gloriously wavy. She wore no makeup, but her cheeks and lips were pink, and the blue dress lit up her eyes and set off her tan arms and legs. Her feet, her small toes, were bare, too. He didn't bother to disguise his interest, and she returned his smile.

"Have anything to drink?" he asked.

"Not much," she admitted. "Some wine, some vodka, and I think I have a bottle of good whiskey one of my clients gave me as a thank-you."

"Let's see it." Jack grasped the small bottle she pulled out of a crowded kitchen cabinet. It was indeed good stuff. "Bourbon. Perfect. All we need is glasses, or we could just swig it."

Judy chortled. "Oh, let's be civilized about it." She pulled a couple of faceted high-ball glasses out of another cabinet and got a few cubes for each out of the freezer. He broke the wax seal on the bottle and poured her a little, and poured himself a little more. They took a few sips, not speaking as they sat at the old, round table. He felt the smooth wood grain under his elbows.

"I have something for you," she said, getting up and plucking what looked like a piece of paper from a coupon-stuffed clip on the side of the refrigerator.

He took it from her as she sat again. It was the picture she shot when she met him that day in Oklahoma. The roiling sky behind him and his car was vast, a universe of sinister mystery.

"That was an amazing day," he said, giving her what he hoped was a significant look. "Thanks."

"I know everyone asks me this," Judy said, "but how did you get into chasing?"

"Well, that story is tied up in other stories," he said, a little reticent, but he saw he was reeling her in. Besides, he liked talking to her. "Stop me if I bore you." She shook her head and smiled, as if she'd never be bored with what he had to say. "After high school, I decided to travel instead of going right to college. I didn't know what I wanted to do, and I knew that not going to college would piss my dad off. So I didn't go. I took a little money I'd saved and started driving around the country. I stayed at a lot of state parks. Sometimes I worked in them. I spent a few months with my aunt and uncle in Florida. I lived in California for almost a year, but there were too damn many people. When I was in New Mexico, I ran into some chasers, and I talked them into letting me tag along a couple of times. I'd always loved storms, of course, but I'd never called my weather-watching chasing, exactly. I took to it right away and decided it was a sign, a direction for me to go. I got my bachelor's at New Mexico Tech and got to help with some neat lightning studies there. I've been in Oklahoma ever since. I'm *this* close to my PhD," he said, holding up an invisible pinch between his thumb and index finger.

"I started as a spotter when I was in high school," Judy said. "I thought about studying meteorology for about half a second, but I'm happier not doing math."

He laughed. "Yeah, there's a lot of math."

"It's not that I can't do it, but I've learned that just because I can do something doesn't mean I should. So I studied art and photography and a little photojournalism, just in case my studio didn't work out, and here I am." She took another sip of her drink. The ice tinkled in the glass, a sound he loved. "What will you do with your degree?"

"More research, I hope," Jack said, "as long as I get to be in the field as much as possible. The problem with forecasting is that you're almost always stuck in the office when there's a big storm event."

"Better than being stuck videotaping a wedding. I can't tell you the torture of being behind the camera, videotaping the thousandth awkward dance to 'Daddy's Little Girl,' while I hear thunder rolling in the distance. It kills me. I try to minimize weddings during chase season, but unfortunately, it's wedding season, too, and I have to make a little money."

"You need to talk them into getting married in front of a supercell, like on your business card."

"One day I will," Judy said, her blue eyes twinkling.

He drained his glass, savoring the sweet burn of the whiskey, and poured himself another. This was fine, he thought. A woman who loved storms with good liquor in her cabinet. He felt his edges blurring away. They were quiet for a moment, in this quiet house, with only the mild murmurs of its grand, wooden dotage around them as it interacted with the wind.

Judy took another sip, more moderate than his, then spoke. "I know this sounds like asking you to see my etchings, but would you like to see some video of my favorite storm from last year?"

"Sure."

They brought their glasses with them into the living room, where the mural seemed to move in the dim light. Judy put a home-burned DVD in the player, then pushed some buttons on the remote.

"Where'd you shoot this?" Jack asked.

"Colorado."

"I didn't chase in Colorado too much last year. Where?"

"Near Trinidad."

"Oh, I know the one you mean," he said, sitting on the soft, red couch, waiting for the show. "I definitely wasn't there. I was doing something for school. I remember, that was a really marginal day."

"I wasn't going to, either," she said, "but I remember I just really wanted to get out that weekend. It was June, too, one of the last days of the season, and I hate to let those go."

She sat next to him and pressed a button on the remote. "I haven't done any fancy editing with this yet," she said. "It's just basically the storm. This was the last one that went up before dusk. There were a bunch that day, all forming in the same place, spinning, moving off the mountains, not quite getting it together. And then there was this one."

It was gloomy on the video. The light in the sky was almost silver. In the scene were the low-topped mountains of eastern Colorado, and over one of them, a gorgeous supercell expanded, slowly rotating, its walls curving up toward heavy mammatus clouds, their pouches almost impossibly round as they hung from the anvil, living up to their suggestive name.

"Nice mammatus," he said, which came out as a double entendre despite his best efforts, and she laughed.

"Thank you," she replied, and then he had to laugh, too. He put his arm around her and ran his fingers up and down her shoulder as they watched the video.

It was almost hypnotic, to see this cell move toward the camera, rotating, slowly building a wall cloud beneath, and almost perfectly forming the downdraft and tornado. This tornado didn't appear violent at all, though of course it was.

They all were, to some degree. In the fading light, it was a narrow, smoothly lowering funnel, quiet, forming a sharp point that seemed to hover just above the trees in the scene. Once Judy had panned up with her camera, and he realized from the angle that she had been nearly under where it spun from the cloud.

"You were close," he whispered, as if they were in some holy place.

"I know."

Blue against black, the tornado spun into a narrower and narrower funnel, a thin rope spiraling as it lifted. Then it dissipated like a suggestion of mist in the descending darkness.

The DVD flickered back to a menu, and Judy shut off the TV. He looked at her, stroking her hair. She smiled, far away, still in the storm. He eased his arms around her and kissed her, delicately, deliberately, tasting the whiskey on her tongue. As she embraced him, he ran his hands across her back, feeling no bra, feeling the drinks and the night and her supple body. He pulled away, ever so slightly.

"I want to go upstairs," he said.

She merely nodded, got up, took his hand, and brought him to her clouds.

JUDY WAS OF TWO MINDS, but one body. She wanted him, even though a little voice told her that, despite their enticing conversations, Jack was holding back parts of himself. Still, her little voice could be wrong. He was smart and intriguing. He loved storms. He had those to-die-for green eyes. She wanted to give him, and them, a chance. Aside from all the practical questions, there was some force pulling them toward each other, something primal tangled up in the storms and their personalities. And sometimes, she thought, it was important to tell the little voice to shut the hell up.

She didn't turn on the light. The moonlight already cast the room aglow. He sat on her bed, and she made a move to join him, but he said: "Wait. I want to see you by the window. You're a moon goddess in this light."

Hyperbolic flattery. She loved it. She knew which window he meant. The moonlight was pouring in, bluish white. She walked slowly over to the window, where the sheers where lifting gracefully on the breeze that wafted through the screen. It was the south wind, bringing back fuel for the storms. She could hear the gurgling of the little fountain as she looked outside. The moonlight filtered through her tree and into her garden like a wash of silver.

She turned back to face him. He didn't say anything as he sat on the bed, propped against the pillows, legs extended, watching her. She returned his gaze levelly at first, evaluating his dark hair and handsome jaw, sharp nose and inviting mouth in the half-shadows. She quickly lost her objectivity. He looked at her with such desire that she felt her own body respond. She knew what he wanted. She reached down to her hem, lifted her dress slowly over her head and dropped it to the floor.

"Mmmm, naked," Jack said, smiling a little.

She had known her yearning would be met tonight, this inevitable night, after so much time alone. Now, her skin alive with the cool breeze, her hair stirring, she was aware of the moonlight behind her and at her feet as she advanced toward him. He was already taking off his shirt, his shorts, his briefs, speed-stripping.

"Easy, big fella," she said. "Let me enjoy the unveiling."

She eased next to him and lay amid the rumpled white comforter and the big pillows, admiring the line of his profile, the hard landscape of his back as it rolled into his hip and legs, but as much as she wanted to touch him, she waited for him to act, wanting him to want her, to possess her. It didn't take long. He leaned on one elbow and ran his other hand over her body, touching her breasts, her ribs, the curve of her hips. Slowly, slowly. She felt him stiffen against her thigh. His fingers traced around her nipples until they hardened and ached, and then he leaned in and sucked at them roughly, a sweet pain, while he reached down to touch her. She was already wet, made more so by the deftness of his fingers.

It had been too long since she'd been with someone. She reached up to embrace him, ran her hands up and down his back, pulling him as close as physics would allow, and met his lips with a hunger equal to his, a hard kiss that softened languorously into a flower of fire. She hated to lose those kisses for even one second as he stopped to slip on a condom he'd pulled out of the pocket of his shorts, which were on the floor — so he'd thought they were a sure thing, too. She didn't care. They were. They lay on their sides, facing each other, caressing, kissing deeply, and she was so lost in the feel of his mouth as he devoured hers that when he entered her, the transition to this new sensation was so smooth and pure that it seemed as if he'd been inside her all along. He pushed against her, grinding himself in deeper, and she lost herself in the ache and pressure of him, the heat of his body.

They rolled, and she was on top, moving slowly against him as he grasped her hips. As the waves of pleasure spread through her, she looked down into his eyes, gray, not green, in the semi-darkness, feeling his gaze bore into her the way his body did, with compulsive intensity. She heard her old analog clock tick-tick-ticking on the dresser, the only sound except for the wind in the tree and the bubbling fountain and the slight creak of the bed and now, in the distance, a train. She imagined it to be thunder, a rolling, longing sound, as the cloudburst opened up within her. She moaned and leaned back, hearing him gasp, too, as he came.

For those long seconds, there was lightning behind her closed eyes, and the ticking stopped. Then it was there again, time, the moment, and she eased herself off him, curled up in the crook of his arm. He didn't speak. He stroked her hair, let his hands linger and then come to rest on her body, and was asleep in a few minutes. She listened to his breathing and the wind and the clock. The wind and the clock. The wind and the clock.

❧

SHE WOKE briefly at 3 a.m. when she heard the motorcycle drive up and the front door open and close. Jack mumbled in her ear, "What's that?"

"Sister," Judy said.

"OK," Jack said, and they both returned to slumber.

When she woke again, it was 8:15, the room was light, and Jack wasn't there. She heard birds outside. She lay there for a few moments, listening, trying to orient herself to the sounds of her house, which was suddenly strange with two other people in it, one of whom she'd just slept with, could fall in love with. Oh, boy. Then she heard the toaster ding downstairs.

Ugh. Thursday, she thought. The photo shoot.

She took a quick shower and put on a slightly more professional outfit than usual, khakis and a white blouse, so she'd be ready for Mrs. Grenoble and whichever little grand-nipper she'd bring by. She braided her hair, too.

Jack and Shannon were at the kitchen table, laughing about something. Jack had the newspaper in his hand and a glass of orange juice in front of him, and Shannon was eating toast spread with apple butter.

"I've never had anyone do dramatic readings of the comics for me before," said Shannon, who wore a flowered sundress and sandals and whose corn-silk hair, unruly and curling just above her shoulders, looked especially luminous in the morning light.

"A man of many talents," Judy remarked, not sure what to make of their interaction. "I see you've met?"

"It was unavoidable," Jack said. "I damn near sat on her when I went to watch TV this morning."

Shannon giggled. "I really should stop sleeping on the couch."

"It's OK," Jack said in response to Judy's raised eyebrows. "I beat a hasty retreat to your back garden, had a smoke and read the paper until it was safe to come back in."

Judy, not knowing what to say, didn't say anything for a minute. She peered into the fridge, trying to see if there was anything she wanted to eat. Jack started reading another comic strip aloud. The punchline was something about business meetings resembling hell.

Shannon broke into peals of laughter. Judy was pretty sure Shannon had never been in a business meeting in her life, but it didn't matter, she supposed. Judy pulled a couple of eggs out of the door of the fridge.

"Eggs, anybody?"

"That would be great," Jack said, giving Judy a smile. There, that was better.

"How do you like 'em?"

"Sunny side up, broken," Jack said.

"Good," Judy said, "because I almost always break them."

She put two more slices of bread in the toaster and got out a wide frying pan, added a little butter and heated it up before cracking the eggs into it. They made a pleasing sizzle.

"God," Shannon said, "that really makes me want bacon, for some reason."

"I didn't think about getting bacon," Judy said.

"Oh, that's OK," Shannon said. "Do you have any bacon bits?"

Now Jack laughed.

"Actually," Judy said, "I think I do."

"I'm serious," Shannon said. "I want bacon bits."

Judy pulled the plastic bottle of bacon-flavored soy pieces out of a cabinet and handed them over. Shannon popped the top and poured herself a handful of the brown bits, then ate them, a bit indelicately, crunching, until she licked her hand to get the last few. Jack watched her flicking tongue with fascination.

"Now *I* want bacon bits," he said, still staring at Shannon.

"In your eggs?" Judy asked, not without a touch of irritation.

"Um, sure," he said, grabbing the bottle off the table and handing it to her. Shannon giggled. Judy sprinkled the bacon bits in the eggs, then pulled the finished toast out of the toaster, buttered it and put it on a plate. She got her breakfast factory going, more toast, more eggs. Jack read the comics silently now, and Shannon hummed a little song as she looked over the obituaries in the news section.

In a few minutes, the plates of eggs were on the table, along with the stack of toast and juice refills all around. Judy began to relax. It was nice to eat breakfast, she thought, and actually have people around to eat with. This was OK.

"Jack, I have an appointment this morning," she said as they ate. "I have to shoot an old lady at ten."

"You really shouldn't have told me," Jack said. "Now I'll have no plausible deniability when the police come around."

Shannon starting laughing again, and Judy smiled. "I'm taking a nice grandmother's photo. I couldn't reschedule. I'm sorry. Will you be OK for about an hour?"

"Sure, I can watch TV, if your sister will let me," Jack said.

"I can watch TV, too!" Shannon said.

"What?" Judy inquired. "No motorcycle test drives today?"

Shannon shook her head. "I've decided that motorcycles are not for me, at least not this week."

"Well," Jack said, "they *are* demanding, and you have to feed them and groom them and make sure their stalls are cleaned out."

"Their riders are even worse," said Shannon, all coquette. "They demand constant attention and devotion, when riding should be enough. I love to ride. I love to feel that animal between my legs. Don't you think riders should just enjoy the ride?"

"Every gentleman knows riding is the ultimate sport," Jack agreed, grinning, and Shannon snickered at the way he played along. Judy wondered why he was so witty all of a sudden. It was Shannon doing her thing again.

Judy was bad at flirting. Shannon got all the flair, along with more beauty, a certain grace in movement and a sometimes embarrassingly good memory. Judy had artistic talent and the ability to balance her checkbook and occasionally wondered if she'd had the short end of the deal, especially when Shannon was treading on her territory. She'd have to deal with it later, after the photo shoot.

She saw Mrs. Grenoble's silver Lincoln pulling into the driveway. It was time.

"OK, guys," Judy said, putting her plate in the sink; then to Jack: "I'll see you in about an hour." He stood up and gave her a quick smooch.

"I'll be here," he said.

She smiled, feeling a little weird and a little worried, and went through the house to the studio in back to meet Mrs. Grenoble.

JUDY HAD NEVER WANTED to finish a job so quickly, but she put on her patient face. The baby, Mrs. Grenoble's grandson, seemed to sense her anxiety, however, and he fidgeted and fussed in the old lady's arms until even the grande dame had to sit down and rest. Judy took little Davy, then, and cooed and rocked him until she forgot about her hurry and the baby settled down. He even smiled beneath his shock of dark brown hair.

"There you go, my dear," said Mrs. Grenoble, elegant in her dark blue pants suit and coiffed white hair. "That is why I come to you. You have the magic."

"You know I do house calls, don't you?" Judy asked, bouncing the baby.

"I know, but there are always my kids and their kids underfoot, and frankly, it's nice to get out of there sometimes."

"He's got a nice head of hair," Judy said, handing Davy back to grandma.

"Oh, he gets that from his father," Mrs. Grenoble said. "Lord knows our family always had a bunch of bald babies. My daughter's going bald now. Don't tell her I told you," she continued, in response to Judy's raised eyebrows. "She's taking a drug for it. Better than joining the Hair Club for Men, or getting a 'do like mine each week. It looks wonderful, doesn't it? But it's completely hollow. It's kind of a bubble of hair. I don't know how Ricardo does it."

"Oh, he cuts my hair, too, on those rare occasions when I get it cut," Judy said of the hairdresser, who was known more dully as Richard when he went to high school with her. "He's really good."

She took dozens and dozens of digital stills, in sync with the bright, diffused light of the pole-mounted flashes, as Mrs. Grenoble moved back and forth in front of the backdrop with little Davy. Then they shot photos by the windows, where the natural light cast gentle, flattering shadows on the woman's furrowed face and the baby's glowing cheeks. They even shot a few photos among the flowers in the garden, with a lens that let the background drop out in a blur of color. Judy would get a sweet portrait of Mrs. Grenoble looking down at her grandson in the sunlight, and everyone would be happy.

The appointment took an hour and ten minutes. Judy helped Mrs. Grenoble strap the baby into his car seat, promised proofs by next week, and waved her on her way. Then she went back into the studio by the side door.

It took her a few minutes to tidy up and compose herself. She looked in the full-length wall mirror, which clients used to get ready for their shoots, to make sure she was still presentable. Yes, she was. Kind of cute. Some might say pretty, in a understated kind of way. She was content enough with that.

She opened the door to the living room and found Jack and Shannon sitting closely on the couch, talking, looking at a laptop computer he'd propped up on the coffee table. Some news channel was playing on the TV, and behind them, on the wall, her mural was a kaleidoscope of chaos.

"You're back!" Jack said. "I hope you don't mind, but I'm using your wireless to check some data. I just got a call from Professor Malik. We're heading out tomorrow. I've got to get back."

"This weather stuff is a lot more interesting than I thought," Shannon said. "I'm learning all about fronts and things." Then lightly, matter-of-factly: "Jack is so nice. He says he'll give me a ride back to OKC."

For a long moment, the only sound was Jack's tapping on the keyboard as Judy felt an invisible two-by-four whack her in the back of the head. She managed to say, "You're leaving?" She wasn't sure to whom her query was directed.

"Yeah," Shannon said. "In fact, I'd better go upstairs and get my bag together."

Shannon went around the corner and up the stairs, leaving Judy and Jack alone. She stood, unmoving, looking at him as he typed and clicked through web pages. He must have felt her eyes on him and looked up.

"I'm sorry about this," he said. "It's just bad timing. Maybe I'll see you out there. This could be a nice storm system."

"Um, good," Judy said, her tone hollow. "I mean, I know you need to go. And I'm not working this weekend, so maybe I'll chase, too."

For once, the storms were the last thing on her mind. She

was caught in a different kind of whirlwind. Shannon came down the stairs, and before Judy knew it, she and Jack were chattering and packed and heading out the door.

Shannon gave her a hug. "Thanks, sis," she said. "I know I can always count on you. I'll try to be better about calling."

Judy wanted to ask Shannon where she would stay, but suddenly, she didn't want to know.

Jack was last to leave. His green duffel and black laptop bag were slung over his left shoulder. With his right hand he reached up and cupped Judy's chin, then gave her a peck on the cheek. "Bad timing," he said again, looking her briefly in the eye. Then he was gone.

POWER SCREWDRIVER IN HAND, glasses sliding down his nose as usual, Marcus perched precariously on the roof of the hail-catcher van, inside the gear-filled hangar they affectionately called the balloon barn, when his cell phone began to ring.

Unfortunately, his cell phone was across the big room, inside his backpack, which sat on a rusting, gray metal desk. There was no way he could make it.

Fortunately, Dennis was sitting in a chair beside the desk, his feet propped up, staring in fascination at Marcus's bag.

"Dennis!" Marcus shouted. "Answer it, for god's sake!"

Dennis jumped, as if awakened from a dream, and began digging in the backpack. It seemed to take forever. Finally, he pulled out the phone and tapped the screen.

"Marcus Heimer's phone," Dennis said in his best perky-secretary voice.

"Shit," Marcus uttered under his breath as he waited to hear the outcome.

"Jack!" Dennis said. "Yeah, he's here. Hang on a second."

Dennis walked over to the van and tossed the phone to Marcus, who had to make a gymnastic catch to prevent it from falling into the nearly repaired hail-catcher net.

"Jack?" Marcus said, pushing his black, curly locks out of his face, trying to sound alert. "What's up? Where are you?"

"I'm on the road, in Kansas, but about to get out, thank god. Anyway, you know that girl Giselle?" Jack said.

"Sure, the French girl," Marcus said. "Are you going to ask her out?"

"Please," Jack said, as if that were the last thing on his mind. "Do you know if they still have a room open in that house? You know, the one where all those girls live."

Marcus only wished he knew more about that house. It seemed to hold eighty percent of the female meteorology majors, of which there just weren't enough, in his opinion. But yes, he did know what Jack was talking about.

"I think they were still looking for another roommate," Marcus said.

"Do me a favor, then," Jack said. "Look up Giselle on the mesonet phone list and call her and tell her I've got a roommate for her."

"I'll make sure I tell her it isn't you," Marcus said.

There was a small laugh on the other end of the line. "Definitely not me, though I'm not saying I've never seen the inner sanctums of Casa Cutie. No, I have a passenger, and she'll be staying there for a while. Her name is Shannon. Tell Giselle to get her French crap out of the spare room."

Marcus laughed. "OK, I'll tell her." Jack sure seemed like he was in a good mood.

"Is the van ready?" Jack asked.

"Just about."

"OK," Jack said. "Tell Dennis to lay off the Oreos. I'll see you tomorrow."

Marcus chuckled as he ended the call.

"What did he want?" Dennis asked from the floor below.

"He said to tell you you're an asshole," Marcus said.

Dennis looked hurt for a second, and then he smirked. "You almost had me," he said. "You're not pimping for him again, are you?"

"Very funny," Marcus said, throwing the phone at Dennis's head. The undergrad caught it, barely.

"That's not the way to treat your electronics." Dennis pushed his brown bangs back from his pasty face.

"No, this is the way to treat your electronics," Marcus said, turning back to the hail catcher, picking up a hammer from the pile of tools on the roof of the van and banging the hell out of the basket's misshapen frame. "It's going to take two tornadoes and a hurricane to blow this thing off by the time I'm done."

"Not that you'll see the tornadoes," Dennis said, rubbing salt into Marcus's sore spot.

"Someday I will. One cannot be king of the hail and master of the funnel at the same time."

"You read way too many comic books," Dennis said, sinking back into the desk chair, putting his feet up and shutting his eyes. "Wake me up when you're done, Hail Man."

Marcus banged on the metal frame a few more times, just to be annoying. Then he got down to work.

"So, is the problem that you can't drive or you just don't want to drive?" Jack asked Shannon as they rolled south on I-35.

"I'm an excellent driver," she said, imitating Dustin Hoffman's nasal tone in *Rain Man*, a remnant of the movie quote game they'd been playing for the past hour as they listened to Jack's rock mix. Then she was herself, her voice lilting. "Of course I can drive, silly. I just don't have a car right now."

"Why not?"

"Sold it," she said, her feet curled under her as she sat sideways on the passenger seat.

"Why?"

"So I could get rides with cute boys like you."

He couldn't suppress his amusement. She was incorrigible. She was easy, lighter than air. Judy was deeper, a river. He felt a twinge of — not guilt, perhaps regret at leaving when he did. He had to leave, for the chase team, but there could have been more time, more goodbyes, more something. There could have been more. It's just that he usually wanted less. Complications were unnecessary at this point in his life. And when he looked at Shannon, it was as if he saw Judy in another form, an idea of Judy, but this was Shannon, her own idea, and when he stopped thinking, the idea was an exhilarating one. He stole a glance at her lovely face, framed by the low, square neck of the sundress. Her cheeks were sprinkled with a few light freckles, and her eyes were icy, pale blue with a glimmer of gray, lighter than her sister's. Shannon wore lustrous eye makeup, pink lipstick and a sparkling barrette in her tousled blond hair. The barrette served no purpose, tamed nary a strand, but oh, did it sparkle.

"So you found a place for me, huh?" she asked.

"Yeah, I think you'll like it. It's a bunch of meteorology majors, girls."

"Aw, all girls?" she pouted, teasing.

"Yes, I'm afraid so."

"It would be so much more fun sleeping with boy meteorology majors."

"You have your own room," Jack said. "You won't be sleeping with the girls, unless, of course, you want to." He let that thought pass briefly, sweetly, through his hungry brain.

"Oh, no, I have to save my energy," she said.

"For what?"

"My first date with you."

He laughed. He couldn't help it. She made him laugh. She had a child's persistence and confidence in getting her lollipop. He kind of enjoyed being the stranger with candy. He didn't even have to offer; there she was, reaching for it.

Jack looked over at her again. "You and your sister aren't close, are you?"

"I know you don't want to talk about my sister," Shannon said. "I think, for the sake of both of our extremely small consciences, we'd better just pretend we met some other way."

"I found you on my doorstep, in a cardboard box, wrapped in a blanket," Jack said innocently, "a kitten in need of a home."

She purred, really purred, and he chuckled again. They were getting into the metro area now. A straight shot south through the city and a quick suburb or two later, and they'd be in Wishwell, the university town where he lived.

"Mind if I smoke?" he asked her.

She shook her head. He kept his left hand on the wheel and used his right to reach into the camera bag between the seats, rummaging for the cigarettes, not finding them right away. She reached in, too, played with his fingers, then pulled out the pack. She slipped the matches out, struck one, and lit the cigarette between those strawberry lips before handing it to him. It still had a trace of pink around the end.

"Thanks," he said, savoring the kiss of nicotine. He opened his window so he wouldn't smoke up the car. "You want one?"

"I don't smoke. I just light 'em up."

"I believe that," he replied.

"So when are you picking me up?"

"What? I still haven't dropped you off yet."

"You know, for our date," she said.

"I can't tonight," Jack said, changing lanes in the heavy traffic. "You heard. I have to get ready for tomorrow."

"Oh, that's fine," she said, seemingly indifferent. "I'm sure I can find some other diversion."

He didn't like to say it, but he thought maybe there should be a grace period of one day between sisters. "I have an idea," he said. "Are you really a good driver? Have your license and everything?"

"Of course I have my license," Shannon said. "Otherwise I'd have nothing to show when the bouncers card me."

"Can you follow orders?"

"I don't often, but I certainly can," she said. "Is this some sort of dominant-submissive exercise?"

"Maybe later," he said, grinning. "I'm trying to ask if you want to drive me tomorrow, in the caravan."

"You mean, on the storm chase?" she asked. "How cool! Really? I can be a storm chaser?"

"It's research," Jack said. "Tomorrow, we aren't chasers. We're researchers. Sometimes they get touchy about that." He was already wondering how he'd explain the addition to

Malik, but the professor usually cut him some slack. Besides, Giselle had been telling everyone on the team that there was no way *she'd* want to drive him again.

"You'll have to do exactly what I tell you when we get in the storm situation," Jack said.

"Really?" Shannon breathed, leaning toward him and grasping his knee, just close enough so her breasts touched his arm.

"And you can't do *that* tomorrow," he said, looking instinctively down her dress.

She sat back in her seat, laughing. "I'm a great driver," she said. "I once did eight months of pizza delivery without so much as a ticket, and that was in a college town, so you know I delivered a lot of pizza."

"Tornadoes are less forgiving than undergraduates," he said, "and they won't respond to your charms."

"I'll be no-nonsense with the tornadoes," Shannon said as Jack exited the highway and headed up Main Street, on the way to the women's house. "My charms are not aimed at the tornadoes."

Jack looked over at her again. Being with her was like eating cotton candy. She wasn't necessarily good for him, but she melted in his mouth. I'm in trouble, he thought, trouble any way you look at it. Either tomorrow will be a disaster, or it'll be great, and if it's great, I'll have no reason to reject her.

Not that he wanted to.

At the door of the one-story brick house, on a quiet, tree-lined side street, he hopped out and got her bag out of the trunk. "This is all you have?" he asked.

"I have some stuff at a friend's place. I'll get it later," Shannon said, taking the bag from him. "I'm sure he'll pick me up."

"I'm sure," Jack said, giving her a sidelong glance as he got back in the car. "Giselle and the others know you're coming. Let me know if there's trouble. Here," he said, and she leaned into the passenger window to take his business card, one he'd printed up to show his research and chasing credentials.

"I can take care of myself," she said.

"I'll come get you tomorrow at 7 a.m."

"That should give me at least three hours' sleep," Shannon said playfully, then turned around, sauntered up the sidewalk and entered the house without even knocking.

"Fearless," Jack said to himself as he watched her go. Then he hit the gas, speeding back toward his apartment.

❧

THAT MORNING, after they left, Judy spent about fifteen minutes sitting on the couch, feeling her mural glowering behind her back and not wanting to touch it. Then she spent about twenty minutes on her swing in the garden, but the place that usually soothed her just annoyed her, and the boy in the fountain seemed to be laughing at her expense.

She spent the whole time trying not to think. She didn't want to think about Jack, about Shannon, about tomorrow, about last night. Finally, the best way to avoid thinking seemed to be working, so she threw herself into it. She grabbed a thumb drive of files and headed to Snap Happy Photo, her old employer. Kyle was working the counter. They went out on a couple of dates in high school, before he figured out he was gay. They'd been friends ever since. He'd never given her a good reason why he still stayed in Pancake. He had even fewer potential mates than she did.

"Judy!" he greeted her. His red hair was buzzed to a whisper, and he wore hoop earrings in both pale ears. "What have you got for me today?"

"I need a few canvas wraps. Portrait jobs."

"You still doing regular prints at home?" Kyle said, taking her drive and writing on the work-order envelope before he dropped it in.

"Up to a certain size. I still come to you for the big ones."

"Hmmm, you have six of them ... I can have them done in a few days, unless you have a rush job. Will that be OK? Oh, and that twenty by thirty frame job will be ready this afternoon."

"Sure. Great," she said, and her low energy made his already arched eyebrows rise.

"Are you sick or something?"

"Maybe I am," she said. "Maybe that's my problem."

"Uh-oh. Sounds like a story."

"For another day, Kyle," she said. "I'll be back in a while to get the big pic, OK?"

"Sure, baby," he said. "Go get yourself a milk shake or something."

That sounded pretty good. She drove to The Filling Station and got herself a vanilla shake, no whipped cream, then drove by the hardware store.

Greg was working, as usual, and her Uncle Ray was in the back office. She waved at her cousin and walked past the gardening supplies and shelves of car gadgets to reach her uncle's lair. His desk was covered with binders and papers, accented by a green toy tractor, a pencil holder made of an old coffee can and a scratched brass and wood nameplate that said "Raymond Hale." The window that let him look out on the store was nearly covered with schedules, flyers and platitudes, taped up and flapping in the breeze of the ancient oscillating fan.

"How are you doing?" she asked.

"I'm not bad." He looked for all the world like his brother, her father, with his paunch and kind gray eyes and thinning brown hair, halfway combed over. "You're a sight for sore eyes. Why don't you come and see us?"

"I come by here all the time."

"I mean come by the house. I've turned into quite a cook, you know." Always, there was that reminder; Aunt Kate had been the cook, and when the tornado took her, Uncle Ray had learned how to do everything and still help Judy's dad run the store. Later, Ray had bought out her dad's share, and here he was, still in Pancake and strangely happy about it.

"I need a concrete invitation," Judy said. "But you know how it is this time of year. I'm busy."

"Yeah, entertaining guests, right?" For a moment, Judy thought he was talking about Jack, and her stomach hurt. "I saw your sister when she dropped by a couple of days ago. Is she still staying with you?"

Judy put on what she hoped was a blank face. "She left."

"Did she buy that motorcycle she was talking about?"

"No," Judy said. "She got a ride back to Oklahoma City."

"Never sits still for long, that one. I never understood how she and my Kate got along so well, but there it was. Of course, Shannon isn't the girl she was then." He looked somber for a moment, then smiled. "Hey, I got in some of them sunflower seeds you like, the mini ones in different colors. Take a packet."

"Oh, I'll buy it," Judy said, stepping out of his office.

"No, no, take a packet," Uncle Ray said, getting up and coming out the door, too. He shouted up to Greg. "Get Judy a packet of them seeds I told you about!" Ray turned back to her and gave her a small, awkward hug. "Don't be a stranger."

Funny he should say that. Her hometown did feel strange to her today. The outside world was encroaching. She took the packet of seeds from Greg, giving him a pained smile, and got back in her car. She drove to the edge of town, to the windmill park, and pulled up in one of the gravel spaces. She couldn't make herself get out of the car. Even this place, her beautiful oasis, was corrupted by the memory of just yesterday and a feeling of failure. Her aversion would pass, she knew, but today, she was too upset to go through those gates. She angled her seat back and dozed off in the warm and spotty sunshine. There were more clouds today, with more moisture ahead of the cold front, and she dreamed she was among them, riding a white and fluffy cumulus, looking down on Jack as he slept naked on another cloud, drifting away from her. She looked far below, where the lakes were blue jewels, and saw Shannon as a child in one of them, out of proportion, nearly filling up the pond. Her sister's hair was fine and bright. She was chubby, happy, the baby Judy remembered. The toddler Shannon splashed as she took a bath in the sapphire water, laughing, playing with plastic dollhouse furniture, it looked like. Judy strained to see. The little white chairs and table and bed were broken into sharp pieces.

Judy awoke with a start. Forty-five minutes gone. It was enough. She headed back to Snap Happy and picked up the framed photo, destined for a nice commission sale, then drove home.

She was in the middle of processing the Grenoble portraits on the high-powered Mac in her studio when her cell phone rang.

"Judy Hale," she said, trying to sound perky. It could be business, and she needed some.

"Well, how the *Hale* are you?" came the male voice. She couldn't quite place it.

"Um, fine," she said. "What can I do for you?"

"You don't know who this is, do you?" he said. "I'm hurt, really hurt."

It dawned on her. "Robinson! I'm sorry. Don't be hurt. I think all my pistons aren't firing today."

"What's wrong with you? It's a gorgeous day, and we're going to have storms tomorrow."

"Where are you?"

"Wichita, but tomorrow, I'm on my way to see you, that is, if you tell me where you live. I remember it's Pancake, but I'm sure I'll never locate you in that vast metropolis. We *have* to go chasing tomorrow."

"Oh, I don't know, Robinson," she said, getting up and walking the phone over to the studio window. Her garden looked peaceful in the late afternoon.

"Come on, Judy. Bruce and Whit stood me up. They said it didn't look that great to them, and they have real jobs, poor bastards."

She smiled a little. "So do you."

"Web designer, freelance writer, man about town ... hardly a real job," he said. "Anyway, I'm on vacation. Are you working a wedding this weekend?"

"Oddly enough, no," she said. "The next few are booked, though. What is it about this year? All the storms are on weekends. Anyway, I have other work to do. I really shouldn't go."

Part of her wanted to, but she didn't feel up to it after having her misplaced hopes crushed.

Robinson persisted. "Something's going on here. You are not your usual self."

"I just feel numb right now, and dumb, to boot." She wasn't sure she wanted to tell him everything, but she felt herself giving in to his friendly interest. She needed a friend.

"Why dumb?"

"I think I've just been the victim of a romantic hit and run," she admitted, "only I think it's partly my fault, because I stepped in front of the car."

"Oh." She could almost hear the wheels turning. "It was that guy, wasn't it?" he asked after a moment. "The one we met in Childress?"

Judy was stunned. "How did you know?"

Robinson laughed. "You two had that googly-eyed vibe. I could tell something was up the next morning when you were so distracted over breakfast."

"You kill me," Judy said. "And here I was thinking that men weren't observant."

"None are as observant as I am, of course," Robinson said, making her chuckle. "Anyway, don't feel dumb. We all do dumb things in the pursuit of love."

"I guess so. I just hate myself for hoping."

"It's either that or kill yourself. Besides, tomorrow, your hope is better spent on the chase. Storms have no emotional hangups. They don't have intentions. They just exist. They arise, they may terrorize, but they are completely beyond our control."

"And definitely not interested in dating," Judy said.

"That's right," he said. "They put us in our place, but you never run into them at a restaurant with someone else hanging on their arm. So come on, you'll feel less dumb if you go chasing with me tomorrow."

"All right, Robinson," Judy said, feeling a little better. "You're very persuasive, you know."

"I'm just channeling Mother Nature," he said. "Email me the address, OK? Mother Nature can't help me with navigation."

BRAD TREAT WAS out for redemption. Thor's Tours was nearing the end of a two-week session, and with a sparkling new windshield, his rented van was ready for whatever nature could throw his way. He just needed to learn to catch.

He had the same tour group, on its last two days of vacation, and they were grouchy after several days without storms and no real tornado to brag about. Two of the tourists, a couple from New York, had left already in disgust. He'd tapped into his limited funds to treat the rest to a day at Six Flags Over Texas, and that had cheered them up a little, except Noel, who spent the day throwing up corn dogs after riding one of the big roller coasters.

At least that was one day Brad had saved money on gas. With prices the way they were, he figured he almost broke even. And he'd had a chance to spend a night at home in Fort Worth while the tourists stayed at yet another cheap motel with a number in the name, though Willa wasn't exactly happy to see him. They'd had robotic sex anyway, which was about all he hoped for anymore.

Now, however, he had to produce a storm. At least a storm. He was no longer hopeful about getting a tornado. Even the most experienced chasers missed them sometimes, but Brad had a plan to enlist the most experienced chasers, though they didn't know it.

He'd found a university student clued in to this year's mesonet experiment, and he'd traded beer for information. In short, Brad had the radio frequency used by the caravan, and he planned to stick with the researchers like glue. He'd made a trip to Oklahoma, to the severe storms lab in the university town where the mesonet was based, in the guise of getting his tourists a look at the Storm Prediction Center. The lab wouldn't let them in. The public affairs lady blamed security in the age of terrorism. They bought T-shirts there instead, then spent a miserable afternoon at the Cowboy Museum. For god's sake, he thought, how many fucking pictures of cowboys can a person look at?

It would all be worth it today. This was the day they were following the chase team into glory.

Brad knew from his source that the chasers' target was the Kansas-Nebraska border, and they were leaving painfully early. He banged on the doors of all his tourists at 6 a.m. so they'd be ready to go. He lingered in the doorway of the room shared by Pinky and her nose-ringed friend, chatting them up and checking out their little sleeper T-shirts and bare legs, then moved on to get his van gassed up and ready for what he expected could be a five-hour trip to the zone.

It was about 7 a.m. when they threw their bags in the back and piled in, rubbing their eyes, some lugging big cups of coffee and doughnuts from the Krispy Kreme. As they sat in the motel parking lot in the early morning light, sleepy and murmuring, Brad turned on the new handheld scanner he'd bought. He realized he'd left the manual at home. The radio had so many buttons. He had no idea what they meant. He didn't want to scan, anyway; he just wanted to get that one frequency. After five minutes of button-pushing and cursing, he finally looked up at Noel, who was riding shotgun and barely containing his amused snorts.

"Well?" Brad said crossly.

"Give it to me," Noel said. "What do you want it to do?"

"Just tune in this channel," Brad said, handing over the scribbled napkin he'd been carrying around in his wallet.

"No problem," Noel said.

In a minute, the radio was tuned, the mag-mount antenna on the roof was clearly working, and Brad was rolling toward the mesonet's staging area. It was easy enough to follow the caravan onto the Interstate. The heavily instrumented cars and vans looked like a mad scientist's road show. Radio chatter was infrequent as they headed north through Oklahoma and into Kansas. The tourists sang "99 Bottles of Beer on the Wall," and Brad seriously considered suicide.

"I need a bathroom break," Juicy said from the back as they exited Wichita. He'd been drinking juice, not coffee like the others, but the coffee drinkers chimed in. They all wanted a rest.

"I can't stop," Brad said, eyeing the caravan in front of him. The university's cars were moving faster than he expected, and he didn't want to lose them.

"What do you want us to do?" asked Pinky. "Pee in our cups?" Her hair, which was dark pink and wet this morning, now was bright pink and sticking straight up as it dried.

"Do you want a good storm," Brad said, "or a crappy one?"

"Do you want a fresh van," Pinky said, "or one that smells like crap?"

Brad weighed the alternatives. "Damn it," he said. "OK, you have five minutes. *Five minutes.*" He pulled off at the next exit and waited for fifteen while they all took turns using the single bathroom at the dingiest gas station he'd ever seen. He ran across the street to the diner and used its restroom, then hurried back to top off the tank. He got back in the van to listen to the scanner. They were losing the research team. "Hurry. Hurry!" he shouted at the tourists still lingering outside, eating their chips and drinking their colas. Great. They'll have to pee again, he thought.

He got them all in, peeled out of the parking lot and took the ramp to the highway. Noel actually seemed interested in what he was hearing on the scanner. The balding meteorologist had started doing his own daily severe-storm forecasts, a twist on the humdrum TV weather scripts he'd been writing in Georgia. This was the first day since last weekend that Noel had been optimistic about their chances. Even though Brad resented that Noel knew more about weather than he did, he took some heart in his forecast.

The problem now was that the caravan could barely be heard at all on the radio. Heading up 135, Brad floored it. For ten minutes, he thought he might actually be gaining on them.

He heard the siren first, then looked in his rearview mirror and saw the blue lights. "Uh-oh," said Old Blue Eyes, the guy in the blue-tinted sunglasses sitting with Juicy in the back.

Ten long minutes later, the $140 ticket stuffed in the glove compartment, Brad continued north on the highway at a more reasonable pace. If they caught up, they caught up. The caravan would have to stop somewhere.

He was right. In an hour, as they neared Salina, the radio chatter began coming in a lot more clearly. The mesonet was in town. He heard them mention the name of the truck stop and pulled off at that exit.

"What, peeing so soon?" Pinky asked. She'd gotten a lot more smart-alecky since the windmill incident.

"Enjoy it while it lasts," Brad said. "In fact, you might want to buy a couple of diapers while we're here, because I don't know when we'll stop again."

Most of the tourists laughed, but Pinky stuck her tongue out at him.

Brad spotted the mesonet's cars as he pulled into the Mega-Oasis truck stop. It was the type that had a big store filled with CB gear, plastic flowers, bobble heads, convenience items, books on tape and CD, porn rentals and junk food. It also had a food court, trucker showers, a lounge and wireless Internet.

Brad parked near the caravan. A few of the university types appeared to be outside. He suspected the rest were inside, strategizing. At least he hoped so. To avoid looking like a complete moocher, he grabbed his laptop bag and headed in to see what he could overhear while he pretended to check data.

❧

"OF ALL THE trucks stops in all the towns in all the world," Judy said to Robinson as he pulled his yellow SUV into the Mega-Oasis in Salina. There it was, the mesonet. And with it, she was sure, Jack.

"It wasn't intentional," Robinson said. "Do you want to try another one?"

"No, of course not. I mean, I'm a grown-up, right?"

"A grown-up who looks kind of like Pippi Longstocking."

"Oh, shut up," she said good-naturedly. "My parents named me after Judy Garland."

"Great Braids Through History," Robinson intoned.

"You know they're cute," she said, steeling herself for the inevitable. "Shall we go in?"

They hopped out and took Robinson's laptop along.

It was good to see him again. Had it been just five days since their last chase? His wavy light-brown hair was tamed by his black film festival hat, and his brown eyes were shaded by hip black sunglasses. He wore a black T-shirt to match, and khaki shorts. When he wasn't smiling, a smile seemed always about to appear, his dimples always emerging. He was fun on a road trip, laid-back and open to everything he saw around him. He had a habit of honking at every cow they saw. It cracked her up.

Inside the truck stop, Judy entered the bathroom and chose the one stall of three that was open. She had an unsettled feeling, and it wasn't just from the dubious cleanliness of the public restroom. She heard an occupant of another stall clump out. As Judy washed her hands in the sink, she checked out her V-neck white T-shirt and khaki shorts in the mirror. Still crisp and clean. She was reaching for a paper towel when the other stall opened and someone familiar emerged.

Judy couldn't quite believe her eyes. It was Shannon, totally out of context.

"Sis!" Shannon said as she washed her hands. "This *is* a coincidence."

"What are you doing here?"

Shannon pulled a white comb out of her pink backpack and started teasing her shiny hair as she looked in the mirror. "I'm a storm chaser today!" she said.

"A storm chaser? By yourself?" Judy asked, knowing that couldn't be true.

"Duh! No, I'm with the university guys," Shannon said, smoothing her little pink tank top and short denim skirt. She put her comb away and gave Judy a quick hug. "Gotta go, sweetie," she said, then disappeared through the door.

Judy was conflicted, not happy knowing that Shannon could only be here because of Jack, but also amazed that Shannon would take an interest in anything Judy loved to do. Strange how things worked out.

She walked into the bustling, brightly lit eating area and spotted Robinson in his cap, sitting at one of the tables, his laptop open. She sat next to him as he flipped through pages of satellite and radar images, forecast discussions and surface maps. "Nice wireless here," he said.

"I just saw my sister."

"What?" He sounded surprised. "You have a sister? Does she work here or something?"

Judy laughed in spite of herself. "No. I guess I didn't tell you the whole story. When, um, when Jack left my place, he took my sister with him."

"No shit. Did she live with you?" Robinson asked.

"No, she was just visiting."

"Huh," Robinson said. "Of all the truck stops in all the towns in all the world."

"Exactly," Judy said. She gave her head a shake, trying to clear the cobwebs, trying not to look around for Jack. "So, how does it look?"

"I'm not sure the timing of this thing is going to be all we hoped," Robinson said. "That upper-level disturbance won't come through until after dark. Until then, we might be fighting the cap, or we might have crap. However, you can see a few clouds starting to bubble along the front." He pointed to just south of the Nebraska border on the gray-and-white satellite image. "We'll know more in a couple of hours, I guess."

"We might want to get farther north," Judy said.

"I don't think there's a big rush yet," Robinson said. "At least here we have data."

"Yeah," Judy said, a bit sarcastically, "and all the discomforts of home."

"Might as well relax. This is chasing. Hurry up and wait."

They ordered a couple of subs and talked about their options. They would wait and check data again here before committing to anything. After they ate, they went out to his car in the big parking lot to hang out for a while. He cranked up Elvis Costello on the sound system, and they leaned back in their seats and watched the movement of people and cars and trucks around them. Judy, especially, watched the mesonet, its people and its cars' anemometers, spinning in the healthy breeze. Southeast wind, at least, she thought.

Then she saw him. She knew she would.

"I just need one minute," she said to Robinson.

"That looks like a lying dog best left sleeping," Robinson replied as he lounged in the driver's seat, "but do you what you have to do."

Judy got out of the car and walked slowly toward Jack, not sure of what to say, only knowing she wanted clarification. He was alone, leaning against one of the cars, smoking, idly looking over the parking lot. A few of his colleagues were milling nearby. He spotted her out of the corner of his eye when she was still several yards away and turned his head to face her, taking a long drag and exhaling as she approached, staring her down with those glittering green eyes.

"Jack."

"Judy," he replied, cordial and cool.

"I ran into Shannon inside."

"Yeah, she wanted to try chasing," Jack said, "so today, she's driving me."

"What?" Judy was taken aback. "Driving? You know she's never done this before."

"It doesn't matter," Jack said nonchalantly. "She can handle it. She's good at following directions."

Judy took a few steps closer to him, close enough so she could smell his smoke and aftershave. She was torn between anger and concern for Shannon, and now, aware of his body, she was disconcerted being this close to him again.

"Be careful, Jack," she said in a low voice, so none of the others around could hear. "I mean it. Be careful."

"How do you mean it?" Jack asked deliberately, looking her dead in the eye, his voice subtly teasing, obviously aware of the sexual charge still between them.

Judy found herself distracted and agitated.

"You know what I mean," she said, then walked away.

Perhaps she meant more than even she realized. She got back into Robinson's car and slammed the door. She was silent for a few minutes. "Welcome to the Working Week" began playing on the stereo. *I hope it doesn't kill me, too, Elvis,* she mentally responded to the lyrics.

"I can't believe he has her driving," she said. "She's never even chased storms before. It's dangerous, you know?"

"I know," Robinson said, his eyes closed and arms crossed as he leaned back and listened to the music. "At least he's chased a lot. As long as she's not making the decisions, she should be OK."

"If I can be sure about anything," Judy said, "it's Shannon's inability to make a decision."

"She'll be all right," Robinson said. He opened his eyes and looked over at Judy. "Will you?"

"I'm just fine," Judy said, her eyes suddenly moist as Robinson's kindness triggered a release she'd resisted. With a deep breath, she sucked in her anger and disappointment and tried to transform her feelings into strength. "Let's check data again. I want to find a storm."

WHEN THE ATMOSPHERE kicked into gear, chasers forgot everything else. Jack saw some unaffiliated chasers leave the truck stop first, and soon after he conferred with Malik and the others, their caravan was on the road again, too. Their target was west of Concordia, where they thought they could intercept the most promising point in the line. It was going to be a line, it appeared from the radar and satellite data. There was too much simultaneous development on the front, which now draped across the northern Kansas border. They had to hope for a cell to dominate, perhaps break away, if they wanted to see a tornado.

They headed north on Route 81. Shannon drove Jack in the lead car, as she had all day. They didn't say much. He suspected neither wanted to admit they'd seen Judy. Instead, Jack pointed out the developing anvils north of them and tried to explain what they were looking for. Shannon didn't seem that interested in the storms, but she was still interested in him. That was clear from her occasional glances, from her body language. It was a language he liked to read.

"That van's following awfully close," she said after a while. "Can you tell them to back off?"

Jack looked over his shoulder. It was a white van, but he didn't recognize the driver, and it didn't have any instruments on the roof. "That's not one of ours," he said. "I think I saw him back at the truck stop. He's got a van full of people. Might be a chase tour."

"People pay to do this?"

"Everyone pays to do this, between the gas and the hotels and the gear. But some people pay a lot more. Some tours are worth it for newbies. A lucky tourist can see more in a week than some veterans see in five years."

"Well, this guy is so close, he can't be seeing anything except my ass."

"And what a magnificent view," Jack joked.

She smiled. "You don't know the half of it."

As they continued north, Jack kept an eye on the van. The driver had a focused expression. Constipated, really. The guy wouldn't pass, and he was tailgating hard.

Jack radioed back to Professor Malik and Sam Rainier and their crew, who were in the van behind the interloper. "FC, any idea who that bozo is behind us?"

Rainier, sounding like the cowboy he was, responded. "It says 'Thor's Tours' on the back. He's a dang idiot for driving that close."

"Cute," Jack said. "I guess he can't find his own way."

"Wouldn't be the first time," Rainier said. "Jack, teams, we're going to angle west on 24. We can always shoot north afterward. The storms are trying, but they still aren't going gangbusters yet. There's one with potential, though. If I had to guess, I'd say we'll meet up with our storm of the day in Smith County, maybe around Harlan."

Rainier rarely guessed. He had an instinct for these things. "Sounds good," Jack said. "Probe 3 out."

Just then, the white tour van whipped around their car and sped ahead of them toward the junction with 24, then zoomed west.

"Holy cow," Shannon said.

"I think he heard us."

"How?"

"Radio. Anyway, I hope he heard us call him an idiot."

"Yeah," Shannon said. "It's probably not the first time he's heard that."

Jack chuckled.

As they turned west, the sky ahead and to their right seemed darker, more ominous, a wall of gray. The storms were developing, but they probably wouldn't get the kind of tornadic supercell Jack wanted. Still, they might get a show, and it would be a good way to break Shannon in.

As they crossed the northern tip of Waconda Lake, Jack looked at the atlas. "You know what's coming up, don't you?" he asked.

"What?"

"Cawker City."

"And why should I care?"

"You're a Kansas girl, aren't you? Surely you've seen the world's largest ball of twine?"

She laughed, a giddy, chiming sound. "That's right!" she said. "I was only about six years old, though. I think it was smaller then."

"Well, you'll have to look quick, because we don't have time to stop," he said. "I think it'll be on the left."

They got into town and slowed down. Shannon and Jack looked for the ball of twine. He'd seen it before, on a slow chase day, but it had been a few years. As they came over a small rise, they saw the funny little pavilion on the left — and several people in the wide street. The white tour van that had passed them earlier was parked on the right.

"Watch out," Jack said.

Shannon slowed a little, thinking the way was clear. It was, for a moment. Then a young woman with pink hair, waving a camera, ran from where she'd been hidden behind the van and dashed right in front of their car, followed closely by a tall, skinny guy Jack recognized as the driver.

Shannon screamed, hit the brakes and turned right all at once. She ended up scooting between the stunned people and the van and bumped over the curb before coming to a halt. Their chase car had three of four wheels in the grass of what looked like an herb and flower garden, in front of a weather-beaten, perhaps once yellow-brick, building that housed the ball of twine gift shop, across the street from the pavilion.

Jack immediately picked up the radio. "Probe 3 to all teams. Slow down, guys. Bunch of people in the street. We ran off the road, but we're OK. We'll catch up in a minute."

He looked at Shannon. She was breathing fast, but she was laughing, too. "You sure know how to show a girl a good time," she said.

"You're OK?"

"We're OK," she said, flashing him that beautiful smile and a thumbs-up, though he thought maybe her hand was shaking. He was captivated by her bravado and suddenly angry. That idiot had put her, him, all of them in danger. He leaned over and kissed her quickly on the cheek, inhaling her perfume, then kissed her again in the same place, more gently. "I'll be right back. Then we'll get out of here."

"OK. I'm just going to learn to breathe again."

Jack was pissed. As the cars of the mesonet whizzed by, he looked across the street and saw his target, the tall guy standing in front of the pavilion with a group of sheepish people he assumed were the tourists, including the pink-haired girl. She hid behind the giant ball of twine when she saw Jack crossing the street, but he didn't care about her. She might be stupid, but the guy in charge was responsible. Jack walked up to the young man and got in his face.

"You need to be a lot more careful," Jack said.

"You were the ones who almost hit us!" the young man said.

"No," Jack said. "You are the ones who ran in front of our goddamn car. What's your name?"

"Brad."

"Brad what?"

"Brad Treat. Why?"

"Just taking note for future reference. I'm Jack Andreas, a name you should also note for future reference. You running a tour here?"

"Yes, I am."

"Then you need to get your head out of your ass and, if possible, keep your people off the road. In fact, you shouldn't be on the road either. You're a hazard."

"We have the same right to be on the road as you do," Brad said, full of nasal indignation. "We're professional storm chasers, too."

Jack gave him The Look, the one that made undergrads quail.

"Do you hear that?" Jack asked. Brad cocked his head, then shook it slowly, not sure what he was supposed to be listening for. "That's the sound of me not giving a fuck. If I ever see you again, if you ever get in my way, I will personally kick your ass."

Brad was only a little slighter than Jack and even an inch or two taller, but he didn't have the steel. "I'm outta here," Brad said, trying to sound tough, then shouted for the tourists to get in the van. In a moment, after carefully looking both ways and walking across the street to their ride, they peeled out, heading west, and Jack exhaled some of his anger in a sigh.

"Are you all right?" he asked Shannon when he got back to the car.

"I'm fine," she said. "Your friend Professor Malik and that cowboy guy were calling on the radio. I told them we were OK. I guess I should just back this out of here, huh?"

"Sure," he said. "You still have one wheel on the street. Not much of a curb. These cars have seen worse. The tires look OK. Just look both ways. Try not to nail any tourists."

Shannon laughed, a little nervously. "If they survived the last five minutes, I think they have a good chance of making it through the day."

"You must be great at dodgeball."

"I told you," she said, "I'm an excellent driver." She backed out the way she'd so suddenly come, then put the car in drive and headed west.

"Good," Jack said. "I'm not letting you off the hook. Now we have to catch up."

"You are really making me work hard to get my first date with you," she said as they drove out of town. He heard thunder.

"You don't think of this as a date? It's got all the elements. Excitement. Danger."

"Sex?" she asked, glancing at him suggestively.

Jack felt a tingle of arousal he would rather put off till later. "At least not while the professor's looking," he said.

"YOU KNOW WHAT THIS IS?" Robinson looked north into the oncoming blast, holding on to his hat, as his baggy khaki shorts and black T-shirt whipped in the wind. He and Judy stood in the center of a desolate intersection of three dusty farm roads that cut through emerald green grass and brown fields. Nearby, a tiny, abandoned stone house with roof and windows gone stood next to a stripped and skeletal tree and a rusted old plow, the only signs of long-gone life here. All this flat spot in northern Kansas needed was a talking scarecrow.

"What would you call it?" Judy, exhilarated, shouted into the growing gusts. Both had their video cameras on tripods, facing the undulating wall of reddish-brown dust moving ominously toward them.

"This is a haboob!" Robinson said.

"Maybe it's a derecho!" Judy replied.

"A gust front?"

"The end of the world?"

"This is *so* Dust Bowl," he shouted back.

The rolling gust front stretched from horizon to horizon, a seething mass of dirt and wind. It was the colossal blowout of the line of storms, which had collapsed all their energy into this rampaging outflow. Now the derecho was gaining power as it rolled south, carrying curtains of earth with it.

Judy's adrenaline rose with the wind. It was the same feeling that made chickens hide and dogs howl, she suspected, a natural reaction to the drop in pressure and nature's keening.

They'd done a quick check on their phones during a stop in the last town, and the radar loop showed the storms melding and expiring, throwing down this violent line. It was nearly all wind. So they hurriedly drove west, away from civilization, and found this photogenic open spot. Here, they would let it overtake them.

As the gust front got closer, Judy began to see more detail — the blue-green in its depths, the ruddy roiling of the dust at its base, the occasional dark gustnadoes it spit out in front of it. It was glorious.

"This would make a great horror movie," Robinson said as he turned his camera to catch a gustnado off to their east.

"The Wicked Wind of the West," Judy said in her best dramatic-narrator voice, snapping still photos of the roofless house with the monster behind it.

"More like northwest," Robinson said. "Hey! You can film me! I've been wanting to make a short film. It'll be funny."

"What are you talking about?" Judy asked. They were getting hit by the first flecks of dirt and pebbles and grass from the gust front. It was nearly upon them.

"Just film me. Your camera is better than mine. You'll know what to do."

"OK," Judy said, already grabbing her camera. She tossed her tripod in the back seat of his car and hopped in the passenger side as the dirt started stinging their bare legs and faces.

"Here!" Robinson said, handing her his camera and hat as she got in. "Stow these somewhere." He tossed his tripod in the back, then slammed the door and stood in front of the car, hands on hips, awaiting the worst of it in the middle of the empty intersection.

"Holy crap," Judy said, amused. "He's nuts." She had a perfect view out the front window, facing into the derecho. The wall of churning dust began to consume the car, peppering it with dirt, gravel, tumbleweeds and almost no rain. Robinson jumped up and down far enough from the car so she could get a good shot out the windshield. He did the mime-fighting-the-wind routine, only it was for real. Then he pretended to flee from it. He ran up to her window, beating on the glass as if he were trying to get in, then ran into the wind and ran away again, feigning terror as bits of grass pelted him. He stuck his arms out like a scarecrow and stood stiffly as the wind whipped his clothes. Then he tried to shield his eyes and flailed blindly in the gale. A couple of small branches from the old tree whipped by, and one smacked him on the arm. Judy could see him mouth "Ow!" as she filmed and had to stifle a giggle. After two minutes, it was too much even for him, and he clambered to the driver's side, struggled to pull the door open against the howling onslaught, and got in. Even in those few moments before he slammed the door, a fine coating of dust blew in and settled on everything.

"Wow!" he said, breathing heavily, delighted and high from the adventure. "What a sandblast! I want to do that again, but I hate grit in my teeth."

Judy laughed. "This video is *awesome*," she said over the persistent pounding of the storm.

"I can't wait to see it. We'll make a short film, OK?"

"We? I thought *you* wanted to make a short film."

"Oh, you know you do," Robinson said. "We just have to figure out the, um—"

"Plot?" Judy asked innocently.

"No, silly, artists don't need plots!" he said. "But it might need a point. I'll think about it."

"OK." Judy filmed out the windows as the wind kept howling, and he picked up his camera and filmed out his side. There was little rain, just the constant barrage of dust and tiny windblown objects.

"Whoa!" he said suddenly. She looked over to see what got

his attention. Down the road that extended west, a couple of power poles suddenly leaned hard, blown half over by the wind. Judy filmed them as a few more down the line listed more and more southward. In a minute, about six crashed onto the road, including one just behind them. In moments, it was over, the wind already dying down.

"Damn!" Judy said. "We are really lucky we're on this side of the road."

"Planning, not luck," Robinson said with an air of authority.

Judy raised an eyebrow at him, and he yielded.

"OK, luck," he admitted. "That was unreal. Let's go see what else this thing did."

They turned around and tried to figure out whether it was safe to cross the downed lines. The strange three-road intersection offered them an out, and after a little diagonal reconnoitering, they were soon back on the main road that would lead them east into the nearby town.

What they found was surprising. The straight-line winds had blown out the glass in the old movie theater marquee and in several other signs. Shingles were everywhere. A drive-in burger place's sign had blown over, along with fences, mailboxes and the like. The power was out, and just on the other side of town, a tractor-trailer truck had been tossed on its side.

"Maybe we should have filmed here," Robinson said.

"Yeah, and you would have had your head taken off by a flying shingle," Judy said.

"Good point," Robinson said. "I need my head."

The sky showed the first pinks of sunset. The chase was over. "You need me to drive for a while, Dust Bowl Boy?" she asked.

"Sure. Let's get to the next town with power and grab dinner and some gas, and then you can drive us home."

"Home? Oh, yeah. My home."

"Sure," Robinson said. "Then we can see if tomorrow's worth chasing. I mean, you don't mind if I camp on your floor or something, do you?"

"I have a guest room," Judy said. "As a matter of fact, I think all men are staying in the guest room from now on."

"That's much better than I expected," Robinson said, trying to wipe dust off his face and shirt as he turned south. "I thought all men would be sleeping in the garage."

"I'm still entertaining that option," Judy said with mock severity. Still, she had to acknowledge to herself that she wasn't all that sulky right now. A good chase went a long way toward putting the whole man thing in perspective. When she found a man as appealing as a storm, she would know that she'd found the right one.

Robinson started singing that cheesy song from *Dirty Dancing*, "She's Like the Wind," in the worst fake opera voice she'd ever heard.

It made her giggle, and as he wailed on, she couldn't stop laughing.

❧

MARCUS SAW that Jack was in a bad mood. None of them were too happy, given how the storms had crapped out, except maybe that new girl who drove Jack today. She always seemed to have a coy remark on her lips. Pretty lips, Marcus thought. And damn, that short skirt. Not the usual field gear. He saw there was something between her and Jack. Shannon Hale was her name.

Marcus had heard of another Hale, another woman who chased, a rare enough thing, but this apparently wasn't her. And it wasn't exactly clear if Shannon was a chaser or just another one of those dalliers who hang around for a while and then can't take the driving and the boredom that filled the long stretches between storms.

They were at a chain restaurant in Salina, the kind that served Mexican and American and whatever you wanted to call big, fatty portions that hit the spot after a long chase. Most of the team had returned to the hotel, but Marcus, Dennis, Jack and Shannon lingered at the restaurant's square bar. It was a little too brightly lit, decorated with mass-purchased, eclectic memorabilia that seemed to have no actual connection with anyone's memory. The TVs were playing old sitcom reruns silently while pop music played. They'd been drinking for almost two hours, hashing over today's and other chases.

"It almost did it today," Jack said, sipping perhaps his seventh glass of beer, not that Marcus was counting. It was one of the darker brews on tap. "That storm was trying to get it together. It had a halfhearted wall cloud. It wanted to."

"But not bad enough," Marcus said, nursing a bottle of Mexican beer. "The updraft was weak. Sad hail core."

"It was pathetic," Jack agreed. "It didn't have time to get its act together. That fucking line overtook it."

"It was a storm, wasn't it?" Shannon asked, looking right at Jack with an interest that made Marcus want to loosen his tie, even though he wasn't wearing one. "You'd think it was a sunny day, the way you were cursing. It's kind of fun to see you pushed to the edge of sanity." Mischief twinkled around her pale, gray-blue eyes as she took another healthy sip of her margarita.

"Perhaps now is not the time to push that particular button," Jack said in a low voice, but he returned her gaze and didn't look away.

"At least the hail catcher stayed on in that wind," said Dennis, staring at Sergeant Friday on the closest TV, oblivious to the mating ritual, quaffing one cola after another. A caffeine addict, he'd recently turned legal but never seemed interested in their occasional stops at the Cloudy Cow, one of their crowd's favorite bars back home. Dennis did look uncomfortable perched on the bar stool. His girth wasn't meant for those little round seats.

"Of course the basket stayed on," Marcus said, pushing his glasses up his nose. "I told you, it's going to take a lot more than a little wind to knock it off now."

"I measured eighty-four miles per hour," Jack said. Tornado strength, Marcus noted silently, only all in a straight line.

"So what's next?" Marcus asked. "Are we going to try again tomorrow?"

"I think we're going to make that decision in the morning," Jack said. He was playing with Shannon's fingers, which were delicately wrapped around the stem of her wet glass. She started moving her fingers slowly up and down the stem as she stared at Jack. *Very* distracting.

"OK," Marcus said, trying to pretend he didn't notice. "I'm calling it a night. You guys OK to drive?"

"I'm stopping with this one," Shannon said, though she sounded a little iffy already. "I'll be fine."

Marcus hesitated. He didn't feel he was in a position to grab Jack's keys. Even though they were friends, there was a pecking order, and Jack was top rooster. Plus he wasn't sure whether an intrusion would be welcome at this point, given the heat emanating from Jack and Shannon's end of the bar.

"I can drive these guys," Dennis said suddenly, to Marcus's relief. "I mean, I've been drinking Coke all night. And I want to get back to the hotel and catch more of this *Dragnet* marathon, where I can hear the sound. This show is hilarious. I think I've memorized every one."

"That explains what you do with your spare time," Marcus said.

Jack looked over at Dennis and seemed to be thinking through the options. "OK, you can drive us," he finally said, breaking his hand away from Shannon's. "I need a cigarette, anyway. This damn no-smoking law is killing me."

They all laughed at the unintended joke.

"Want to go now?" Dennis asked.

Jack smiled at Dennis's brute force. "Sure, we're coming."

"Don't make any promises you can't keep," Shannon said to Jack. Marcus put his money down and walked toward the door, only then allowing himself to roll his eyes so they wouldn't see.

❧

DENNIS TOOK the keys from Shannon, then got in the driver's side and unlocked the doors. Shannon gave Jack a questioning look, as if to say, *Where do you want me?*

"Go ahead. Sit up front," Jack said. He got into the back seat. He had to admit, those beers had definitely taken the edge off. The lousy storm didn't seem so important right now. And god, Shannon was pretty. The street lights shone in flashes in her blond hair as they traveled across town toward the cluster of hotels by the highway. It didn't really matter what she said or did. She was beautiful. And impossible.

"Dennis, do you have a girlfriend?" she asked their driver.

Jack didn't know those kinds of details about Dennis, even after their April chase, only that he was a geek and dedicated enough to help Marcus tinker with the hail-catcher, process data or whatever he needed, whenever he needed. He'd be a perfect grad-assistant slave when he got to that level.

Dennis let out a chuckle at Shannon's inquiry. "I don't need a girlfriend. I barely have enough time for porn."

Jack laughed.

"Porn?" Shannon echoed. "I bet you didn't know this, but a real girlfriend can make it a lot more interesting to watch porn."

"You mean watch it with a girl?" Dennis said. He sounded uncomfortable. "Not many girls are interested."

"Some are." Shannon leaned toward Dennis a little. "It's great for ideas," she stage-whispered into his ear.

Dennis clearly couldn't believe this woman was actually flirting with him. "Maybe you could recommend some titles," he said after a moment, sneaking a peek at Shannon as he drove, "or recommend a girl." Then Dennis glanced in the rearview mirror, saw Jack and lost his nerve. Perhaps he had an inkling that the gorgeous creature next to him was previously claimed territory.

Jack chuckled to himself. She was a flirt. It was her nature. She loved using her power, getting a reaction. He wondered if he should be annoyed. The beer made him mellow, and he wasn't. She was like some comet whose orbit could be nudged by whatever planet she was near. Jack, who wasn't new to spinning from body to body, was confident his pull was strong. But tonight, he wasn't sure they would manage the collision he was starting to crave.

They got to the hotel, a medium-rate, three-story affair, and Dennis tossed the keys to Jack before disappearing as fast as he could. In the darkness of this far end of the parking lot, they both watched him quick-step across the pavement until he got to the lobby doors and went inside.

"I think he was in over his head," Shannon said, smiling as she wandered over to Jack and put her arms around his waist.

"You're definitely off the deep end," Jack said, meaning it as a compliment.

"Is this our first date yet?"

"God knows it should be," Jack said. "We're drunk enough." He slipped his arms around her and leaned over her to taste her mouth, finally, a first kiss that melted away every thought and tension, delicious, tinged with tequila, and almost entirely free of emotional anticipation. With Shannon, he didn't expect expectations. She floated in front of him, impossibly light, or was that the beer? He liked the sensation.

He released her. A little shorter than he, she looked up at him, still holding him around the waist. Her eyes were liquid jewels, watery blue, in the scant light that reached them through the glass of the distant hotel doors.

"Not tonight," he said quietly, reading her mind.

She let go. "I know you're kidding now."

"We both have roommates. I'm not getting another room. It'll be too obvious."

"You're going to tell me you've never managed a meeting on the road before? Maybe with someone we both know?"

He let the allusion to her sister pass. "It's easier if that someone has her own place or her own car," he said. "You and I have issues. Malik wouldn't approve. And this car is out of the question, not to mention damn uncomfortable," he said when she gave the research vehicle a suggestive glance. The truth was, he could always find a way to fuck, and bed-hopping was not uncommon among the teams of hot-blooded college students, but the one thing he didn't want to do was endanger his reputation with Malik or Rainier or the university. Shannon, with her constant presence, threatened to be more of an entanglement than a quick diversion, and he couldn't afford that on the road.

"You don't really care if Professor Malik approves," she said. Her tone wasn't accusatory, just a statement. She was almost teasing him. "You strike me as someone who doesn't care about anything in particular."

"Storms," he said. Then, more softly: "Pretty girls." He touched her chin and kissed her on the lips, then let go.

"Maybe Dennis is available," she said, definitely teasing now.

"Whatever you need, baby," he said, equally mocking. God, she looked like Judy in this light. He shook the thought. "OK, let me make it formal." He was only a little sardonic. "Will you go out with me when we get home?"

"I'll have to think about it," she said, before she leaned into him and kissed him hard. She grabbed his crotch for a good second before pulling away her hand and walking briskly toward the lobby door.

"Holy shit," he muttered under his breath, staggering back a half step. He watched her walk away, her hips swinging. The pleasant pain of her touch made him crazy. Now he'd be without her all night. "I must be stupid or something," he muttered, then lit a cigarette and strolled slowly through the dark parking lot toward the hotel, letting the steam blow off before he had to step into the light.

SHANNON WANTED to drive them home, even though Jack volunteered. After their dusty gust-out experience, she'd driven for another whole day of fruitless chasing and equally fruitless flirting. He thought it should be his turn to drive. He had no weather or readings to pay attention to today. But she said she didn't mind, actually liked handling this clunky sedan, and he didn't feel like arguing. This way, he could study her as they drove back through eastern Kansas and Oklahoma to I-40, then headed west. It was a warm day, irritating in its storm-free splendor, and they had the windows open so he could smoke and she could let her platinum-blond hair dry. It fluffed in the wind and flew back from her creamy face, the candy-pink lips, the rose-tinted sunglasses that shielded her from the late-afternoon sun. She gripped the steering wheel with silver-ringed fingers, her fingernails pink, too. He followed the line of her slender arms from her hands to her sloping shoulders and the little yellow shirt with a temptingly deep V-neck. She wore short denim shorts and brown sandals.

"How do you do it?" he asked, turned a little sideways in his seat, his sunglasses perched up on his head so he could observe her without a filter.

"What?"

"Look beautiful all the time."

She tossed her head, basking in the compliment. "I would say it's inner beauty, but you would know I was fibbing."

"Why not inner beauty? You don't kill puppies or anything, do you?"

"Only if I have to," she said.

"I can't imagine a situation in which you would have to kill a puppy," Jack said.

"Oh, don't get me started," Shannon said, as if she were about to launch into a terrible tale, but she was smiling.

"I killed a bird once."

"Ew, am I going to not like this story?"

"Too bad. I think our date has started."

"Really?" She turned her face toward him now, smiling more broadly, then looked back at the road. "I guess we have to exchange embarrassing stories, then."

"So I hit this bird with my car," he said.

"Oh, well, we've all done that sometime."

"No, not like this," he said. "It didn't kill it, when I hit it. When I stopped the car, there it was, wedged into the grille. A sparrow, I think. It was hurt bad but still alive. I broke its neck, just like that. I didn't even think about it."

Shannon didn't say anything for a minute. "I guess that's what you do to things that suffer," she said. "At least things that have no choice about it."

"Do you choose not to suffer?"

"You could say that."

Jack couldn't resist asking the next question as they reached the eastern edges of Oklahoma City. "Where were you during the tornado?"

"I don't talk about the tornado," she said flatly.

"I want to know."

"I don't talk about it." Her voice was sharp, impatient, eclipsing her carefree cheer for the first time. "Have I asked you anything? Anything like that? Do you want me to?"

He was uncomfortable then. He didn't answer. One thing he liked about her was that she didn't ask questions he didn't want to answer. It was as if she knew he didn't want to go there, or maybe she just wanted to keep it light.

"Then we're agreed," Jack finally said.

"Right."

"So you choose not to suffer," he said. "At least we've established that."

"I don't think about it," Shannon said. "I don't think about yesterday and tomorrow. That's for suckers. That's for people who believe some fantasy story about how it's all going to be all right after they're dead."

He wanted to reach out, run a hand through her hair. But he just sat in his seat, half-turned toward her as he'd been, and watched her drive. "I still think you're beautiful."

"Just keep looking skin-deep," she said, with a bright smile. "I like that in a man."

He turned on the radio and they chatted about music and other trivia on the way to the university in Wishwell. They parked the cars, secured the gear, and then it was time, finally, to go home.

"Guess I'm driving you now," Jack said, yawning. They'd had little sleep, even if they were sleeping in separate rooms. It was late to bed and early to rise on the road. They walked to his light-gold sedan.

"It looks so funny without pipes and spinny things on the roof," she said, looking over his little no-frills car, a stark contrast to the mesonet vehicles.

He laughed. "I have a kit with all that," he said. "Sometimes I put it on."

They got in, and he drove to his apartment as the sunset turned the sky orange and set alight the car washes and fast-food restaurants that lined the streets. He didn't even think about it until he got to his door and realized he hadn't dropped her off.

"Our date really *has* begun," she said, looking him in the eye as he turned off the engine.

"I guess it has," he said.

They grabbed their bags and walked into the breezeway. He got his mail out of his metal box, in the middle of the row of eight, noticing in the bills and junk what looked like another typed postcard from his father, something about pieces of the Antarctic ice shelf breaking off. Maybe he would read it later. They went up the stairs of the dark-wood, two-story building. Number 203, said the brass numbers on the brown door. He opened it, stepping aside to let Shannon enter first.

Jack hardly ever had anyone visit his place. It was an uneasy opportunity to look at it through someone else's eyes. Spartan. White walls, tan carpet, the *de rigueur* decor for cheap apartment complexes. It was almost clean, with a pair of sneakers thrown here, a jacket thrown there, lots of magazines and some books, mostly weather stuff. No bric-a-brac, except a brick on his black metal bookcase that he told her came from Wakita, the Oklahoma town the filmmakers trashed in *Twister*. A few of his tornado photos, in cheap frames, adorned the living room wall. In front of a couch and cushy chair, there was a TV and a DVD player, along with a stereo, on plain black shelves. Glass sliding doors led out to a balcony where one director's chair sat under a dead hanging plant, just visible in the vanishing twilight. The galley kitchen didn't even have a toaster or canisters, though his microwave had seen a lot of use.

"How about I order a pizza?" he asked.

"Sure," Shannon said. "I'm suddenly starving. Any kind is good." She plopped down on the denim-covered couch and curled against the red pillows piled up on one side. She grabbed the remote off the beat-up wooden coffee table and turned on the TV. "We are *not* watching the weather," she informed him as she turned to one of the women's channels, where the movie of the moment revealed a housewife trying to sort out the puzzle of her murderous, bigamous husband.

"You like that garbage?" Jack asked, looking at the pizza magnet on the fridge and pushing the numbers on his phone.

"I find it's a good reminder of what I never, ever want to be," Shannon said. "If I ever get this stupid, shoot me."

How bright was she? Pretty smart, he guessed. Or pretty and smart enough. It didn't have to matter. He could worry about that kind of thing if he ever became Dr. Andreas. The pizza place put him on hold, and he pushed past some science experiments in the fridge to grab a beer.

"Want a drink?" he asked her, still on hold, half listening to the recorded chatter about dinner specials that would feed an entire football team.

"Definitely," she said, eyes never leaving the TV. "Can you do a vodka martini? I like them very dirty."

Jack smiled and opened the fridge again, putting the unopened beer back in its place. "Let me see if I have olives." He did, thank god, and vermouth. "Oh," he said when the pizza man came back on the phone. "Yeah, the large special with pepperoni and mushrooms and the two-liter Coke," he said. "OK," he acknowledged the price, and hung up.

"Coke?" she asked. "No Coke. You'd better be drinking with me."

"I might need it to go with rum later," he said, only half joking. "Anyway, I think I'll have martinis with you."

It was about 2 a.m. when he woke up on the couch, Shannon wrapped in his arms, the TV quietly droning on some sports channel as the dim, amber glow of the street lights filtered in through the balcony doors. They'd fallen asleep? He couldn't believe it. Some date. The pizza, the martinis, they were potent when mixed with exhaustion.

Shannon sensed his movement and shifted, opening her eyes. He looked down into her face. His body was slow to wake to her, so close to him, as he climbed out of sleep. She wiggled up slowly to kiss his neck, nibble on his ear, kiss his chin, and he began to remember why she had so attracted him. She was raw, direct. She pulled off his T-shirt and kept moving her lips down his torso, nibbling his nipples, licking his chest, kissing him all the way down to his shorts. She unbuttoned them smoothly, pulled them and the briefs down, off, and he lay there naked and hard under her, watching her as she caressed him. She hadn't removed a stitch of her own clothing. She was in total control as she kissed his thighs, then took him in her mouth, awakening the sensations he lived for. For those few minutes, it was enough to lose all rational, even irrational, thought. This girl who didn't want to remember could make him forget. He let himself fall into beautiful blankness.

❧

JUDY WASN'T sure when she noticed that Robinson was calling her every night. At first, it seemed random. They'd gone on a halfhearted chase the day after the derecho, and they'd seen some nice structure, a white cell bubbling over a green field, sculpted with striations, accented by a rainbow, but little else. Then he was on his way and calling, asking her about her day, her garden, her photos, her favorite movies, the weddings she was filming. Sometimes a postcard would arrive. He had a couple more weeks in the Plains, and as he traveled, he dropped lines from The Big Texan in Amarillo, Carhenge in

Alliance, Nebraska, and the mysterious land of UFOs in Roswell, New Mexico. He even saw a slender tornado in eastern Colorado one day when she was working — of course she was working — and he emailed the pictures. She was jealous as hell, but he made it OK. He was so funny about it. "Remember, you get to live here all year round," he said. "Sometime in summer or fall, you'll get some amazing high plains storm, and I'll be trapped in the eastern metropolis, land of mushy summer showers, grilling veggie burgers and dreaming of a big Kansas tornado and the steak to go with it."

It was true. Within two weeks of him leaving the Plains, she'd chased a couple of good storms in western Kansas and Nebraska; the first produced an almost transparent white tornado, while the latter evolved into a beautiful, low-precip supercell, a graceful, spinning top, with some of the best lightning she'd ever seen. The weddings kept her busy, too, and she even managed to get a storm in the background as she shot a portrait of a giddy couple on their big day. It wasn't much of a storm, but it made her feel better to think it was possible to chase virtually and work at the same time.

Sometimes, she found her thoughts turning to Shannon and Jack. She wondered if he had left her sister as fast as he'd left Judy, but then again, it was almost impossible to break that record. And Judy knew Shannon had an uncanny ability to keep the men she wanted and ditch the rest. "I like to dump guys," Shannon had once told her when she was just a freshman in high school and Judy was about to graduate. Judy had few dates in school. Shannon was one of those freshman girls the senior guys couldn't get enough of. She went to all the dances and proms with dates, real dates — football players and cute, smart guys she turned dumb on the spot. Judy and her few friends, the art crowd who dressed oddly and sat by themselves outside at lunch, never even crossed into that circle, much less rolled with it.

Before the tornado, it was different between them. Shannon had loved hanging out with Judy. As kids, they'd gone to almost every movie that came to their one-horse town and breathlessly imagined what that world outside of Pancake was like. Shannon followed Judy around as her older sister used their dad's old camera to take photos of flowers, fences, everything. They read books to each other. Well, Judy mostly read to Shannon, but sometimes Shannon would return the favor, going through the old-time Nancy Drews their mom kept around, the ones where the cars still had running boards. Judy got too old for them, but she loved hearing Shannon read, seeing her happy, as her girlish voice became fast and breathless when Nancy and her friends got stuck in a rising tide in a cave or crept around a spooky mansion.

Shannon was ten when the tornado hit; Judy was fourteen. Where was Shannon that day? Judy usually put it out of her mind. Shannon was with Aunt Kate, of course, bugging her between piano lessons as she often did after school. Aunt Kate taught lots of piano lessons. Greg was at the store with his father. When the siren sounded, their aunt had stuffed Shannon in the storm cellar, then went upstairs to try to close the windows. That's when it hit—no ceremony, just the blast. Shannon told Judy the story that night, when, homeless, they camped out in the hardware store with their parents, Uncle Ray, and Greg; it was the only time Judy remembered her sister talking about it.

Judy had been just a few doors down, at their own little house, which had no storm cellar. The siren sent her running to her bedroom closet, huddled with the childish stuffed animals she had finally put away but hadn't been able to throw out. Her mother, a kindergarten teacher, was still at school, her father still at the store. While she hugged herself in the closet, thinking it was just another false alarm, the hail banging on the roof tapered off to nothing. Then she heard the terrifying sound, the noise people said was like a freight train but was really like the cracking of a thousand bones when a twister tore through the heart of a town. The cacophony was incredible, a hungry, choppy roar. The roof lifted off above her head, and half the walls collapsed around her — but not her closet. She was so paralyzed with fear that she stayed there for maybe ten minutes after it went by, trembling, breathing hard in the spitting rain, even though it took no more than thirty seconds to destroy their lives. When she emerged, among the first things she saw lying in the debris were the soggy blue spines of the Nancy Drew books, splayed amid the remains of their living room. Then she ran down the street to the splinters of Aunt Kate's house. She saw no one but heard screams from inside the cellar. She got a neighbor to help pull pieces of wood and other debris off the door and opened it to find a hysterical Shannon and no Aunt Kate. Their aunt's body was discovered a hundred yards away, near the wreckage of another house. The twister had carried her there. The baby-grand piano that had been in Ray and Kate's living room was the only thing in the house left standing, battered but still adorned with the art-glass vase that for years had sat on top.

What followed, Judy wasn't sure she remembered and didn't like to think about. Some memories fade for a reason. Their family, once so sure of its place in the world, began to creak and sway. Her parents fought and stressed about money and everything else. Her mother drank more and more. It was a while before Judy noticed that Shannon had become a different person, and it wasn't just because she was growing up. She had thrown the old Shannon away. Judy, who had found her only solace in photography and art after the tornado, missed her.

Now, it was the other Shannon that Judy thought about, or tried not to think about, the sister-stranger who connected with people the way a butterfly connected with a flower, momentarily, prettily, gone.

"Robinson, do you have any siblings besides that sister you told me about?" she asked one evening when he called. He was back home in Maryland, complaining about the work he had to do, though he was excited by one assignment, a web article on a local rock band he liked. She was on her mobile phone, sitting on the wooden swing in her garden, which by now, mid-June, was in full and heady blossom. The tangle of scents was divine as the purple evening twilight insinuated itself into the pathways and her bubbling fountain in the corner. The elfin boy still tossed the glistening stream of water from one hand to another, playing his magical game of catch. He was entrancing in the fading glow, and she watched him as Robinson spoke.

"I have two brothers and two sisters," he said.

"Are they all like you?" Judy asked. "Your poor mother."

"Hey! My mom is a high-energy person! She appreciates attention-deficit disorder in her children."

Judy chuckled. "So you all got along, then?"

"Except for Silas, the black sheep. He used to steal stuff out of our Christmas stockings when we were kids. Now he's a day trader. Ugh."

"Silas?" she asked. "What did your parents call the rest of you?"

"Oh, there's Tess, Elizabeth, and Lance."

Judy took a second to digest the names. "English lit freaks, huh?"

"Yeah," he said. "My mom fell in love with her English professor, and then she married him. Us having the last name of Marvell only compounded the problem. You know Marvell? 'Let us roll all our strength, and all our sweetness, up into one ball; and tear our pleasures with rough strife …' "

"Ooo, nice." More than nice. Poetry, sweet and seductive, in Robinson's usually merry voice. Rather than dwell on the thought, she hastened to continue. "Those seventeenth-century guys knew how to get the girl. I had a crush on an art professor once. Very embarrassing. Thank god he had morals, because mine went out the window every time I saw him illuminated by the slide projector."

"Egads," Robinson said. "You probably would have had kids named Leonardo and Raffaelo."

"Leonardo's not bad," Judy said. "And we might have gone more contemporary. You know, 'Andy.'"

"Maybe we should stick with Leonardo. Write it down."

"We're going to need that name down the road, huh?" Judy asked, amused and wondering where the conversation was going.

"You never know," he said, and she could hear him smile.

"My sister and I got along great when we were kids, little kids," Judy said, "and then it was like she disappeared."

"She was never around?"

"Oh, she was around — it just wasn't her anymore."

"Was that after—?" he didn't finish his question.

"Yes, everything is divided into before and after."

"Can you remember what you were like before?"

Judy thought about it for a minute. "No. It's like I'm

looking at a different person. Oh. D'oh," she said, realizing what he was getting at.

"Even I was like a different person when I was a kid," Robinson said. "I mean, every five or ten years, I look back, and I'm a different person. You're probably even more different from the way you were then. I never had anything happen to me like that, not like you're talking about, but I still have to introduce myself to myself once in a while, and we go on from there. Maybe you can kind of reintroduce yourself to your sister."

"There's a lot of water under that bridge," Judy said.

"No worries," he said. "There's nothing wrong with being estranged from your family. There's a long and proud tradition. Maybe *you're* the black sheep."

She thought about it for a second. "I like that idea," she said. "It makes me feel like a rebel."

"Very sexy," Robinson said.

"I know. I need a black leather jacket."

"You've got enough cows out there," he said. "Maybe you can kill your own jacket."

"Ugh," she said. "You've just ruined my image of black leather jackets."

"How about black leather pants?" he asked hopefully.

She laughed. "Good night, Robinson."

"Good night, rebel."

She pressed the hangup button and listened to the burbling water and humming insects in the growing darkness. It was a calm night, and warm. There wouldn't be many more storms. The season was getting on.

THERE WERE a few times when Jack thought Shannon was gone. He wouldn't see her for three or four days. Then she'd be there, in his apartment, using the key he'd given her in a moment of weakness. Their reunion each time was heated, hungry, single-minded. Once, they didn't leave his place for two days. Then she'd disappear again. Each vanishing seemed to be a way of telling him that she didn't want him, that she wasn't a threat to his damn isolation. At least that was the way he heard the message, and it only made him want her more, on the generous terms she had defined — no limits, no obligation. At the moments she arrived, she was just what he desired, the sweetest diversion, the dirtiest martini. And so it came to be, after the spring chases were over, that he offered to take her to Florida for a couple of weeks of tropical turpitude. His aunt and uncle were spending the summer in the North Carolina mountains, he told her, and their beach condo was waiting.

It was July, when the best chance of Plains storms was somewhere in the Dakotas or in the convergence zone east of Denver. Jack had chased storms this time of year in the lonely high plains, but they meant a lot of work, a lot of driving. And Florida, he reminded himself, had lightning.

They left Wishwell late at night, to avoid the traffic, and dropped south on the Interstate, the radio playing softly, the windows open. They didn't talk much, just enough to make sure the other was awake. Jack drove. They were somewhere in that open space north of the Oklahoma border, enveloped in inky blackness in the long, rough country between the urban islands of Oklahoma City and the Dallas metroplex, when a rush of feathers flashed in their headlights, an instantaneous gleam of predatory eye and terrible talon. Just as quickly, before Jack had time to draw a breath in astonishment and tap the brakes, it whooshed away into the night.

"Owl," he whispered as he drove on, picking up speed again.

"Are you sure?" Shannon asked, also quietly. She was curled up as best she could on the passenger seat, a fluffy white bed pillow under her head.

"There's no mistaking that face," he murmured.

"Why are we whispering?" She began to giggle.

"Maybe because owls aren't like other birds," he said, more emphatically. "They're rare. They mean something."

"They mean some mouse is dying a horrible death," Shannon scoffed.

"The Cherokee say the owl cries for its lost love, not that I believe in that kind of thing."

"Owls don't seem like the type."

"I don't think of them as sad, either," he said. "More like powerful and solitary. But in the story, apparently, the owl masqueraded as a man so he could marry a very pretty woman, only he didn't tell her that he turned into an owl every night. When she found out, she got angry and kicked him out because he couldn't bring home enough meat."

"It's very important for a man to give his woman big meat," Shannon said, teasing as always.

Jack didn't bite. His mind was still on the great bird, now somewhere in the darkness, beating on the clouds with its wings. "I like owls."

Shannon didn't reply, just closed her eyes and settled into her pillow. Jack leaned back and pressed the accelerator, watching the stars for feathery shadows.

It was late the next night when they arrived at the old white condo building, five stories high, in south Cocoa Beach.

They had each driven multiple shifts, alternately napping, so they wouldn't have to stop before they got there.

"I hear it!" Shannon said when they got out of the car. Jack looked around in the weak parking lot lights, not sure what she meant. "The ocean!" she said. "I hear it!"

"I guess we're really at the beach, then."

"You don't get it, dummy. I've never been to the ocean."

Jack looked at her incredulously. "I'm really tired," he said. "But before we go to bed, you have to dip your toes in."

Then walked through the breezeway that cut through the heart of the condo building and out onto the walkway that bridged the dune line. A slender moon was enough to limn the little waves with silver as they rolled into the shore. At the bottom of the wooden steps, Shannon took off her sandals, and before Jack knew it, she was stripping off everything. "Come on!" she said, running into the water.

He kicked off his leather sandals — a nod to their destination — and walked to the water's edge, letting the waves wash over his feet. He stood there and watched her splash, unable to match her energy. The water streamed down her body as she dropped and rolled in one of the waves and jumped up again. "Aren't you getting in?" she asked.

"Tomorrow," he said. "But fear not. Tonight, I'll dream of mermaids."

She crossed her arms over her round little breasts and pouted at him for a moment, then realized he was calling her a mermaid and emerged to hug him, getting his clothes thoroughly damp in the process. He wrapped his arms around her and kissed her. Salty.

He let her go so she could put her clothes back on and looked around. No one on the beach. Amazing. He loved it. It wasn't like the Mid-Atlantic, where he grew up. Every time he came here he was pleasantly surprised that it hadn't all gone to hell yet, though from the increasing number of strip malls and condos they passed on the way in, he saw the train to Hades was pulling into the station.

Once they got their suitcases and his camera bags up to the little two-bedroom condo on the third floor and found Aunt Maxie's hidden key, they both stripped and fell into bed, and into slumber, beat.

When Jack awoke with the dawn the next morning, he realized it was the first night they'd slept together without making love. The main bedroom had a sliding door that led out to a large balcony, and a sapphire and diamond glow stole across the walls as the sun rose over the Atlantic. Shannon, who was closer to the door, moaned and turned her face away from the light, burying her head in his chest. He held her, letting her sleep, as the sound of the ocean filled his ears and light saturated his vision. Then he let his eyes drift shut, awash in waves of dreamless slumber.

❦

AT A BEACHFRONT BAR, Jack settled back in his deck chair, enjoying the daily bikini contest. He and Shannon were drinking banana daiquiris under the meager shade of the table's umbrella, letting the subtropical heat soak through their skins. The summer sun and drenching humidity transformed any motivations for action they might have had into molten indolence.

Shannon, in a black bikini top and tiny black shorts, tossed her evaluations to Jack as the contestants strutted across the small stage to the drunken cheers of a meager lunchtime crowd. "Boob job," she said. "Terrible hair color. Boob job. Oh, I think those are real."

"Mmm, real," he said, half-drunk, evaluating the dark-haired beauty showing off an itsy-bitsy ruby-red bikini. Probably a stripper trying to pick up a few bucks in her off-hours. Most of them were. The drunken tourist contestants were easy to spot, in contrast — sometimes they were shy, and they just didn't have the walk, or the four-inch-high heels.

Shannon looked at him through her sunglasses, sucking her straw, white between her pink lips, till it made that *pffffft* sound in the clear plastic cup. *What is she thinking? Maybe nothing, like me.* Nothing would be good. He didn't want Shannon thinking too much about him, getting attached to him.

"That waitress is slow. I'm going to get us some refills," she said, picking up her little pink purse.

"OK," Jack said, as Shannon walked to the thatched-roofed bar on the other side of the deck. He was lost in the contest for several minutes before he realized she wasn't back yet. He looked in the direction of the bar and saw her in what he quickly recognized as her flirt posture, leaning in, talking closely with a deeply tan, Spanish-looking guy behind the bar with slick black hair and an earring. The bartender was eating it up, showing his teeth, as Shannon read his palm. Jack had a strange and uncomfortable feeling. He thought it might be jealousy.

After a few minutes, Shannon returned and set the daiquiris on the table. "On the house." She smiled.

Jack almost said something but realized there was nothing to say. There was nothing between them, nothing spoken. No point starting now.

They spent the mornings swimming or walking. Once, they rented bikes and went from bar to bar, up and down the beach highway. "To fitness," he toasted her with a rum runner at one open-air dive.

Sometimes, in the afternoons, he'd check out the radar and see what the sea breeze was bringing in. They went on a few chases. Most of the storms overran them with low-hanging, layered shelf clouds, long, elaborate structures of white and green and gray shadows that swept over the Indian River Lagoon and the barrier islands and out to sea. He got her to come out with him when the lightning was hot one night. She complained of the mosquitoes and stayed in the car, painting her toenails red by the light of a flashlight she held under her chin, while he stood on the banks of the St. Johns River and took time exposures of the fabulous, forked strokes illuminating the water and the distant power lines. It was like a tropical prairie out here, with a stormy allure all its own.

One night, they tried the jazz bar in Cocoa Beach. Shannon put on a little black dress and pinned sparkly barrettes in her hair, and he wore shorts and a retro tropical shirt, a muted green accented with two parallel columns of red and white flowers and hula girls. It was flashier than his Oklahoma wardrobe, but he'd bought it in a moment of drunkenness at a beach emporium when Shannon said it brought out his eyes.

With dark red walls adorned with playful art, the bar seemed almost too classy and urban for this kitschy town. They sat at a table and drank martinis and watched half-toasted big-band wannabes get up and do Frank Sinatra imitations during the open-mike hour. Then the house band came on — an ancient bass player, a peppy drummer, a gruff piano player — good stuff, evocative of his mother's record collection, the one his father never wanted to listen to, afterward. Jack and Shannon closed the bar down, feeling warm and tipsy, and as the last patrons were leaving, long after the band quit, Shannon told him, "I play a little piano."

"Go ahead."

She sat at the baby grand and began to play a few notes, hesitant at first, then settled into a beautiful, simple melody. It wasn't jazz, but it was haunting. She stopped halfway through, abruptly. "I forget the rest," she said quietly. Her lie was transparent. He knew better than to ask why.

"What's that song called?" he asked.

"'Walking in the Air.'" But he saw there was nothing so light about her at that moment. Shannon walked on the ground. He helped her as she leaned against him, drunk, on their way out of the bar.

The day before they had to leave, they decided to hang out at the condo, where Jack's aunt and uncle had strung a big hammock across the balcony. They kept their drinks handy, on the table next to them, as they let themselves be cradled by the hammock's dense white weave. It was hypnotic, the gentle motion, the sound of the ocean and the light glittering blue off the water, the puffy cumulus building white mountains out over the sea.

"It's really too bad I can't fall in love with anyone," Shannon said. Her eyes were half-closed as they lay entangled, facing each other in the hammock, she in a white bikini, Jack in his black swim trunks.

"You never have?"

"It's against my policy," Shannon said. "I'm not saying a boy or two never made me consider it or even think I was there for a day or two. But I soon came to my senses. Suppose I ended up with someone like you?"

"That would be terrible," he said, pulling her closer and kissing her. "Make sure that doesn't happen."

She kissed him without reserve, openly and passionately, as she always did, and he really didn't care if he were the only one or one of many. He'd walked a similar path for so long; why waste time thinking about the future, the past? Sex filled empty moments and anticipation helped fill the rest, when there weren't storms. The occasions were rare when he'd stayed with a woman long enough to wonder what lasting love would be like — usually when the woman in question saw more in him than Shannon did, or paid the rent for a while, or looked the other way when he inevitably strayed. He didn't know what Shannon saw in him, except maybe herself. Yet there was something in her pulling him. Why else was he here with her?

His stickiest relationships had been too real to endure as he found himself drawn to, then repelled by, their once-seductive complications. Shannon was more complicated than she usually let on; he knew this, but so far, she'd kept things simple. In the short time he'd known Judy, he'd seen nothing was simple with her. Shannon was different, and she'd been right there, for the taking, a fast escape. He let his mind wander further, fantasizing, as their mouths touched and tongues explored; imagined a woman who was both, the sisters entwined into one, the lips moving against his expressing another heart, another soul. For a moment, he felt he was a better man for wanting both, without guilt, immersed in pleasure. Doubly aroused, he let the specter go, reminding himself of what Shannon offered, the simple now: languorous kisses on a hot afternoon; the hug of the hammock; the sound of the ocean; blue-sky reflections; rum and Cokes and ice in sweating glasses on the white plastic table. Captured by the hammock, he melted with her into the lengthening shadows, working off his trunks and her bikini bottom so he could push himself inside her, moving in excruciating, agonizing slow motion so they wouldn't fall.

❧

JACK AND SHANNON packed up the car the next morning and began their drive. It seemed harder this time, maybe because the sun was so bright and Jack still had a little headache from the drinks and dehydration of the day before. He swilled a sports drink, even though he hated the stuff, hoping it would help. They switched off every few hours as they traveled the length of Florida, north, then west.

As night began to fall and it started raining, they stopped near Mobile for dinner at a cheap steak house. Over every booth hung a decades-old light fixture dripping with amber prisms, and their sandwiches came with pale, sad fries.

Shannon made a face as she took another bite of her burger. "Kind of makes me miss Oklahoma cow," she said.

"You'll have it before you know it. And I'll have to get back to work on my dissertation," Jack said, none too happily, trying to get through his cold grilled-cheese sandwich.

"I guess it's time for me to hit the job market again," Shannon said.

"Maybe you could take some classes," Jack said.

"Self-improvement? Horrors."

"Have you ever taken any?"

"I guess I got about halfway to a degree," she said. "I kept changing majors. I had a hard time picking one thing I'd be doomed to do for the rest of my life, you know?"

Jack took a sip of his cola. "You need to find something you're passionate about."

"I really don't think there is anything," Shannon said.

"Sometimes I've felt that about people, you know, guys, but it's never lasted." She chewed and looked at him, or through him, as if she were asking herself a question and having trouble coming up with the answer.

Watching her small and pretty form, feeling her uncertainty, he felt an unfamiliar and overwhelming desire to protect her, to wrap her in his arms. He reached across the table and took her hand, and she looked down at it, surprised, then smiled and returned his gaze. With affection or amusement, he wasn't sure.

He volunteered to take the next shift, and he drove north on a minor highway that cut north from Alabama into Mississippi. They were quiet, a little sleepy, as the misty rain fell in the nearly complete darkness. The road glistened, and the trees lining the highway became black shapes, hard to make out. Now and again, a car would approach from the other direction, headlights beaming through the mist.

Jack wasn't ready to go back. Unbidden, thoughts of the days ahead crowded in, the work he had to do, the time he might spend with Shannon. Or maybe he'd go out with friends, break this pattern. She was habit-forming.

What a crappy night it was. No storms, just rain, the worst kind of driving. He loved chasing, but he hated driving in the rain. Its hushed sounds cast a dark spell on this dismal highway.

It happened in an instant, a deer, leaping across the road from the right. Jack slammed on the brakes, instinctively, and the car began to slide. He wrestled with the steering wheel and somehow missed the deer. Halfway off the right shoulder and still moving, he pulled the sedan back onto the highway and kept going, barely missing a beat. His heart was in his mouth. Shannon laughed out loud, a happy burst of relief.

Shaken, he was just about to say something, something funny, when everything went wrong, like a nightmare that hadn't ended but just tricked him into thinking he was awake. "Shit!" he said as two more deer sprang into the headlights. It was too late. His brakes couldn't stop them or the car. He slammed into one deer, and then the car began to spin. It wouldn't slow down on the slick road. He saw the oncoming headlights, heard the squealing brakes and a horn, loud, a dump truck. Shannon screamed. The truck slammed into the passenger side as they crossed the line, and he had the sick sensation of flipping, turning, airborne. His head thumped into the side window as the car smashed back to earth, coming to a halt, miraculously right-side up, in the grassy ditch. Through a fog, he recalled the flash of a deer's eye. Then, in the sputtering gloom, oblivion.

3

STORM SEASON

J udy sat in bed in her cotton pajamas, reading a desert epic by the light of her nightstand lamp, when her phone rang. She ignored it for a moment, twirling her unbraided hair, trying to make out who might be calling this late. Robinson had already called, but maybe it was him again. Sometimes he called just to wish her good night.

She didn't recognize the number, but the caller ID said … hospital?

She didn't take time to process the details. "Hello?"

"Judy Hale?" It was a woman's voice, authoritative, as the voice rattled off her name and a title.

"Yes?"

"Miss Hale, I'm so sorry to bother you again, but we're looking for the contact information for Mr. and Mrs. Hale—your parents?"

Judy was suspicious of anyone wanting that kind of information, but there was something about the woman's tone that put her on edge.

"Bother me again? What's this about?"

She heard mumbling on the other end of the line. "No one has spoken with you yet, Miss Hale?" the woman asked.

"No. What is this about?"

There was more murmuring. "Wait a moment, Miss Hale. There's someone here who would like to talk to you."

She heard the phone being handed off. "Judy?" The voice was deep and raspy.

She took a moment to let it sink in. She knew who this was. She knew it was Jack. She knew something had happened to Shannon, all in a second.

"Jack, what is it?"

"I thought they called you earlier. I ... I was out for a while. I can barely think straight right now. I'm sorry."

Judy had already dropped her book to the floor, and now she grabbed for a pillow with her free hand, as if it would help. "Shannon?"

"I'm sorry. There was an accident." He sounded disbelieving, shaken. She didn't think he could sound like that.

"Are you sure?" It was what people always asked, she knew, a stupid question, but the words slipped out anyway.

"It happened so fast," Jack said. "She's gone."

Judy clutched the phone to her chest, breathing fast and hard. The tears wouldn't come. They were all there, within her head, her heart, about to burst.

She dimly heard Jack's voice. "Judy? Judy?"

She put the phone to her ear again. "What the hell happened? Were you chasing?"

"No. We were coming back from Florida. I ... I was driving. The road was wet. We were in Mississippi, we were fine, you know, but these deer ran in front of the car. They say there was a truck. I don't remember that part very well. They told me they need to talk to your parents."

"Why? I'll tell them." He wasn't making sense.

"Her license says organ donor. They say they need to notify the legal next of kin. And get permission for ... for cremation. I would have called you—they must have thought I—"

"Oh, god," Judy said. She would have to call her parents and tell them, her sensitive father, her tight-lipped mother. *No.*

"I wanted to handle this," Jack said, "but they insisted on some stupid formality, and I didn't know how to reach your parents."

Judy felt sick, dizzy. "OK," she said after a long pause to regain her composure. "I'll tell my parents to call." She paused. "They can ship the ashes here. I've heard of that. They can do that, can't they?"

"I'll bring them."

"I'm sure they can ship them," she said. "You don't need to be involved."

"Christ, I am involved!"

She was shocked by his angry tone. Then she understood. Jack had been the last person to see Shannon alive — had been with her all this time. And there was something else in his voice. Pain. "Were you injured?"

"Concussion," Jack said dully. "Broken ribs, collarbone. It's nothing. It will hurt more tomorrow, they said. They don't have to operate. I'm walking wounded. It's nothing."

Judy tried to picture him there in the hospital, tried to picture Shannon in her last moments, then pushed the image away. Ashes. He was bringing her ashes. "How can you drive?"

"They said I can if I have to."

"Then I guess I'll see you when you ... Call if you need to," she said. "Be careful." She didn't know why she said it. Maybe because it seemed like nothing was safe right now.

Jack gave her the number for the hospital contact, and she wrote it on the notepad she kept on the nightstand. "I'll be there in a few days," he said.

She ended the call. Before she could give in to hysterics, she took a deep breath and forced herself to call her parents' number. The rings went out into the darkness and through the wires, a forlorn sound that seemed to hover in the air forever, not long enough. Her mother answered, and at the sound of her voice, Judy lost all the composure she'd tried to preserve. "Mom," she said, crying now as she hadn't since she was a young girl. "It's me. About Shannon."

Judy knew that her voice betrayed everything, that April Hale would sense the worst. "Something happened to Shannon?"

"Yes." Judy caught her breath. "We've lost her."

"What? How?" the older woman said, her voice brittle with shock.

"She was on a trip with a friend." Judy didn't want to get into the details. "It was a car accident. I guess they took her to a Mississippi hospital."

"But what happened?"

"I think they skidded on the wet road and a truck hit them. It was all very quick," Judy said, trying to comfort her, knowing the words sounded hollow, as if *quick* made it all right.

"How do you know about this?" She could hear her mother grasping for anything that might make it untrue.

"Her friend called me. They were trying to get in touch with you, the hospital was, I mean. Oh, Mom. Shannon was an organ donor, and they want to make sure you know about it, I guess. And they want to discuss — arrangements. Her friend said he'd bring the ashes here, if you're OK with it."

"Oh, my god. My little Shannon," her mother whispered. She didn't say anything for a minute or two, and Judy thought she might be crying. Then she spoke, as if from a dream. "An organ donor? At least she can help someone." The words seemed poor consolation. "I have to tell your father," her mother continued in dismay, going through the same realizations Judy had experienced a moment before.

"I know, Mom," Judy said. "I know."

She gave her mother the number, and they promised to talk in the morning. Then Judy put down the phone and curled up on the bed, arms crossed, eyes wide open. A chill ran through her, and she trembled in the silence of the house, in the reflection of the lamp off her room's blue walls. She didn't want to turn out the light.

❧

SLEEP DIDN'T MAKE anything better for Judy over the next couple of days. It was all nightmares, sudden awakenings, sweat and chills. Her parents said they would come to Pancake for the service, and at their request, she arranged everything. She hadn't cried again. But two days after she learned Shannon was gone, she got a call from Robinson. His "How are you doing, Judy?" did what the memories could not.

"Robinson," she croaked. She couldn't hide the tears in her voice. She couldn't say anything.

"Judy." His voice was soothing. "I didn't know how soon to call. I know. I know what happened. One of the university guys posted something on Storm Track. I'm so sorry, sweetie."

"Oh, Robinson," Judy said, then without thinking: "God, I wish you were here."

"You do?" He sounded pleased. "Listen. You have some stuff to get through now, but when this is over, I'm going to get you out of there. We'll go chase the monsoon in Arizona. I've always wanted to do that. It would be great for you. Imagine the photographic possibilities."

Judy recovered herself with a sniffle, wondering if she could escape the nightmares there. "Nothing like the desert to dry up tears, right?"

"I know it seems like a lot to think about right now, but you're going to want to do something when this is over, something other than stare at your windmills."

"How'd you know?" She'd spent two hours that morning in the windmill park, hugging her knees as she sat on a bench, trying to make sense of the creaking and clattering of the wind in the great metal blades as they chopped through the air, unstoppable.

"How many times have you told me about your windmills?" Robinson chided. "Judy, listen to me. I'm right here. Are you OK?"

"It's getting better," she said. "I don't want to talk about it now, though. You know?"

"I know," he said. "I'll call you tomorrow."

"Thank you, Robinson."

Late that afternoon, there was a knock on her door. For a second, she had the crazy thought that it might be Robinson, then realized it was probably the florist. A few of her parents' friends in Arizona had already sent stiff, formal arrangements that she'd stuck in the kitchen. There hadn't been a word from anyone in Pancake, even after the obituary ran, only Uncle Ray and Greg offering to do what they could. Uncle Ray was as shaken as anyone by the news, no doubt recalling past losses and the endearing child Shannon once was.

She opened the door. There, his left arm in a sling, his forehead bruised, his face lined with fatigue, was Jack. He clutched a box under his good arm. His eyes locked on hers, and she couldn't say anything.

He stood silent for a moment, too. He seemed to be searching her face. A wave of emotions shifted over his features, almost too quickly to catch, only she was sensitive to it, like a subtle change of the wind in the trees. What was it? A strange recognition, of blood, of grief.

"I came as soon as I could," he said.

"I didn't expect you until tomorrow. The service is the day after that."

"I can't come. I won't. I don't think she would have wanted me there, anyway."

"I don't think she'd have wanted any of us there," Judy said. "She'd probably want us to go off and have a party and forget about it."

He granted her a half smile and extended his good arm toward her with the box, wincing as he stretched.

She took it, not dwelling on it, noticing it was sealed with the label of some Mississippi crematorium. "What do we owe you?"

"Nothing. Your parents took care of it, anyway."

She paused. "You look like you're hurting."

"I'm OK." His voice was rougher than she remembered. "It's the collarbone. The ribs, too, though not so much. Three months of this, they said. Everything I do hurts."

"Maybe you should come in for a minute," Judy said, hoping he wouldn't. She felt a simmering and, she realized, pointless anger toward him, along with curiosity, a desire to understand how she could have misread him so badly, how a brief and joyful meeting could have ended up somewhere so wrong.

Jack seemed to consider her offer, then shook his head. "I have to get back. Are you coming for her things, or do you want me to send them? I talked to her roommates. They said they'd pack everything up. I don't think there's much. I don't think you need to come down."

He was trying to make it easy on her. "If you really think there isn't much, then give it to charity," Judy said. "She's been living like a nomad for years. I think all she had was clothes. She hated things. Do you mind sending along papers, that kind of stuff? My parents might need those. Or call me and I'll come down to deal with it if it's any trouble at all. I really should. She's my sister."

"I know," he said. Those green eyes, the eyes that had so attracted her that day on the dusty road in Oklahoma, held her gaze again.

Judy flashed back to the moment when he stood in her doorway and touched her chin and kissed her on the cheek, dismissing her in an instant. He raised his hand now, slowly, and touched her cheek again. His eyes conveyed a suggestion of sympathy, an echo of desire, but was it her he was seeing? She shivered and shifted almost imperceptibly away. He lowered his arm.

"I'm going," he said, brusque again, in control.

"Thank you for making the effort to come here," Judy said.

"I owed her that."

She looked toward the driveway, where a two-door, burgundy car was parked. Jack followed her gaze. "Rental," he said. Of course. The other car was gone.

"At least you can get a new car." It sounded more harsh than she meant it.

He didn't answer for a second. "Tell your parents I'm sorry, too."

"OK," Judy said, her voice softer. "I'll tell them."

He walked slowly, awkwardly down the sidewalk, his posture stiff to protect his shoulder and ribs. He lowered himself carefully into the driver's seat, then backed out of the driveway, past her big wooden flowers, and headed east down Main Street.

Judy realized she still had the box under her arm. She looked down. It was just a box. It held no emotion for her. Her sister was really gone. It was just a box.

ON THE EVE of Shannon's service, Judy stayed up half the night repainting part of her mural. It was a corner that she'd never been able to get right, a collage of different attempts. Tonight, hovering on a stepstool above the tornadoes and patchwork fields and indeterminate shapes and colors of the mural's landscape, she got out her palette of acrylics and painted the corner black, as if it were a night sky, a clear hole in the clouds, and dabbed in yellow and white stars. Around the hole in the sky, she painted clouds over clouds, puffy and purple and green, with hints of a golden lining, not the sun, something else. Perhaps the veiled moon, reflected light, or fire, hidden and consuming. She dabbed on the clouds, repainted them, changed colors and painted them again with increasing frustration, slapping on the pigment with thick and messy strokes. She could not express her feelings about what happened. Before the night was over, she'd given up, and the corner of the sky remained muddled, blurred shades of midnight.

She was bleary-eyed at the memorial, which was flat and impersonal, saying nothing of the real Shannon, that is, either Shannon that Judy had known. Her parents, who had stayed the night before with Uncle Ray and Greg, seemed grim and lost. The only one who cried, strangely, was Uncle Ray, and Judy wondered if he was far away and long ago, reliving Aunt Kate's funeral.

That evening, at Uncle Ray's house, rebuilt in a more modern style on the spot where it had been destroyed all those years ago, Judy sat with her mother at the glass-topped kitchen table and drank iced tea while Ray, Greg and her father talked in the living room. Or at least, Judy drank iced tea; her mother sipped a glass of brandy. The men looked at photo albums, something that always seemed to happen after funerals, and talked with a peculiar sense of nostalgia about Ray's pictures of the tornado damage. It was odd how the tornado could bring up so many wrenching memories and yet still fascinate them, all of them. Judy thought maybe Ray and Greg were trying to distract her father a little, help him think through what happened. Every once in a while, he seemed to look off into space, disconsolate, until his brother nudged him and asked him a question or showed him another photo.

"Dad seems so upset," Judy said quietly. Like her mother, she had her elbows on the table, but that was where the resemblance ended. Judy had always taken after her father. Her mother's short, white hair framed a rounder face and gray eyes, and she was a no-nonsense woman. Judy's sensitivity had always mystified her.

"He hasn't been that well, Judy," April Hale said. "The doctor said it might have been a mini-stroke. He's just a little confused sometimes, a little unsteady. And then this happened. I don't know if he'll ever be the same."

"Why didn't you tell me?" asked Judy, alarmed at this news.

"The change was so subtle, I didn't even notice it for a long time, or maybe I didn't want to. I didn't want to trouble you."

"You never did trouble me. You should have."

"Why start now?" her mother asked, sipping her drink, and Judy saw she was making an awkward joke.

"I guess you're right." Judy raised her eyebrows, not laughing, and took a sip of tea. They had never talked about real things in their house. They'd never talked about love or art or what life had to offer, inside or outside of Pancake. They weren't a huggy family. Perhaps that was why they had so much trouble dealing with the tornado. All their emotion gurgled under the surface, like a hidden spring, while mold grew on the cave walls. "Listen, Shannon's friend, the one who was in the accident with her, he said to say he was sorry."

"She was dating him, wasn't she?" her mother asked. "Last time we talked with her, she said she was dating one of your storm chaser friends."

"She said that, did she?" Judy still didn't want to picture them together.

"I've asked myself over and over whether he might have been to blame." This was what her mother did, looked for someone or something to blame. After the tornado, frustrated when she couldn't find one focus for her anger, she spread it around, like machine-gun fire.

"I don't think anybody's to blame," Judy said, though she also was conflicted about the accident. She felt her sister's absence keenly, in every empty chair, in every family quirk that would have been greeted by Shannon's giddy laughter. But she also recognized the chasm between them. If Shannon were alive, Judy would be doing her best to ignore her and her affair with Jack. It seemed pointless to forgive her, for she understood that Shannon's behavior was not born of malice. It was just Shannon. Now that her sister was dead, the only one left to forgive was Jack, yet she found him a poor focus for a grudge. He had left her reeling, but he had left her life; only Shannon's death had brought him back.

"That service today was awful," she said, trying to change the course of the conversation. "That preacher didn't seem to understand Shannon at all."

"Did you?"

"No," Judy admitted. "But I understood she was bright, in the sense of light, you know? She was full of energy."

"If she was light, you were fire," April Hale said. "You had all the talent. She always wanted to be as smart as you. She was always competing with you, even if you didn't know it."

"Was she?" Judy was bewildered. "She seemed to have everything she wanted. Everything I didn't have."

"She had what she could get," her mother said.

Later, when their parents had gone to bed, Judy and Greg sat in the green rocking chairs on the white front porch and worked on a big bottle of bargain wine, looking out on the red and pink rose bushes and the nearly dark, empty street in the warm summer night. Though insects hummed, it was late enough that the mosquitoes had thinned out, and it was still and clear. A couple of citronella candles in glass globes sat on the flat porch railing and cast a flickering, yellow light on their glasses, adding luster to the red liquid.

"We'd better not lose any more Hales for a while," Greg

said, rocking. The chair made a squeak-squeak sound on the wooden planks.

"Are we going to run out?" asked Judy, a little tipsy, feeling some of her tension flow away in the cabernet.

"We just never seem to lose them in any kind of normal way."

"I don't think any death seems normal to people who are alive," Judy said, reaching over to give his arm a friendly squeeze, right below the "Wheat Me" tattoo. "I hate to see our parents getting older. I mean, the ones we have left. Ugh, I'm sorry. That was a stupid thing to say."

"It's fine," her cousin said. "That was so long ago. I'm moving on. I'm getting my computer degree and getting out of here."

"Will that be the end of Hale Hardware?" Judy asked, sticking her legs out and watching her sandaled feet move up and down, slowly, with the rocking chair.

"Dad's worried one of the big chain stores will come in and push him out. I wouldn't be surprised if he went to Arizona, too."

Judy smiled, knowing her cousin was just being grouchy. "Never," she said.

"I know," Greg said, rolling his eyes. "Why does he love it here so much?"

"Because it's the goddamn beautiful prairie in the goddamn heart of America," Judy said, knowing she sounded tipsy and not caring. "Time has forgotten us, but we still remember."

"What does that mean?" Greg scoffed. "Remember what?"

"The smell of roses and wheat and storms."

"Bullshit," Greg said, but Judy meant it, in a fuzzy, three-glasses-of-wine kind of way. It was easier to think about this place, the land she loved, than it was to think about her sister, whom she had once loved, in some primal way would always love, but had lost even before the accident. Her eyes filled up, and she tried to wipe the tears away without Greg seeing.

Greg leaned over the side of his chair, grabbed the bottle off the porch floor and refilled their glasses. Then he raised his.

"To Shannon," he said.

"To Shannon," she replied, clinking her glass against his and tipping a wave of wine into her mouth, a complex song that played on her tongue and in her throat as she swallowed. Then she sighed and closed her eyes, rocking, rocking. In the distance, a train whistle blew, and somewhere, far away, a motorcycle droned into the night.

THE PLASTIC BOTTLE of pain pills lay on the floor of Jack's kitchen, where it had rolled under the edge of the cabinet. He had tried twice already to pick it up, amid the crumbs and the dust bunnies. Now, with all the discipline and denial he could muster, he lowered himself gingerly to a crouch, trying to keep his back vertical, his shoulder steady. He reached out with his right hand and grasped the plastic bottle, only to feel the wrenching of the broken bones in his left shoulder. He let out a small cry of pain. By the time he stood up again, his eyes were watering.

He'd spent days on the couch or in bed, watching TV and storm videos, trying to rest, to get the bones to heal. Nothing but time would do it. It had been a week. He thought maybe it was getting a little better, and then he'd do something stupid like drop the bottle and have to stress the collarbone all over again.

The truth was, the pain pills made him feel a little queasy. Some days, he just drank whiskey. It was medicinal, he told himself.

At the end of the second week, it was getting a little better. He tried to sleep on his good side, but sometimes, in the morning, he could feel the collarbone had slipped out of place. He had to snap it back in before his body awoke to the pain. Sometimes, when he breathed, he thought he heard the bones clicking inside. He carried himself carefully, coddling his ribs, dimly aware that they were healing, too. In time, he started to think a little less about Shannon, and a little less about his mother. Her loss had become fresh and raw again after the accident, a wound reopened as his foggy memory forced him to relive a long-imagined scene on a dark road, late at night.

"Jack, are you sure you want this one?" Marcus said one steamy day as they stood in the middle of a used car lot. It smelled of asphalt and oil. After one test drive, Jack had chosen a beat-up, olive-green station wagon as his new, old car.

"It's fine. It runs OK. It's perfect for hail. I can't make it any worse," Jack said, taking a draw on a cigarette, holding himself straight as an arrow. Standing this way made his shoulder feel better, made him feel taller.

"But it's — it's —" Marcus groped for a diplomatic way to say it.

"A P.O.S.?" Jack finished. "Yes, it's a piece of shit. But it'll be my piece of shit. And it's about all I can afford right now."

The salesman, his mustache trim, his tie red, his impeccably white shirt wet under the armpits, approached them from the office, smiling. "My manager says, for you, one thousand five hundred dollars for this beautiful car and its wonderful mileage." His English was too crisp to be anything but foreign.

"Eight hundred cash, and I drive this eyesore off your lot today, saving you the embarrassment of foisting it on some other moron," Jack said.

The salesman didn't even blink. "I will draw up the papers," he said.

One day, Jack felt well enough to run his errand, to release the last vestiges of Shannon. He grabbed the envelope on the kitchen counter, the fat one addressed to Judy, and drove himself to the post office.

STORMS LOOKED different from inside the sky.

Robinson's handwritten poem about the desert, a lightning postcard, and his voice, on the phone night after night, finally coaxed Judy onto the plane to Phoenix, where she would meet him. From here, with burning blue above her, she could look down and clearly see the children of the monsoon. In the August heat, with moisture streaming in from the Pacific and spinning around the Four Corners high, storms blossomed over the desert. Their anvils were gleaming white discs, stretching out like misty parasols that cast huge shadows over the brown landscape below. The pilot eased the plane around the deceptively lovely storms, avoiding their potent updrafts.

It felt strange, not driving to a chase. Her carry-on bags were a nightmare of camera gear that got her stopped at nearly every security checkpoint. She had a digital camera, a video camera, two tripods and extra gadgets. In her backpack, she had the envelope for her parents.

She hadn't wanted to look in there. It was hard to believe Shannon's life had been boiled down to this packet of papers. Now, though, with a half hour until they landed, she decided she owed it to herself, to Shannon, to glance at the contents before handing them over.

It was a fat, brown envelope. Instead of pulling the tab and showering herself with the gray padding, she worked out the staples and popped open the end.

There wasn't much in there. A checkbook, some car insurance stuff, a few forms and bills she figured her parents would throw out anyway. And amid the papers, there was another envelope, a yellow one, folded over something thick. She pulled it out and wondered if she should open it. Of course she should. Jack had addressed the whole thing to her. She unfolded the envelope, reached inside and felt the familiar cloth of a worn hardbound book. She pulled it out, slowly. It was *The Mystery of the Tolling Bell*, one of the Nancy Drew books she and Shannon used to read together. The spine was broken, and many of the pages had brown splotches where the rain had stained them. Inside the front cover, their names were scrawled, *Judy Hale, Shannon Hale,* in purple pen.

Judy traced her finger along the names, written in the stilted cursive of children, and shook her head. A sob caught in her throat. She couldn't believe Shannon had kept this, all this time. Judy stowed the novel in its envelope in her bag, separate from the papers. She looked at the return address on the packet — *J. Andrecs,* in neat, printed letters, slanted in black ink, far away, sending her sister back to her.

"Thank you," she murmured.

"Are your parents always that, um, friendly?" Robinson asked. He and Judy had parked next to a narrow, rural road in a desolate area south of Phoenix. Their red rental car was a convertible, but they kept the tan roof in place while they ran the motor and blasted the air conditioning to fend off the 109-degree heat. There were no storms yet, though they eyed a few wan clouds with hope.

"I'm sorry about that," Judy said, tapping the steering wheel as she stared through the windshield at the scrubby, harshly lit landscape and the pointy little mountains. "My mother sometimes can't help being rude. I think she's decided to hate storm chasers. I think it has something to do with what happened."

"She doesn't hate *you*," he said as he tinkered with his video camera. His face was shadowed by his trusty cap. "It was just when she said, 'Why don't you get a hobby that doesn't kill people?' that gave me pause."

Judy snorted. "Storm chasing had nothing to do with it, but that hardly matters to her. I think she wants someone to blame. I guess it was a good idea not to stay there. We'd never hear the end of it."

"Maybe tomorrow we should try farther north, Flagstaff, if the storms don't pop here," Robinson said.

"At least we'd see the state," she said. "Oh, look! A dust devil!"

She opened the car door, stepped out and was smacked by the blast furnace of the desert. "Hellacious," she said, breathing in the hot, dry air as she opened the back door and pulled out her tripod. And delicious, she thought.

She clicked her video camera into the mount and zoomed in on the base of the dust devil. It kicked up amber dirt and weeds beyond a stretch of gray-green vegetation, and then it spiraled upward, responding to the light winds, rising with the heat, sending out thin tendrils of dust like ethereal arms, embracing itself. Robinson hopped out of the car, too, and panned across the scene, the flat land, the mountains.

"Look, two more!" he said.

Conditions were perfect here, where the hills met the plain. The three dust devils grew tall and majestic, all moving slowly in the same direction, swinging their indeterminate hips with deliberate grace. They trekked for hundreds of yards, rivaling in form, if not in violence, small tornadoes Judy had seen. After ten minutes or so, they thinned to smudges against the blue sky, and then they were gone.

"As light as angels," she said in wonder.

They tried heading east of the city at sunset, where a few storms formed on the high ground. One gave them a lightning show for a while, turning orange and purple as the sun slipped away behind them, and then it died as the air cooled. There would be no evening chase. After some tasty Mexican food and a couple of Coronas, they retired to the hotel, beat from the heat.

They had decided to share a suite, to save money, and now Judy wondered if it was a good idea. She and Robinson had become close, through their phone calls, through everything that had happened, but now, his nearness raised questions she wasn't sure she was ready to answer. They sat on the comfy couch for a while, laughing at an old Bill Murray movie on TV. During the commercials, he scribbled in what looked like a journal.

"What is that?" she asked. "Your diary?"

"Not exactly. You might call it thoughts or essays. Sometimes it's poems. It's mostly about nature, about the storms.

I'm thinking of putting it together with some pictures and making a book out of it."

"Really? That sounds like something I'd read."

"Maybe it's something we should do together," he said. "You're a better photographer than I am. I can write; you can illustrate."

"This isn't going to be like the short film we were going to do together, the one of you getting hammered by the gust front, is it?" she asked, ribbing him.

"No." He looked her in the eye. "This time I'm serious. I want to do something with you."

She felt his rare earnestness, was drawn to it. Then the movie came back on, and he smiled and put his journal aside. They settled back into watching and laughing, subject dropped.

"I'm exhausted," she said when it was over. "I love getting the extra hour when I come west, but it wears me out."

"Then it must be time for bed," he said, turning toward her, resting his elbow on the back of the couch and twirling a curl of his short, wavy hair. The look in his brown eyes was playful, inviting. She gazed back and smiled, silent, not ready to respond. After a long pause, he smiled, too. "You get the bedroom," he said. "I'll fold out the couch."

"You're sweet," she said, moving a little closer to him on the fat cushions of the sofa. "Robinson, I want to tell you something. It's kind of embarrassing."

"Really? How embarrassing?" he asked with mock anticipation.

"Not in a fun way," Judy said, smiling, then not. "It's kind of stupid, really. I want to tell you, first, that I am so glad you got me out here. I'm having a really good time."

"I knew you would."

"And it's helping me think through things, you know? You know what I'm talking about. My sister. Years ago, we were best friends, we really were, when we were kids. Sometimes the best friends you have as kids don't last, and we were dealing with some pretty unusual circumstances. But it was like, when I lost her as a friend, which is really what happened, I didn't trust that kind of friendship anymore. I had friends but not many. Once in a while, I'd have one of those conversations that really made me think I had made a connection with someone again, but it was always fleeting. It was like I'd lost the ability to have a really good, deep friend. That's what embarrasses me, that I've been so lousy at making that connection. I grew away from everyone I knew, especially Shannon. Yet somehow, in the back of my mind, even with all the strangeness between us, I thought she and I might be friends again someday. Sisters and friends. And then — then there was no chance of that ever happening. And I thought I might never have a best friend again. But I was talking with you every night, and especially since then, I've realized something. You're my best friend, Robinson."

On his face, pleasure mixed with puzzlement. "I'm trying to decide if this is the 'you're just a friend' speech or the 'you've got a friend' speech, which is really kind of a nice song, or ..."

"You're too funny, Robinson," she said. "Don't think about this too much. I'm just trying to say this means something to me. You and me, it means something. It means more than anything has in a really long time."

He put an arm around her. "I think that's good, then," he said. "So you're not going to, like, never talk to me now, right?"

"Why would you think that?"

"A lot of women have said nice things to me right before they started ignoring my phone messages."

"This isn't a blowoff, Robinson. It's more like, I don't know, I want you to know that you are really important to me. And that's all I can say for now."

"So maybe you'll say more later."

"Maybe." She smiled.

"You know what? I have a best friend already."

She feigned shock. "So you're blowing *me* off?"

"Oh, you're different. I mean, I have a guy best friend. You know, we hang out and do guy stuff. Drink beer and go see the Orioles. I'm really very normal. I'm always afraid you're going to decide I'm too boring to talk to. My college roommate said I was too well-adjusted to write anything creative. Maybe that's why I'm a journalist."

She laughed. "You seem pretty creative to me. And I don't think you're all that normal, if it makes you feel any better."

"That's the nicest thing anyone's ever said to me," he said, and she grinned. She lay her head on his shoulder, nestling into the crook of his arm, and he gently, slowly kissed her forehead. She knew there could be more, that they could be more, but she wasn't sure she was ready. Her body stirred, unbidden, at the touch of his lips on her skin, at the feel of his warmth next to hers, but at this moment, she needed his comfort more. She didn't want to break the spell. She stayed still, breathing slowly, until he lay his head against hers. They dozed off that way, for a while, and when a distant siren woke her, she extricated herself, put a blanket over him as he sleepily curled up on the couch, turned off the light and retired to the bedroom.

They started the next day at a nearby cafe with pancakes, which reminded Judy of home. Then they slathered sunscreen on themselves, donned sunglasses and folded down the car roof before starting the drive north. By midafternoon, they found themselves on the long, empty road out to Meteor Crater, aiming to be tourists if they couldn't be chasers.

Judy didn't linger in the visitor center. While Robinson read about the impact fifty thousand years ago, she made a beeline for the rim with her camera. But after a few minutes of taking pictures, she found her lenses could not do the crater justice. This grassy bowl, smashed into the desert, was too vast for her camera, and her mind, to comprehend.

She was sitting on the gnarly rocks at the crater's edge, feeling tiny in the universe, when Robinson emerged from the building and sat next to her. The temperature had eased as the clouds above them thickened and filtered the sun. In the distance, they could see a couple of rain shafts but no lightning yet.

"Do you know what they used to call this place?" Robinson asked.

"What?"

"Franklin's Hole."

Judy giggled. "It's a hole, all right."

"After that," he said, "it was Coon Butte."

"Even more poetic."

"They thought it was a volcano for a long time."

"Really? It seems so different to me. So exotic. So, 'Holy crap, a great big rock is about to fall on our heads!'"

A welcome breeze swept across them and the rocks. A trio of tourists nearby chattered in German. Below, the bowl seemed impossibly green. Erosion channels that etched the sides of the crater told the story; when it rained, water drained into the depression and quenched the desert's thirst.

"So," Judy said, "are you chasing with Bruce and Whit next spring?"

"I don't think so. They've had kind of a falling out."

"I hadn't heard about that. They're such good friends."

"Yeah, but you remember that tornado that went through the truck stop near Abilene in late May? The one that sucked up the tractor trailers? The video was all over The Weather Channel."

"Oh, yeah, I hated missing that one," Judy said.

"Bruce shot that video," he said. "Whit was there, too, but you know Whit. He just turns his video over to the National Weather Service. Not Bruce. After it got all over TV, he hired a PR guy and tried to get on all these talk shows. He started ragging on all the other chasers who missed it. He used the footage in his car dealership commercials, too, though I'm not sure how. Whit said the ads screamed something about 'extreme deals' to replace your storm-damaged vehicles. It was all pretty tacky. Bruce got a really big head. He started to believe in his own mythology."

"I thought he already had a really big head," Judy said.

"Now it won't even fit in the door of his SUV."

Judy laughed. "And that's a big SUV. So they're not getting along, huh?"

"No, and Whit doesn't think his office will let him off during peak storm season again. So I'm looking for a chase partner." He wiggled his eyebrows at her.

"You know you can count on me," she said, happy to get the invitation.

"I was hoping you'd say that," he said. "And you even have a home base right in the heart of it all!"

"Pancake, vacation capital of the world."

After a quiet night in Flagstaff, they headed back to

Phoenix for two more days of chasing, including a spectacular evening of lightning over the desert. Each vivid bolt stitched itself across the black velvet sky like molten silver threads. Amid the cacti in the middle of nowhere, they ran into another chaser who gave them tips on the terrain. She was a lightning specialist, a kindred spirit, and she and Judy exchanged cards, promising to write. Back at the suite that night, Judy and Robinson retired to their separate quarters, and Judy did not dream of Jack or Shannon or Robinson. Instead, she dreamt of lightning, and was at peace.

At the airport the next day, Judy set down her luggage so she could bid Robinson farewell at his gate. His plane was leaving first.

"I'll see you next storm season," he said. "I'm coming out early, start of May."

"Good," she said. "I can't wait till spring."

She could have been talking about the storms, but she wasn't sure that she was. He put his bags down and enfolded her in his arms. She returned his long, lingering hug, trying to soak up his warmth, knowing she would miss it. He rubbed his face gently against her hair, breathing her in, then disentangled himself. She found herself flushed, anxious at his leaving.

Robinson grabbed the ends of her braids and gave them a little tug. "Spring," he whispered, with his trademark impish smile. Then he picked up his bags and disappeared into the line and down the long corridor that would lead him back to the sky.

"Every day from here on out brings us a minute or two closer to spring," Sam Rainier said. "I love the solstice."

Professor Malik, Jack and Marcus sat around the glow of the stone fireplace in the great room of Rainier's ranch house, notebooks on their laps, beers in their hands, watching Rainier admiring the world beyond him. He stood in front of the large windows, hands on his hips, in jeans and a Western shirt. Dusk was already settling on this shortest day of the year. Beyond him were softly rolling hills, a red horse barn and fields, starting to fill in with white as it snowed. The dizzily falling flakes caught the last gleams of cloudy light. His long, snowy-white hair made him seem like a king of this winter world. He reigned here. The occasional girlfriend came and went, but always, he stayed, enjoying the isolation. The city was beginning to creep out this way, but he had enough land that he could maintain an island of what the old Red Earth Country used to be.

"A little more daylight every day," said Malik, who looked tan even now, on the official cusp of winter. "A little more sun, a little more heat. It'll be storm season before we know it."

"Will we be ready?" Rainier asked.

"We've gone over just about everything. We've got the cars. It's a two-year grant, so we've got the funding," Malik said. "But here's the thing. The university is really looking for results this year. I mean, we always have results, but they want more, better. We'll have to maximize every storm we get, get closer, get better data, learn more about how the tornado forms. They want something they can put out a press release on," he said to groans. "Maybe actually prove something."

Rainier laughed. "Anything but that," he said. "This is academia!"

"I'm not saying we do anything different," Malik said, "but

we need some good luck, wisely used. Last year was too spotty. And the government grants are harder and harder to get, all the more reason to make sure everything goes according to plan with the mesonet. I guess they're spending too much money on tanks."

"I'd love to have one of those for core-punching," Marcus said wistfully.

Professor Malik laughed. "You'll have the government van. We're lucky it's not being shipped to some desert halfway across the world."

"A perfect place for catching hail," Jack cracked, sipping his beer. He felt the season changing, felt it in his mostly healed body, in his clearing head as the darkest day spun away with the orbiting Earth. The autumn had seemed more oppressive than usual. He'd been working a lot, drinking a little. His dissertation was almost in hand. He'd seen a lot of the inside of the offices at the meteorology building and almost nothing of the land and sky he craved, but he hadn't felt ready to experience those raw sensations as the few and speedy autumn storms screamed through. This spring, he knew, he would need to chase, would need to get out, get into the supercells, attempt to expunge the experiences of the past year. He'd get close to the tornadoes. Malik wouldn't be disappointed.

"Those ribs ready yet?" Marcus asked hopefully.

"They feel fine," Jack joked.

Marcus frowned. "You know what I mean."

Rainier broke himself away from the view. "Let me check. Smell is torturing you, isn't it?" he said, grinning. He stomped off toward the kitchen and to a back patio where a gas-powered meat smoker had been wafting delicious enticements all afternoon.

"I need another beer. Anyone?" Jack asked as he got up.

"I'll come with you," Malik said.

"I'm fine," said Marcus, who took Rainier's place at the window, scanning the snowy tableau.

In the large kitchen, with its long marble island and stainless-steel appliances and electric wine cellar — he'd always thought Rainier had some money tucked away somewhere — Jack poked through the fridge, getting out the potato salad they were going to have with their ribs. Malik popped a can of biscuit dough, put the rubbery pucks on a tray and into the oven for their transformation into buttery bread, and took out the bubbling apple crisp Rainier had put in earlier. Then he dropped corncobs, fresh from Florida via the grocery store, into the pot boiling on the stove. Not bad for freezing weather.

Jack found what he was looking for and pulled out the bottle.

"Check it out," he said to Malik. The label said "Tornado Alley Amber Ale."

"I didn't know he had that in there!" Malik said. "Where'd he get that?"

"Arkansas, I think."

"Give me one of those. Maybe it will bring us luck."

"God, scientists are the worst when it comes to superstition," Jack said, handing him the bottle, and Malik chortled. They opened their beers and took healthy swigs.

"Mmm," Malik said. "You know, Jack, I've noticed you've been around the lab a lot more. You're doing good work, of course, and I never thought I'd be saying this to you, but — you just haven't seemed like the old Jack. Maybe you need to get out more."

"I am the old Jack. I just turned thirty," he said.

"Puh-leeeze," Malik said. "You're making me feel decrepit."

"I'm fine. I just want to get the dissertation done, move onward and upward. I have plenty of fun," Jack said.

Malik looked skeptical. "I used to have fun," he said. "Then I got married. Actually, don't tell my wife this, but it's even more fun now. She chases with me sometimes, though most of the time, she tells me I'm crazy. I think it's just what I need."

"I think you're more domesticated than I am, professor," Jack said.

"I hope so. I'm painfully dull."

Just then, Rainier elbowed open the sliding door that led from the patio to the dining area and came in with a steaming platter of seasoned pork ribs.

"I smell that!" Marcus shouted from the other room, and the others laughed.

After they'd sated themselves, Malik and Rainier talked over budget details by the fire, while Jack and Marcus went outside to the patio to drink more beer and watch the snow falling in the dark. Slats of dim light shone through the vertical blinds of the sliding doors and onto their Adirondack chairs.

"I even love snow," Jack said, reaching out to catch some flakes on his brown suede gloves. He wore a black toque on his head and a brown leather jacket, which barely kept out the cold. "I love rain. I love thunder. It's almost all I think about. Am I a freak?"

"You're asking the wrong person," Marcus said, "though you seem more focused than anyone I've ever met."

"So am I a freak?" Jack was uncomfortable asking but suddenly wanted to know.

"Not everyone has the same level of obsession," Marcus said. "You have a talent. It might be a freakish talent, but I don't think you're a freak for following it. If you're not sure, I guess you have to ask yourself why you got into storm chasing in the first place."

Jack mulled the question for a moment. "Because I love the storms," he said. "Because they do for me what nothing else can. They're a new mystery, every time out. They don't destroy because they want to. They aren't beautiful because someone made them that way. They just are. They're powerful. They're magnificent, in infinite ways. They can't be fucked up by people. Really … they're all that matters. Mattered."

"Don't they still matter?" Marcus asked.

"Yes, but I'm not sure they should."

"Because of what happened? That had nothing to do with storms."

"It had to do with me," Jack said. "I didn't know what I was doing with that girl."

Marcus chuckled. "I never thought I'd hear you say that. I thought you always knew what you were doing."

Jack allowed himself a rueful smile. "So did I. I think her sister got to me first. And then, there she was, this pretty thing — an escape from her sister, or an extension. Or just another in a long chain. I wasn't sure. I thought I would have more time to find out."

"You'll sort it out. Maybe your head takes longer to heal than your bones," Marcus said. He took a sip of beer and pulled his black pea coat more tightly around him. The snowflakes fell on his long, dark curls and onto his glasses, where they melted, leaving the lenses speckled like a windshield. "I don't know anything about women, unfortunately, but I know they can't get enough of you. When you're ready for them, they'll be there. For now, just worry about what you need."

"I don't even know what that is."

"The storms, stupid," Marcus said with good humor. "It's all about the storms."

Jack flashed back to the storms he'd seen over the years, filtering out his encyclopedic memory of dates and places and Fujita scale ratings and letting himself remember only the color and sensation of each moment, the storms of his childhood, the lightning of New Mexico, the tornado when he first met Judy, the amazing supercells that saved him from misery, that carried him through year after year, always transcendent, even when the rest of his life seemed brittle and hard. It was the time in between that made him hesitate, suddenly. He didn't want to think about the rest. That's what beer and women had always been, filler, sometimes delightfully delusional filler.

"You know the best women to go out with? Married women," Jack told Marcus. "They don't expect anything. If they decide to fool around, they don't want anything but sex. It's fantastic."

"Now there's the Jack I know and despise," Marcus said.

"I don't know if I have the energy for it anymore."

"The sex?"

"I think I'll always have the energy for sex," Jack said in a wry tone. "It's the stuff that sometimes follows that concerns me."

"I know you're not talking about feelings."

"No, not mine," Jack said. "Everyone else's."

Marcus laughed. "What is this, an attack of conscience? I'm sure it's temporary. You're going to forget about all of this when you see another tornado."

"Four or five months from now," Jack said. "Christ." He took another sip of beer and rallied, tired of introspection. "Fuck it. It's all that matters. You're right. It's all about the storms."

JUDY EMERGED from the house with a couple of glasses of iced tea. "This wireless connection rocks," Robinson said from the swing in the garden, where he was tapping on the keyboard of his laptop computer.

It was May third, in the golden light of early evening, and her flowers were blooming again.

It had been a long winter, with more snow than Judy remembered seeing since her childhood. It had muted the land, smooth and white, softening the trees' stark, leafless branches. The only thing that bloomed in her house during those gray months was a tropical splash of color, the paphiopedilum orchid she'd been ready to abandon to the compost. Relocated near a southern window, it flourished. Its leaves grew bright, and it sent up a long, slender spike that in slow motion unfolded a furry-winged, round-lipped yellow slipper, a tiny sun that led her into spring.

Now, everything was growing madly, green and sweet, and the fountain bubbled in the corner. Judy set Robinson's glass on the small wrought-iron table next to the swing, then took a seat by him. He was flipping fast through pages of data for tomorrow's chase. She looked over his shoulder at the computer model he was perusing and let out a low whistle.

"Holy cow, that CAPE's over five thousand," she said.

"Nuclear," Robinson said of the potential for convection. "Just west of here, tomorrow afternoon."

"What about winds?" she asked.

"That low coming in is going to back everything nicely. Dewpoints are already looking good. And feel that south wind."

The warm, moist breeze sailed through her blooms and ivy, spreading the roses' heady scent, stirring the old oak branches above their heads. It was the moisture train, transporting tropical Gulf of Mexico air into the Plains.

"Helicity?" she asked.

"Dreamy."

"Lifted index?"

"Minus eight or so, right now," he said. "It'll all change a little by the morning, but we've got a serious storm situation on our hands. It'll be PDS watch boxes by tomorrow afternoon."

"Don't curse it," Judy replied, but she wondered. PDS meant *particularly dangerous situation* or, as she sometimes thought of it, pretty damn scary. The thing is, when the Storm Prediction Center went that far with a tornado watch, it usually ended up being what chasers called a "PDS bust box." Too much of a good thing. Anyway, that wasn't until tomorrow, and there was no way to foresee whether all the elements would come together as spectacularly as the computer predictions suggested. They rarely did.

One thing seemed certain. They wouldn't have to go far.

"Just when I thought Pancake was pre-disastered," she said.

"I wouldn't worry." Robinson closed his laptop and put an arm casually around her shoulders as they swung gently. "The thing about tornadoes is that a couple of miles can make all the difference in the world. Let's hope we see a dozen tomorrow, all in the middle of abandoned fields."

"Sounds good to me," Judy said, though part of her was thinking, with creepy ambivalence, *I may finally get to see what it was like, all those years ago.*

"At least we won't have a long drive, and we can check data up until the last minute," Robinson said. "This close, it's going to be a real gentleman's chase."

Judy studied his face, his curly hair and his brown eyes, which lit up like amber as he looked at the sky. He was clearly happy to have returned to the Plains, to the freedom of chase season, as he gazed through the branches, content in the moment, in the comforting motion of the swing. Then she glanced at her fountain, the bubbling, elfin boy who still looked skyward, tossing the stream of water from hand to hand, spilling his joy into the basin below, into her garden. The resemblance was remarkable.

❧

"THIS IS a hell of a way to break in a new team," said Jack, looking around at the mesonet drivers and passengers in the meteorology building's parking lot. It was chilly this morning, and he wore a gray university sweatshirt over his white T-shirt and long khaki shorts. He took a long draw on a cigarette as he leaned against the lead van, next to the snappy-yet-casual Professor Malik. They'd just spent an hour going over the data. It looked as if nature was about to lay a good whipping on west-central Kansas.

"It's likely to be a very busy day," Malik acknowledged. "But it's not all newbies. We have some of the experienced people back. I'm putting a new one with you, though, Jack. He's a promising student. Grew up in Texas. Loves storms. He'll be a senior next year."

"I don't want a kid," Jack said.

"He's good. Ice water in his veins."

"And you know this how?"

"I'm just making it up," Malik confessed, grinning. "The stuff about the ice water, anyway. But he's a great student. He'll be fine, *Doctor* Andreas."

"Hmph." Jack took another drag and wondered if he should have had breakfast. He was hungry and cranky. He'd rushed out of his apartment that morning, stopping only to dash off a postcard telling his father that his dissertation had been accepted. He hadn't been sure about sending it, but then thought, what the hell, maybe he'll die of shock when he sees it.

Jack looked around and counted the mesonet vehicles. One was missing. "Where is my car, anyway?"

"You mean the green machine?" Malik asked.

"Obviously, I know where that is," Jack said, gesturing to his defiantly ugly station wagon. "I mean the probe."

"I think the boys have been working on it."

Jack gave him a look. "Working on it?"

"You'll see," Malik said, a twinkle in his brown eyes.

Jack scowled and pulled out his phone. He punched in the number. "Marcus!" he barked at the hello on the other end. "Where's my car?"

"We're about to deliver your probe," Marcus said.

"That sounds painful. Just get it over here. We're leaving in twenty minutes."

In five, Probe 3 came around the corner, then rocked to a halt a few feet away. It looked about the same as Jack remembered, only —

"What is that?" Jack asked as the red-plaid-clad Marcus and unruly Dennis got out of the car.

"Loudspeaker system!" Dennis said.

"You're kidding." Jack leaned forward to examine the speakers on the roof. "Very Blues Brothers."

"Not quite as big. Anyway, it was easy," said Marcus. "And now you can yell at us without getting into a coughing fit."

"Very funny," Jack said, though he could barely suppress a smile. "What else?"

"There's a siren. Well, an air horn, really. And the lights," Marcus said.

"Oh, yeah," Jack said, noticing a bar of amber spin-lights on the top of the car. They weren't on.

"You just flip a switch on the dash," Marcus said.

"Convenient," Jack said, "in case I need to lead a presidential motorcade or something."

Marcus rolled his eyes behind his glasses. "When it gets hairy, it's good to be visible."

"You're just trying to butter me up with gadgets," Jack said.

"Is it working?" Dennis asked.

"I'll tell you if we survive today." Jack turned to Malik. "Shall I rally the troops?"

"Please do," Malik said. "I'll see if I can find my earplugs." He walked away, waving at Sam Rainier, who'd just arrived in his slick German sedan.

Jack dropped his cigarette on the pavement and crushed it under his high-top sneaker, then sat in the driver's seat of the car, flipped the radio to external and keyed the mike. "All probes, we leave in fifteen minutes!" he boomed. Marcus and Dennis jumped at the reverberating blast of sound. The others on the team stopped what they were doing and gaped. Jack laughed as he got out. "Hey, I could learn to like this thing!"

"Good," said Marcus, tapping his head with the heel of one

hand, trying to get his ears working again. "I needed something to tinker with after I got the van where I wanted it."

"The hail-catcher might get a good workout today," Jack said.

"Maybe. I almost don't care," Marcus said. "All I know is, this is the year I'm going to see a tornado. One way or another, I'm going to see a tornado."

"Not if we send you into the hail core all season," Jack said, enjoying the tormented look on Marcus's face.

"One way or another, I swear to god," Marcus muttered. He and a chuckling Dennis walked off to the other side of the parking lot, where the hail van was parked.

A clean-cut young man with dark brown hair, in jeans and a white severe-storms-lab golf shirt, walked hesitantly toward Jack. "Jack?" he asked, holding out his hand. "I'm Renny Ramirez. I'm supposed to drive you today."

Renny was dressed like Malik, Jack noted with amusement. Another brilliant, untested protege.

"Ever get a speeding ticket?" Jack asked, shaking the undergrad's hand.

For a second, Renny looked as if he didn't want to answer. "A couple," he finally admitted.

"Good," Jack said. "Get in."

✎

A LEVEL LANDSCAPE can look the same for years, with subtle variations — rain washes out its color, snow purifies it, fog obscures it, sun etches it in sharp shadow. But one day, the familiar, flat land is transformed. A giant has pushed a mountain into view, built it up from the essence of air. Suddenly, everything is dwarfed by its imposing mass, its rough, vertical walls. The mountain is the new focus of every eye, the dominant presence that rules what came before. The world has changed.

This was the new mountain west of Pancake, a growing and morphing monster that took over the late-afternoon sky and made the land of Judy's childhood seem foreign and vulnerable. It looked like something to ski down, to climb up, to watch warily for an eruption of nature's wrath.

She and Robinson had traveled just fifty miles southwest of town around midafternoon, chasing a puff on the satellite image. By the time they got near it, it was a rising tower, developing clusters and fists of hard, white convection that built the mountain handful by handful, rapidly, faster than the imagination of geology. The evolving features rolled up the sides of the mountain, expanding like an explosion, becoming darker and more forbidding until the anvil began to spread out above their heads, shadowing the people in its path.

"We don't need data now," Judy said, gazing raptly at the flattening base of the storm. There were stirrings there, hints of rotation as tendrils of cloud lowered and lifted. Both she and Robinson had their video cameras on tripods, aimed at this swirling heart.

"This bad boy means business," Robinson said, tugging down on the bill of his baseball cap as the wind intensified. "I don't think we need a radar image to tell us that."

He'd driven his bright yellow SUV. She'd stashed her car in her garage, just in case there was hail. It was a safe bet there already was. As the strong updraft threw the ice particles skyward into the freezing zone, and as they dropped and were picked up and cycled through again, those that didn't hit the ground grew with every minute. Judy and Robinson were directly east of the developing mesocyclone; to their north, a stunning, white shaft of precipitation fell, its color almost certainly the reflection of falling balls of ice.

Judy felt nervous, more than the usual prickle of anticipation she experienced during a chase. The storm had already moved thirty or so miles east-northeast of where it had been born as an insignificant shower. At her back was Pancake, not far away, and this mountain was sliding toward it, threatening to engulf it. Somehow, the chase felt different when her home was in the path. She never wanted a town hit, but her town? As much as she wanted to remember, to re-create that terrible day sixteen years ago so she could finally understand its cruel mechanics, the reality of it was almost too much to endure. It was like recognizing a sequence of events as something she'd once dreamed about, a frightening invasion of her subconscious.

They got into the car and moved a little farther down the road so the storm wouldn't overtake them, then hopped out and set up their cameras again. A distinct wall cloud had lowered from the base. The supercell dominated the sky, dark, laced with green light, and lightning zipped through the anvil above their heads. It wasn't the safest thing, being outside the car with bolts threatening, but their adrenaline had taken over. They were in the perfect spot, out of the hail and in the cell's sights.

"You know sometimes you get a feeling about a storm, when you know everything is clicking?" Robinson asked. The rotation was more visible now, undeniable.

Judy knew exactly what he was talking about. "It feels just like this. Look over there. Dust. I think it's RFD."

What appeared to be a rear-flank downdraft was kicking up dust under the base, near the back side of the meso. The descending air began to cut a slot in the clouds, setting up the magical interaction between updraft and downdraft. The slot curled into the storm, appearing to carve out a slender funnel that began to poke its nose toward the ground.

"It's doing it. It's doing it!" Robinson said. They were less than a mile away, and the view was so clear, it almost didn't feel real. As her video rolled, Judy snapped a few shots with her still camera. The shutter sounded sluggish as it responded to the low light, so she cranked up the ISO to compensate. It shot faster this time, and she took about twenty more frames as the slender, white funnel connected with the dust now spinning on the ground. The tornado was a delicate conduit from the earth to the gods, its vaporous texture defying its power. Its snowy color shifted to russet as it ripped through a freshly plowed field northwest of them. At least there are no houses here, Judy thought, as the tornado eased northeast until it came nearly parallel with their position. It didn't get big, just darker, and then it became more wispy until only a sinuous snake of condensation lifted away from the ground and spiraled into the clouds.

"Wow," Robinson breathed when it was over. "Talk about all the big wedges you want, but that's one of the most beautiful tornadoes I've ever seen!"

Judy was already packing up, putting her tripod in the back seat and her cameras in the front. "Now's not the time to have a stormgasm," she said, getting in. "It isn't over. That looks like a new meso just east. We're going to have to catch up."

"I know, I know. I just hated to leave this one." He, too, stowed his tripod and gear, then sat in the driver's seat and popped his video camera into the dash mount. He tapped on the laptop mounted between the seats to check the radar. "I think we've lost signal," he said, then took a moment to reach out and lay a hand on her shoulder. "Don't worry."

She nodded. He knew what she was thinking.

He wheeled the vehicle around, driving east, eyeing the mesocyclone ahead and to the left. A few golf-ball-size hailstones hit the car, banging loudly on the roof as they sped up, trying to get back into position. They passed a sign that said "Pancake, 6 miles."

"Here's where it gets interesting," he said, giving Judy a sidelong glance. "Are you ready?"

"Ready as I can be."

"Why don't you call Whit, see if he can help us get a track on this thing," Robinson said. Whit was working at his National Weather Service office in Texas, two states away and out of the firing zone.

Judy picked up her cell, glanced at her slow-to-load radar app, then scrolled to Whit's office number and hit dial. She was transferred once, then put on hold. At long last, he came on.

"Whit? It's Judy."

"Judy!" came back that delicious drawl. "Are you with Robinson? He said he might call."

"Yeah. We just saw the prettiest tornado. It lasted about eight minutes. It shifted from white to yellow to red. It was wild. Can you pass it on to the local NWS?"

"Sure. You want some radar data?"

"Please," Judy said. "We're headed toward Pancake. It's headed toward Pancake. I live in Pancake — you do the math. We want to get a better sense of its path."

"OK, let me look at the loop." Whit was quiet for a moment, and Judy heard the murmur of the other people in the office and the clicking of his keyboard. "You're going to be cutting it close, Judy," he said. "If it's any comfort, I think it's headed for the south side. It might miss. But there are already warnings out."

"I know. We heard the warnings. We got a half-baked radar image. I just wanted a third opinion. This thing looks like it has a wicked new meso on it."

"The shear is impressive," he said. "So is the hail. Pancake's going to lose some windows, if nothing else."

"OK," Judy said. "Just trying to breathe here. What's your best guess?"

"South side of town," Whit said. "Maybe southeast. Just stay safe. Stay ahead of it. Good luck, Judy. Let me know what happens."

"I will. Thanks, Whit." She pressed the button to end the call.

Robinson reached over and stroked her hair, tugged on a braid. "Judy, honey?"

She smiled at the endearment. "South side of town, maybe southeast," she said. "Let's just catch up, get ahead a little. There's not much we can do. I'm going to call Greg, make sure he and Uncle Ray are safe."

They were on an east-west road that ran south of town. A few outlying buildings were visible to the north as they got ahead of the storm and its rain and hail. They'd have to press east, then jog north to get into a good intercept position and see what this great, spinning mountain of cloud had in store. A new wall cloud lowered from the meso, its rotation obvious. It wouldn't take long.

Judy opened her window a little to sample the air. There was still a stout southeast wind, smelling strongly of the moist earth, rushing like water through the grasses that lined the road. And there was another sound. It was Pancake's tornado siren.

BRAD TREAT WAS EXPANDING his empire. Not only had he launched his second year of Thor's Tours; now he was brokering video, gathering the fruits of other chasers' labor and selling it for a significant cut. It wasn't a lot of money, but it was starting to be enough that he often didn't have to work his other job, as a car stereo salesman and installer at the electronic warehouse store down the street in Fort Worth. He had paid a few of the chasers to use their tornado photos, too, so he could post them on his website to lure more tourists.

High on his entrepreneurial bender and hungry for more acquisitions, Brad had proposed to Willa at Christmas, and she had said yes, though he wasn't sure why. He suspected that she liked the ring, a showy, antique-looking number he'd snagged at a pawn shop, though he told her it was his great-grandmother's. He said great-grandma was a pioneer from the early days of Texas, and her spirit reminded him of Willa. He made all that up, but sometimes a good story made questionable jewelry go down more easily.

To improve his chances on the road, Brad had even hired a forecaster: Noel. The Georgian hadn't been thrilled with returning — none of the other tourists from last spring came back — but with assurances that he would be able to call the weather shots and get paid, too, he had agreed.

Equipped with a new laptop, mobile hotspot and ham radio, Brad had a feeling his investment would pay off today. The Storm Prediction Center had made a doomsday forecast, and he'd been watching clouds build all afternoon as he waffled between targets. The convection was already well underway when Noel finally convinced him to go after a particularly menacing storm.

They were in western Kansas, in a big rental van loaded with six tourists, speeding east toward an honest-to-goodness supercell. Brad was excited. The tourists — a middle-aged couple, a retired Navy man, a college girl, and two young guys from England — were chattering excitedly at the tornado warnings streaming over the weather radio. This storm was the real thing, dramatically rotating, its dark form filling the whole sky. But just when it seemed the chase couldn't be any more promising, Noel broke the news.

"We're on the wrong side of it," he said from the passenger seat, looking at a radar image.

"I'm hearing tornado warnings," Brad said. "Don't tell me that."

"It's got a hook, no question," Noel said. "We're just not going to see crap from here. We're on the back side, northwest of it. Somehow, we're going to have to get around it. Punch the core, maybe. Catch it once it gets past Pancake."

"But Pancake's in the tornado warning," Brad said peevishly. He shuddered at the thought of punching the core, as he remembered all too well the fruitless slog through the rain and hail last year that ended with a toy windmill shattering his windshield. He had to find a tornado, prove his mettle. At this point, he would do anything to deliver one.

"It can't be helped," Noel said, poring over a Kansas gazetteer and occasionally referring to GPS software on the laptop. "We have no road options. There's the road that goes right into Pancake, but we can't get there from here. To catch a south road, we either have to go forty miles back or get past it. If we go past it, go east, we can catch the cell as it gets near the next town. It looks like it's heading kind of northeast anyway."

"What's the next town?" Brad asked, resigning himself to Noel's strategy.

"Prairie Rock," Noel said. "God help them."

THE MESONET HAD BEEN CAUGHT out of position, too far east to intercept the first tornado that descended from the massive supercell steamrolling toward Pancake. Jack was annoyed. They'd probably catch it just outside of Pancake, and then they'd have to deploy on a horrible road network before it reached the next town.

Pancake. It seemed as if everything came back to Pancake, the flat little place where disturbingly big things happened. He remembered something he'd read, some silly scientific study. Despite the hills to the east and the slow rise to the west, Kansas really was flatter than a pancake. If Kansas were more like a pancake, all the roads would have killer potholes, as big as houses. They'd have beautiful women inside them, ready to trap him and fuck with his mind.

"Jack? Jack?" Renny was saying.

Jack heard his driver even as he registered in his subconscious that someone had been speaking on the radio. He had no idea who. "What is it?" he asked Renny, doubly annoyed to be caught in his distractions.

"What do I tell the professor?"

"Nothing. Let me talk to him." Jack picked up the mike. "FC, this is Probe 3. Where do you want us again? You kind of broke up there." He gave Renny a look that told him to be quiet about his momentary lapse of attention.

"Probe 3, go straight ahead. Do not take the north road into town. I'm going to deploy some of the probes farther east and north, but I don't want anybody getting tangled up in town traffic."

"But it's not a very big town," Jack joked.

"You heard me, Jack," Malik said. "This could be a real mess. Get as close as you can but not in the middle of flying debris, OK?"

"Is there any other kind?" Jack said. "OK, FC. Fear not. Probe 3 is on the case. Over."

They were getting close. To the north, he could see buildings, the east end of Pancake. Just a few houses were on this road. Here, they were beyond the outskirts, in farm country. They passed a smelly feed lot on their left. The cows stared and chewed, unaware of the elements about to be unleashed.

"Check this out," Jack said. He reached for the mike again, switching the system to loudspeaker mode. "Mooooooo!" he boomed.

One cow of dozens turned its head toward the road.

"Dummies," Jack said. Renny laughed.

Ahead, the massive supercell spun ominously, spectacularly, perhaps five miles away. Jack could detect the wall cloud and what looked like the beginnings of a twister.

"A little faster, Renny," Jack said. "We're not missing this."

"But we're not supposed to go into town."

"Where we're going, there might not be any town left," Jack said. "Don't worry. We'll just get close enough to get our grant money's worth."

The motor picked up, and so did Jack's pulse. He thought briefly of Judy and her house and wondered if they were out of harm's way. Then the past year faded mercifully into a blur and the color of the sky, all swirled and subsumed into this, the birth of a tornado.

"I THINK this highway is going to keep us out of the hail core," Noel said, "but we're going to have to try to drop south before we get to Prairie Rock if we're going to see anything."

"We're going to see tornadoes!" Brad almost screamed.

The automated voice on the weather radio blared the news: "Trained storm spotters have confirmed a developing tornado south of Pancake. A tornado has already been sighted with this storm. This is an extremely dangerous situation. Seek shelter in an interior room on the lowest floor of your house," and so on and so on, *ad nauseam*.

"Noel, I will do whatever it takes. Figure it out. Figure out which road will get us there," Brad said.

"Why can't we see the tornado?" one of the British guys said.

"Because it's on the other side of all that rain," Noel said. "We're going to catch the storm a little farther up the road. We'll see something. I don't think it's done yet."

"We will definitely see a tornado!" Brad said, his eyebrows lifting to new heights, his voice attaining a rabid pitch as he addressed his six tourists. "People, I can promise you this. No matter what, even if everything else goes wrong today, we are going to see a tornado."

ROBINSON PULLED the car into the parking lot of a gas station on the southern edge of Pancake. A woman and man inside the glass doors stared in horror at the approaching storm. Though Robinson and Judy weren't near the center of town, the tornado siren was still loud, inciting the same monkey-screech brain alarms as fingernails on a chalkboard, wrenching their ears with its wail as they rolled down their windows to listen to the howl and thunder.

Robinson angled his car so it faced west. Across the street, what looked like a closed soda stand and a shed and a small, white house huddled, framed by a gate painted like a rainbow. The empty driveway was painted yellow.

"What the hell is that?" Robinson asked.

"The *Wizard of Oz* house," Judy said.

"You're kidding. Is Dorothy in there?"

Judy laughed, half out of fear. "I hope not, because she's about to return to Oz if she is."

Looming beyond the house, perhaps a mile away, was the new and violently rotating mesocyclone and, descending from it, a ragged wall cloud. It looked darker, meaner than the last one. Judy had mixed feelings. This budding tornado had already missed half of her town, including her house and her uncle's —though she wondered how much of her garden had been shredded by hail — yet it was still a threat, about to make a point on Pancake's south end, approaching the railroad tracks and buildings here. She realized that she wanted to see her garden live, her town survive, its children grow up without the memory that haunted her. She no longer needed to relive the tornado. She wanted to see the tornadoes, yes; photograph them, experience them for a lifetime; but she also wanted a future.

The spinning lowering became smoother as it descended. As they watched, a rust-spotted white pickup truck whizzed by them and parked under the roof that shaded the gas pumps on the opposite side of the station. The redheaded driver, a wiry man in grubby jeans and T-shirt, jumped out of the truck, leaving the door open, and ran into the station's convenience store.

"Dust! It's on the ground!" Robinson said as he turned back to the storm.

"Robinson —" Judy started to say.

"Backing off, backing off," he said, already pressing the accelerator. He took a quick left. "Hey!" he exclaimed as his hat suddenly flew off and out the open window. "I love that hat!"

"We'll look for it later in Iowa," Judy said.

He got to a reasonably safe distance, turned around fast and parked alongside the road, where they could face the tornado. It grew in size and violence as it crawled toward the cluster of buildings. It didn't look good for Pancake's tourist district.

They both saw it coming. The tornado, now a thick, fluid pillar, picked up speed it as churned forward, heading toward the Oz house.

"You've got to be kidding," Robinson said.

They both had video cameras rolling when the outer edges of the circulation embraced the already weathered buildings. Judy set hers on the dash and opened her door into the howling inflow, stepping out of the car to snap a succession of stills, the shutter going *zap-zap-zap-zap* as she caught the stunning sequence. The dark trunk of the funnel had not even touched the house when the fierce winds at the base started to sweep through, lifting off the Oz house's roof. The whole complex disintegrated in an instant as the tornado devoured the structures, and debris flew high into the air.

"God *damn*," Robinson said. "Off to see the wizard!"

"The gas station!" Judy said as she jumped back in the car.

But the funnel was already moving on a more northward

angle. Boards and insulation rained down on the gas station where they'd just been, and the T-shaped roof structure over the pumps teetered. The empty truck beneath didn't have a chance as the pavilion collapsed, but the building somehow survived. A flutter of shingles flew off its roof.

A brilliant bolt of lightning slammed into the ground between Robinson's car and the tornado, and the instantaneous crash of thunder made both of them jump. Judy watched in wonder as the tornado ambled across the road, nearing the tracks, where a train engine and two railroad cars sat idle. Beyond the tracks, there were a couple of railroad shacks, then a few houses. Homes became more dense farther north.

"Stop, stop," Judy whispered under her breath.

The train was the first station on the twister's whistlestop tour. Defying gravity, the engine lifted up as the swirling tornado overtook it and heaved it around the funnel, then dashed it to the ground fifty yards away, knocking down a couple of power poles in the process. The other cars were tossed aside like toys. Next, the twister plowed through the shacks.

Robinson eased his SUV forward, following slowly, driving carefully around boards lying in the road. He glanced in his rearview mirror. "There's a car coming up fast," he said.

Judy turned and looked through the back window. It was one of the mesonet cars. She didn't think hard about who it might be, just faced front. "So it is," she said. "I'm more worried about those houses."

The tornado was getting closer to the first house and thinner, too, leaning, an S-shaped shadow of its former self.

"I think it's weakening," Robinson said. "It's a freakin' miracle."

"It's strong enough," Judy said. The now-slim tornado bore down on the dwelling, traveling about as fast as a leisurely grandma on her Sunday drive. Judy saw the round swimming pool in the little blue house's backyard, the trees in spring leaf. The twister never altered its pace as it ripped through the yard and sideswiped the house. A piece of the roof flew off. Two trees lashed from side to side in a frenetic dance before crashing to the ground. The pool collapsed, gushing water everywhere. In seconds, its damage done, the tornado lifted.

Judy leaned back in her seat, drained, and rubbed her forehead. "You're right," she said. "It is a freakin' miracle."

"Let's make sure they're all right," Robinson said. "Then we have to decide what to do."

"Sounds good." As he drove forward, she pulled out her phone and dialed the fire department, telling them about the house. She stole a glance in the side mirror as she hung up. The mesonet car was already speeding away, in the other direction.

They turned right and pulled up next to a fallen tree, just as the front door of the half-smashed house opened and a woman with short brown hair and what appeared to be her teenage daughter came out into the yard. They cried and laughed as light rain fell on their heads. Judy rolled down her window. The siren was still blaring. "Are you OK? Is anyone else inside?" she shouted.

"We're fine!" the woman said in a giddy tone. Judy thought she recognized her from the bakery. "We're great! We're alive." The woman's spirits seemed to sag, though, as she looked back toward her house, where one corner was a crumbling mess of splintered two-by-fours and aluminum siding. Her daughter hugged her.

"You're all right, Mom," the girl said. "We're OK."

Relieved, Judy waved, rolled up her window, then wiped away a tear. She hadn't realized she was crying, too. The teenager, the girl, she was so strong. If only she'd been like that, for Shannon, for herself. She had to make up for lost time.

She glanced over at Robinson. A strange light was in his eyes. "What is it?" she asked.

He leaned close. Before she could object, he grasped her shoulders and kissed her on the mouth, sweetly, hotly, with measured and devoted attention. In her yellow rain jacket, Judy thought she might melt into a pool of butter right there.

"Robinson," she breathed when he pulled away.

He smiled his impish smile. "Are we going to do this thing or what?"

She looked into his lively gaze, seeing delight and adventure there, and then she looked up. The storm was getting away from them. They would need to backtrack, head north and east. They would need to hurry.

"Let's do it," she said, flashing him a smile she knew was full of light. She felt full of light. She would take it into the darkness.

❧

"I ALMOST DON'T MIND NOT SEEING a tornado right now," Marcus shouted over the din of hail slamming into the van. Nature's percussion section, he thought. He sat behind the wheel, paging through data on the laptop mounted between the front seats.

The hail van, parked on the road that a few miles west became Pancake's Main Street, was experiencing its finest moment, immersed in the supercell's dense core. While four-inch-plus hailstones made craters in the hood, the hail catcher sucked massive stones into its guts. Dennis sat on the stool in the back, doing the honors, making sure the jars didn't get too full before he switched them out. It was just the two of them today in the van. Marcus was glad, because he was a bit concerned about their safety. He didn't voice it to Dennis, but if a gust of wind caught one of those big stones and sailed it sideways, they could easily lose a window. The metal grate that extended forward from the roof was saving their windshield from destruction.

Marcus scanned the radar and checked out the vertical integrated liquid. He did some quick calculations. "The VIL Density is well over six on this thing," he said, impressed.

"I must have missed class that day," Dennis said as he eyed another big stone tumbling into the jar of hexane at the end of the tube. "What exactly does that mean?"

"Well, it's not conclusive, but given what we're seeing fall into the bucket, I'd say it means big stones," Marcus said. "*Bigger* stones. We probably aren't in the worst of it."

Dennis looked up at Marcus, one eyebrow raised. "That would do a number on a cow," he said. "Are we going to try it?"

"I'm already going to hear shit about the dents," Marcus said. "They know it's a hail van, but I don't know if they really want me totaling it."

"It could be fun," Dennis said. He jumped as another hailstone rolled down the tube and into the jar.

"If your nerves can take it," Marcus said.

"Probe 6, this is FC!" the radio blared. It was turned up loud so they could hear it over the racket.

"Probe 6 here," Marcus responded.

"We're sending you east, then north," Professor Malik

said. Even he sounded tense. This kind of operation was easier when they didn't have to chase around towns. "We need to get you in position, Marcus. Go north on Wagon Road to the highway that leads to Prairie Rock Road and wait for orders." He rattled off some GPS coordinates.

"Ten-four," Marcus replied. "We've got some great samples here, anyway."

"Excellent," Malik said. "I can't wait to see the dents."

❧

"I WANT *exact* POSITIONS," Brad said as he drove the Thor's Tours van northeast on the barren two-lane highway that had led them into the northern fringes of the storm.

"This is a cellular link," said Noel, "and the signal sucks right now. If you invest in that satellite data stuff, then we'll have exact positions. As it is, I can only load a new image about every five minutes, and loops are almost impossible. Maybe the tornado took out a tower."

Brad beat his right thumb against the steering wheel as he drove fast and tried to think. He realized he'd been doing it a lot. His thumb actually hurt. He looked at it, then sucked it for a moment. "Give me some ideas, here, Noel."

"We have to get east of the meso. We can't risk driving into it. I say we stay northeast on this highway and get way ahead of it before it hits Prairie Rock."

"Not acceptable. I want to get it as it approaches," Brad said. "I don't want the show to be over by the time we see it. Show me the data."

Noel turned the laptop toward him so Brad could get a look at the radar loop as he drove. Brad's quick glances did little to dispel the fog in his brain.

"What are our road options?" he asked Noel.

"The only paved road that will work is the one we're on."

"Ah, now we're getting somewhere," Brad said. "There's an unpaved road?"

"Uh, you don't want to do that, Brad," Noel said. "It's already raining. It might be trouble."

"This is a big van. It can handle it. Where does it go?"

"You'd drop south a bit on the next paved road, then head east on the unpaved road. It should go straight. If it works, it will get us east of the meso before the worst of it gets to Prairie Rock. But I'm really not sure it's a good idea."

The chattier of the two British guys piped up again. "Where's the tornado then, mate?"

"That does it," Brad said to Noel. "Show me the other road."

"Brad. You have a van full of —"

"Show me the other road!" Brad shouted. The tourists, who had been buzzing about their prospects as they pointed video cameras out the windows, shut up and stared forward to see how the conflict would play itself out.

Noel looked back at their hopeful faces, then glanced at the quivering Brad. Thor's Tours' captain would not be denied. Noel turned to the laptop and switched over to the GPS software. *Click, click.* "Turn right in two miles," he said in a defeated tone.

Brad sped up. The rain was getting heavier, and small hailstones smacked the van. It was hard to make out any storm structure when he looked south toward the dark core of the storm, but as soon as they got east, the meso would reveal itself. He would deliver a tornado, he was sure of it. This thing had already dropped two twisters, and the warnings hadn't stopped. It was his turn.

The turn! There it was, at a stop sign. He veered south. This road was paved.

"Left in half a mile," Noel said. He didn't sound pleased. Brad didn't care.

"Is this it?" Brad asked as they approached what appeared to be a gravel road that *T*'d into the paved road.

Noel zoomed in on the GPS map on the laptop. "Looks to be it," he said.

Brad made the turn east and held his breath for several yards. Then he let it out a bit. The road was mostly covered with fine gravel — a little bumpy, with cavernous potholes here and there, but it held together. He thought he saw the sky getting lighter ahead. Soon, they would be in the open, and they would get a visual on the mesocyclone. "See, no problem!"

"It's about twelve miles to a paved north-south option," Noel said.

"We won't need it," Brad said. But the rocks under his wheels were becoming more scattered in the muck, and he felt the van resist as he pushed it ahead. He pressed the gas harder. A little mud never killed anybody.

JUDY AND ROBINSON picked their way out of the debris field and drove north into Pancake. Wherever there were trees, shredded leaves littered the ground. A few glass signs were broken, and along the side of the road, small piles of hail lingered, not fully melted. As Judy suspected, the roads were nearly empty. It wouldn't take long to get through and back on the storm's trail. When the siren died away, she knew the worst of the storm had cleared town. It also meant they had a lot of catching up to do.

In the circle at the center of town, the bronze statue of the Great Pioneer stood on a marble pedestal, dressed in rustic clothes, gun and satchel slung over one shoulder, one arm raised and pointing toward the west, where he looked to the promise of America. A bronze dog was at his heels, gazing up at him devotedly.

"You're pointing the wrong way, dude," Robinson said.

Judy laughed. "They ought to turn him into a weather-vane," she said. "Turn right here, then right again."

As Robinson drove around the circle, Judy looked just north of the intersection. There, Hale Hardware stood, only its ripped awning betraying the storm it had survived. Part of her wanted to stop, go in, hug Uncle Ray and Greg, but now she had other business.

It didn't take long for the east road to turn into rural Kansas again — farm fields, pastures and occasional hedgerows. They were getting east of the storm but too far south.

"We're going to have to go north. Where?" Robinson asked.

They hadn't needed the GPS all day, Judy knew the area so well. "There's a good north road just ahead," she said. "It should take us right into the path of this thing."

"And that's good, right?" Robinson asked, grinning.

"I hope so."

They finally reached Wagon Road and turned left. After fifteen minutes or so, they started to draw parallel with the meso. The storm was definitely on a northeast course, headed toward Prairie Rock. Its new wall cloud had already evolved into a large bowl — in reality, a huge funnel, spinning smoothly and with deceptive and deliberate calm.

"That's going to be one big mo-fo," Robinson said.

"It sure is. What do you think?" Judy asked. "Stay even with it like this? I'm a little worried that we'll be cut off. Maybe we should get up to the highway that goes northeast past Prairie Rock Road — then we can stay ahead of it. We still have at least a couple of hours of daylight left, and this looks like it could go and go and go."

"That'll be good if we can stay out of the hail core."

"Yeah, Whit said it had big hail," Judy said. "I knew a guy once whose car just conked out in the middle of a hailstorm. The car thought it was in an accident. Killed the fuel switch."

"No kidding."

Judy was silent for a minute, pondering the options, enjoying the view of the storm and getting a few shots as she looked past Robinson, out the driver's side window. They hadn't slowed down, and it seemed they were still roughly parallel with the funnel, only it was getting closer. "It's your car, Robinson, so it's your choice," she said. "The only other east-west option between here and there is a road that I know is mostly mud, even on dry days. And there were storms last week, so it's probably bad. I would vote no on that. So it's either we hang here, enjoy a good view till it passes, then give up the rest of the day — or we press ahead, try to get east and see the whole show."

Robinson didn't hesitate. "Let's go. We can always bail somewhere and find a hail shelter, right?"

"This is Kansas, Robinson, not the metropolis. But yeah, we might find a barn or something. Just don't count on it."

"We'll be OK," he said. "And you'll be with me. That's all I need." He beamed her a warm smile, then turned back toward the road. His tone was light, charming. She believed him. This was crazy. A tornadic storm was bearing down, and they were flirting. Well, it was about time, she admitted to herself, letting her eyes rove over his curly brown hair and ski-slope nose. Then her gaze was drawn again to the funnel. She picked up her camera and videotaped the storm, a beautiful, scary shot framed by Robinson and the window.

The funnel lowered farther, the most substantial she'd ever seen, with a collar of spinning, ragged cloud above it. A bowl of dust began to spin underneath, not quite connecting, but it made it official: This was a tornado, an infant monster, just a few miles away.

As they started to get ahead of it, they crossed the intersection with the dirt road. It looked like chocolate soup. Yet Judy almost swore she saw a white van to her left, laboring down it. As she looked farther back, she saw the tornado looming. Next to the intersection was parked one of the white mesonet cars, its anemometer spinning fast with the inflow, the warm air the storm was inhaling. Judy wondered: Was it Jack?

Robinson's car started to shake a little with the inflow, too. The tornado filled in, becoming a fat, spinning cylinder, munching through the fields and tossing the occasional tree. They watched it rotate, part of a great and misty machine, as they pushed ahead toward the northeast highway. How something so large and violent could be so graceful was a miracle of nature. It was mesmerizing, and for a few miles, they didn't speak.

What looked like a mesonet van with a big net on the top sped past them, going the opposite way. Judy suddenly wondered if they should follow.

"It's moving pretty fast," she said of the storm. "Maybe thirty, thirty-five miles per hour. I'm not sure."

"We'll beat it," Robinson said. His tone wasn't as confident as she'd like. They had pulled northeast of the beast, but considering the tornado's path and proximity to the road, they would have to get to the highway soon. It wasn't far. She felt him accelerate. They were almost at the turn. Then she saw the glint of white in the rain ahead.

It was not rain.

"Shit!" Robinson said when the first baseball hit. The sound of the hail was sick and loud, metallic.

"We still have the window," Judy said, and just then, the second big stone smashed into the glass. She yelped. It left a spider-web crack in front of her, but the window hung together. The noise began to intensify, *bang, bang!*

"We've got to get out of here," Robinson said, slowing down to minimize the impacts.

"We can't go back." The tornado was too close for comfort. Go back, and it might run them over. Go forward? They were at the intersection. "We can't turn right. There's no shelter on the highway, and if the car is disabled, we'll be right in its path," she said. "Go straight." *Wham! Wham!* Huge stones, like the softballs smashing on the road in front of them, slammed into Robinson's vehicle.

"What's straight?" he asked, alarm in his voice.

"There's a little airport," Judy said quickly. "There might be something. Go!"

They crossed the highway and continued straight, crawling, and the road narrowed. *Wham!* Another big hailstone hit the windshield, smashing another spider web. "Damn," Robinson muttered.

"Prairie Rock Airfield, 1 mile," the sign said.

It was a very, very long mile. The banging noise was tremendous as softballs, baseballs, golf balls, an entire sports arena of ice hurtled into the car. With one thud on the roof that sounded like a bowling ball, the cover of the dome light fell off the ceiling. "Shit!" Robinson said. He sped up. It was too late to save his front window, but he might save the rest. Ahead was the airfield.

"Look!" Judy said. "Up in there!"

Up a bank on the left was a corrugated metal shelter, facing away from them. A driveway ran between the shelter and a small building. Robinson turned left onto the grassy drive and up the bank, then left to see what he could find. Airplanes. All the slots under the shelter — just a roof supported by poles — were filled with a dozen or so airplanes. In the field to their west, big hailstones were bouncing high off the grass. They were getting bigger. And they were still slamming onto the car, with increasing frequency.

Judy saw it first, barely, through the cracks in the windshield. "Four planes down!" she said. As he drove toward the empty spot, Judy looked past the planes, through the open shelter and the hail, and barely made out the shape of the tornado. It would miss them. And, unfortunately, they would miss it. Robinson wheeled his car into the gap, between two small planes, then turned off the engine and rested his head on the steering wheel. The noise was still overwhelming, but now it was from hailstones hitting the metal roof over the car.

"FUCK!" he screamed.

Judy let him have a moment. "Feel better?"

He lifted his head. "Actually, I do. Want to get out?"

She laughed. "I don't know if you want to."

"Bring your camera," he said. "I'll need good pictures for the insurance."

꙰

JACK AND RENNY observed the tornado from a comfortable perch to the east of the meso. They saw the yellow SUV speed by. Chasers. There were a few out but not as many as Jack thought he would see. He noted their course and hoped they drove fast.

"Probes," Malik's voice came over the radio, "keep to your waypoints as instructed but, obviously, move to get out of harm's way. The radar on this thing is classic, and it's very, very nasty."

"I like them nasty," Jack replied.

"Probe 3, I presume," Malik said dryly.

Earlier, Jack had noticed the white van approaching on the dirt road that intersected theirs. He didn't pay much attention to it until he heard the motor whining, saw the clods of mud the van's wheels were kicking up. It was stuck. Oh, boy, was it stuck, not fifty yards from the paved road. The images flashed through his head like a flip book. Tornado. Van. They were going to need help. Then the radio crackled to life again.

"Hey, um, can you hear me? You guys in the white car?"

The voice sounded familiar. Then he heard Malik. "Probes, are you calling?"

"I think I know who it is, FC," Jack said. "OK, guy," he addressed the interloper, "you're on our channel. I hope it's just you in there. You'd better run to our car."

"Um, we're a tour," the voice said. "There are eight of us."

"*Eight?*" Jack exclaimed. He thought quickly. "FC, I need to divert Marcus. Any problem with that?"

"Sounds like you have a situation," Malik said. "I trust you, Jack."

Jack didn't hesitate. "Probe 6, Marcus, come south, now. We need you. I think you're finally going to see a tornado."

MARCUS HAD BEEN AWAITING the worst of the hail core on the highway that went northeast. He had already seen more of the storm's structure than he usually did, but there was enough rain and hail where he was to keep visibility low, and the precipitation was intensifying. Jack's call felt like a lightning bolt.

"On my way!" Marcus shouted, then put down the mike. "Woo-hoo! Strap in, Dennis!"

"You act like you've never seen a tornado before," said the bulky co-pilot as he climbed into the front and clicked in the seat belt. Marcus pulled off the shoulder, headed west to the intersection, then zoomed south. After a few minutes, he saw a yellow SUV pass him going the other way. "They sure don't have hail guards," he noted.

"They'll find that out pretty quick," Dennis said.

They cleared a tree line, and suddenly, Marcus saw it.

"Destroyer of worlds," he whispered in awe, recalling a quote he'd once heard. The tornado was beyond his imagination, a fantastical monster that would trump anything in his comic books, a gigantic, revolving, perilous spectacle. "It's going to be hard to top this."

"Virgins always say that," Dennis teased. "But I see what you mean."

It didn't take long to come upon Jack, who stood outside his probe with a group of eight slightly damp and anxious people watching the approaching tornado. The van in question was still stuck in the mud several yards away. Marcus pulled up, left the motor running and jumped out.

"Get in!" Jack ordered the crowd. Dennis opened the van's side door and the tourists crammed themselves inside among the tubes, coolers and other equipment. Before the tall, skinny guy with the Thor's Tours golf shirt could get aboard, Jack collared him for a second. "You're lucky I don't leave you here," he said.

"Yeah, real lucky," the sullen Brad said, then shrugged off Jack and got into the van.

"Jack, what do I do with them?" Marcus asked.

"South is safe. I think we're going to go north."

"You'd better go now." Winds were picking up. The tornado was getting close.

The radios crackled again. "FC for Probe 3. Jack, are you there?"

Jack leaned into the open passenger window and grabbed the mike Renny handed to him. "Here, FC. Marcus is doing a little rescue. We're going to move fast, intercept."

"Jack, if you see anyone on the highway, try to wave them off. Sirens are out in Prairie Rock. The Weather Service says lightning hit them last week, and they aren't working."

No sirens? Marcus saw the disaster in the making. Mother Nature was out for a gallop, and Prairie Rock was in the way.

Jack paused. "I'll do you one better," he said, but not into the mike. "Renny, get into the van," he told his driver. His tone brooked no refusal, and Renny, looking bewildered, climbed out of the car and into the van.

Marcus knew in a second what Jack planned to do. "The Prairie Rock Road is just that, Jack. There is no road north of

Prairie Rock. It just dead-ends into the town. You know that, right?"

"Then I'd better hurry so I can get in and out, right?" Jack said. "That's my specialty." He grinned. He and Marcus shook hands. Then Jack got into the car's driver's seat, wheeled around and zoomed north, his taillights quickly lost in the blowing dust.

The tornado's watery roar was audible now. Marcus clambered behind the wheel of the now-packed van, slammed his door and sped south. Dennis sat in the co-pilot's chair, with Renny on the floor between the seats. The other eight were stuffed in ridiculous poses among the gear.

Marcus glanced in the side mirror and pushed his glasses up his nose. "You guys might be interested in the view out the back," he announced.

They all turned, straining as best they could to see the tornado. It was massive and ugly now, this close, and it sucked up Brad's van and snorted it out again like a booger in the nose of a giant.

There was a collective gasp from the tourists, many of whom were still clutching and using their video cameras as best they could under the armpits and over the shoulders of their fellow passengers. Brad, who'd been looking through the periscope, whimpered.

◣

THE CORRUGATED METAL roof that sheltered the airplanes sloped gently upward from east to west, or back to front. The airplanes all pointed out, ready to taxi onto the grassy airfield. Robinson's battered car pointed in, where he'd managed to save it from the worst of the onslaught. Still, the finish was dimpled with round dents big and small, so it looked like a deformed golf ball. In a few spots, the hailstones had actually stripped away the yellow paint. A couple of the side windows were busted. The windshield, taillights, headlights and plastic parts all over the car were fractured or smashed.

Still falling, hail accumulated fast on the grass like textured snow, some of it bouncing high, some of it …

"Goddamn *huge*," Robinson said as he watched a five-inch-plus hailstone boing off the ground. "Gorilla hail!"

"King Kong hail, more like," Judy said in amazement.

They overcame the shock of his car's makeover long enough to set up tripods and get video rolling on the unbelievable hailstorm. Now they stood next to each other, shivering in their shorts in the chilly air, watching the hail fog rise above the drifts of round stones, its white breath licking at their knees, ghostly and cold. Some hail bounced under the shelter, accumulating at their feet. More balls of ice zinged loudly on the roof above. Judy looked up. She heard a particularly loud bang overhead at the same time a softball-size bump appeared in the ceiling. "Uh-oh," she said. "How strong do you think this roof is?"

"What do you mean?" Robinson asked.

She pointed up. A wrinkle appeared in his brow as he watched another dent materialize. Like fists punching into the roof, more bumps appeared with each impact. The metal cracked in spots; in some of the fractures, the white of the hail peeked through. Each blow made Judy flinch. Robinson put an arm around her. *Bang! Bang! Bang!*

"Do you want to get in the car?" he asked.

"No way!" Judy said, caught up in the show. "The roof will slow 'em down."

He laughed, then spun her around to face him. "You're beautiful in a storm."

She searched his eyes, his animated face. "If that's all you're looking for, you're looking at the wrong girl," she said.

"Ah, but you're beautiful in a storm, beautiful in the sun, beautiful *inside*." He almost looked embarrassed to say it but exhilarated, too, elated to tell her, finally. He pulled her close and kissed her, more subtly, more sensuously than he did before. His arms wrapped around her and she lost herself in the heat of his mouth, his touch. In the thundering hail, it took her a moment to hear her own heart.

She pulled away for a second. "Geek love," she joked, and he laughed, kissed her again. The bright moments of the dark year past revealed themselves as a pattern she should have sketched out long ago, the long talks and shared storms and sad confidences and absurd laughter, the attraction she'd been afraid to acknowledge, to trust. She ran her hands through his hair and embraced him, feeling her worries fall away, feeling his strength, confident the roof would hold as fast as he held her. This was real, she thought, as he felt her respond and enfolded her more tightly, kissing her neck, her hair, her face, her mouth again. He was real. And it was wonderful.

ONE OR TWO miles can make all the difference between dodging icy softballs or breathing in the dirt of a tornado. Jack was enjoying the latter. Driving under the edge of the meso, he flirted with the tornado and any satellite vortices it decided to drop, but he also stayed out of the worst hail. Thick waves of windblown dust buffeted the car as Jack pushed ahead of the twister's reach. He hit the intersection just right and had to endure only a few baseball-size hailstones and one crack in his windshield as he sped out of the bear's cage and off toward the northeast, putting a little distance between himself and the funnel.

He glanced over at the laptop. The GPS showed Prairie Rock Road just a few miles ahead. A livestock truck headed toward him, the first traffic in miles, and he flashed his headlights. Then he remembered the amber lights. He flipped the switch so they would spin and flash, an even better alarm, and he sounded the air horn as the truck passed. In his rearview mirror, he saw the truck's brake lights go on as its driver realized what lay ahead. It began the laborious process of turning around.

Jack felt almost cheerful. He had a purpose. He was intercepting one of the most impressive tornadoes of his life. He had a great excuse to drive fast. For once, it was a good day to be in Kansas.

A lightning bolt zapped a power pole not two hundred yards away, and sparks flew as he heard the *crack-bang* of the too-close strike. Above and ahead, amid the pouchy mammatus of the anvil, zits of lightning played. The radio whined. This storm was intensely electrical.

The tornado was still in his rearview mirror, a little farther away, slowly crossing the road, its path on a more northern angle than the two-lane highway as the twister headed toward the heart of Prairie Rock. He blinked at a power flash as the twister took out some poles. He had a few minutes. Not many, but a few.

A small sign with an arrow heralded the turn in a mile. It took him less than a minute to get there, and as he turned left on Prairie Rock Road, a bigger, hand-painted sign greeted him. "Prairie Rock — Fantastic Future Ahead — Come Grow With

Us!" The elaborate letters, painted over a fanciful field of wheat, were faded and weathered.

After five more miles of flat fields, another sign awaited, this one more weatherbeaten than the last. "Prairie Rock — Home of the Pickers!" it said, next to a cartoon of an angry-looking horse wearing a football helmet and carrying a ball.

"The Pickers?" Jack said to himself. "Now that's a name that inspires fear."

Prairie Rock was about half the size of Pancake and half as modern. It expanded only one or two blocks off its main street. Jack rolled down his window as he approached the first buildings. There was no siren. Yet, to his left, he could make out the tornado approaching. The town already lay under the shadow of the anvil. An inexperienced observer might see only a dark storm, rain. He knew better. Still, he'd never done anything like this before. He hoped it would do some good for the people who didn't have weather radios. He flipped the switch to turn on the external speakers and picked up the mike as he approached the first buildings.

"The National Weather Service has issued a tornado warning for Prairie Rock." No need to shout. His voice was magnified to godlike proportions as it reverberated off the houses and brick storefronts. "A tornado is approaching! Take cover now!" As he cruised slowly down the street, sounding the horn and repeating the warning, the few people outside looked startled, then genuinely alarmed as they regarded his official-looking car with its instruments and flashing lights and looked up to see the ominous storm approaching from the west. Some people opened their doors to see what the fuss was about and slammed them shut when they realized what approached. A little boy walking his beagle saw the mesonet car, picked up the dog and ran screaming down the street,

"Storm chaser! Storm chaser!" as if the sight itself was enough to bring Armageddon to town.

Jack saw a policeman going door to door on the main street, banging and shouting the warning, too. He waved down Jack and ran over to his car. "Thanks," the cop said. He was young, several years younger than Jack. "We already warned the school. They have a shelter. I appreciate what you're doing, mister, but you should get out of here."

"It looks like you need the help," Jack said.

"I'm not saying we don't, but I can't be responsible for you."

"You need to watch out for yourself," Jack said. "Don't worry about me."

The cop nodded, then ran to the next house and banged on the door.

Jack kept going, repeating his warnings, sounding the air horn. He couldn't see past the buildings very well and wasn't sure how close the tornado was. He was getting near the end of the main street. It really did dead-end; beyond it was a creek, then fields. The end of Prairie Rock, he thought. It was time to turn around and get out.

He flipped around at the circle at the end and started the drive back. At the first intersection, he looked southwest.

"Holy shit," he said.

It was close. Too close. He would not be able to get out in time. All of Prairie Rock lay between him and escape. He could make out debris on the ground as the massive tornado ripped into trees on the west side of town. He looked around, trying to think. There were no east roads, either, at least none that didn't dead-end. He needed a shelter, a substantial building. He drove faster, looking for something, anything that would work. Then he saw the bank on the other side of the street.

He pulled a highly illegal U-turn, screeching tires in the now-empty road, and pulled up in front of it. He grabbed his video camera, the new one he'd had to buy after the accident, and shoved it in the camera bag with the Nikon that had somehow survived. He almost took the laptop, then thought better of it and pushed it under the passenger seat, making sure its wires were still attached. If Malik wanted a probe, he was going to get one.

Jack jumped out with the bag and ran up to the heavy old wooden door. He pulled it open.

Inside, it was hushed, like a church, with marble floors and stone walls, a relic of a time when even Prairie Rock might have had hopes for prosperity. Apparently, in this tomblike old building, they had not heard his warnings. There was one customer, a woman with her toddler in a stroller, dealing with a diminutive blond clerk. An older woman sat at a desk behind the counter, a schoolmarm type with wavy gray hair. A second clerk, glasses perched on the end of her nose, her brown hair twisted up on her head, a fussy silk scarf around her neck, counted money at her window. Jack walked right up to her.

"Do you have a safe?" he asked.

"Just a moment, sir," she said, never stopping her count.

"Do you have a safe?" he asked, louder.

His tone cut through her indifference. She stopped counting and looked up. "Are you going to rob us?" she asked, fear creeping into her voice. Everyone was looking at him now.

"No, lady. I want to deposit myself. You have bigger problems than crime," he said, pointing out the barred, west-facing windows at the front of the bank. They were just large enough to reveal the seething churn of black, swirling dirt and debris and chaos. There was no mistaking it now. The tornado was near enough that everyone in the bank abruptly understood what was coming.

The clerk screamed. It wasn't the reaction he expected. The bloodcurdling sound was enough to push the rest of them into instantaneous action. The older woman at the desk — the manager, Jack guessed from her tone of authority — got up and shouted: "To the safe! To the safe!"

It was in the back, around the corner, not immediately visible from the front. They ran through the swinging gate at the counter — Jack, the two clerks, the manager and the customer, an attractive young woman with short, dark hair who grabbed her little boy out of his stroller and hauled him to her shoulder.

"Teddy!" the boy cried.

"Hurry!" the blond clerk called to the boy's mother as she turned back for a moment to pick up her child's dropped teddy bear.

The safe's door was rectangular, more than a foot thick, with a stair-stepped metal seal punctuated with what looked like gigantic bolts. Jack didn't know how it worked, but he knew it was substantial. The safe itself was no bigger than a walk-in closet, lined with safety-deposit boxes and a few bigger vaults. They squeezed in.

The manager grabbed the handle on the inside of the door and pulled. It moved slowly. Jack grabbed it, too, helping draw it shut.

"Does this thing lock?" he asked.

"Not from the inside," the manager said. "It's a safety thing."

"Is there air in here?" he asked, suddenly feeling claustrophobic.

"There's a vent to the outside. There's a phone. There's battery-powered emergency lighting, if it comes to that," she said.

"OK. I'm more worried about the lock," Jack said. "Let's just hope that door has enough inertia to hold tight."

They all stood looking at one other, hearing the others' breathing, and then they heard the sound — the cracking, crushing, throbbing sound of their town being torn apart.

They dropped down on their haunches, instinctively, and looked at the door, trying to see what they could only hear. It was getting louder, and louder still, accompanied by a groaning change in pressure, as if a giant were peeling the top off a towering can in whose depths they were hiding.

The woman with the child let out a sob. The little boy, already squeezing the life out of his tattered brown teddy bear, sensed her alarm and started to get that scrunched-up, pre-wail face. It was the last thing Jack wanted, a screaming kid while they waited to die.

He put his hand on the woman's shoulder. "Don't worry," he said. "This little guy is going to have a great story to tell someday, when this is over." The woman calmed under his touch, gave Jack a pretty smile, and her boy seemed to swallow his sniffles as he clung to her. At least I've still got it, Jack thought. And he was surrounded by women. There were worse ways to go. He became conscious of his bag next to him and remembered the video camera, pulled it out, set it on the bag on the floor, and turned it on. There would be a record.

The sound was louder, probably debris hitting the building. More alarming was the rumble, the trembling that seemed to grow through the floor. Then everything started shaking. The lights flickered, went out, and the jittery blue-white emergency light sputtered on. The safe suddenly shuddered as if from a violent impact, and the clerk that had screamed before let out a yelp. Jack looked around at the terrified faces. The two clerks clung to each other. They were all being shaken, in a bottle of soda about to explode. The manager had her eyes closed as she leaned back against the rows of small, numbered doors to the deposit boxes, and she mouthed words—a prayer, Jack thought. He had no prayers. Nothing would stop the tornado. The only question was whether it would let them live another day.

The cacophony was a palpable thing, and the walls almost felt as if they were shifting. His ears popped. The huge, heavy door started to move, to open. He felt the air and dust pushing in the slender gap. Maybe this is it, he thought. He jumped up and grabbed the handle and pulled it, hard, trying to seal the fragile shell between this cocoon of life and the beast on the outside.

As he braced himself, feeling the adrenaline, he looked into the little boy's eyes and saw, to his surprise, not fear but an eager curiosity. It was a feeling he understood as the pressure shifted again and the terrible noise dropped off. The safe seemed to settle in place with a weary groan.

It was over.

Jack released the handle, and the door creaked subtly open. The rest followed his lead, got up slowly, and looked toward the hint of air, at whatever awaited them. He helped the manager get off the floor. "Do you want to do the honors?" he asked her.

She looked at him with weariness, then pushed the door open the rest of the way. Daylight and the smell of earth and rain and freshly broken wood greeted them. Daylight. The bank was gone.

They walked in wonder across the stone floor, past the pieces of counter that remained, through the piles of stone blocks and wiring and other debris dropped by the tornado. Jack looked around. There was little to impede his view. Most of the main street had suffered some level of devastation. The tornado's path must have been nearly a mile wide.

Jack still had his camera bag slung over his shoulder. He opened it, stowed the video camera, then spotted his cigarettes and grabbed the pack. He pulled out one and struck a match. He noted, as if from a distance, that his hand was trembling as he held the flame close, touched the paper with it, breathed in the comforting, noxious fumes as it caught.

He looked around again as his pulse slowed. A few lingering raindrops fell on his face, his arms, refreshing. Where was the probe? It seemed to be nowhere in front of him. He looked back toward the bank, or what was left of it. There, leaning against the miraculously upright safe, was the crumpled car.

He picked his way back through the debris and found a door that would open, the passenger-side front, and fished for the laptop. It was there, under the seat, and somehow, still on. He snapped it shut, stuffed it in his bag and walked back to the road.

Down the street, a couple of fire trucks had appeared, labeled Pancake Volunteer Fire Department. They must have been following the storm, waiting to help, he thought. If Prairie Rock had a fire truck, it was probably history by now. The firefighters were checking where they could for survivors. People started to appear all over the street, and they helped, moving aside debris, hugging one another.

Jack's cell phone, forgotten on his belt clip, suddenly rang.

He pulled it out, looked at the caller ID, then answered. "Professor?"

"Damn it, Jack," Malik said. "I've been talking to Marcus. I know what you've been up to. I've been trying to raise you for twenty minutes. We lost your GPS signal. Where in the hell are you?"

"The town formerly known as Prairie Rock," Jack said.

UNDER THE SHELTER of the airfield's metal roof, Judy and Robinson's storm-chasing instincts took over. They disengaged, a bit disheveled, then checked their cameras and filmed the hail as it piled up and gradually dropped off. When only light rain and a few icy peas still fell, Robinson dashed out of their shelter and grabbed a couple of enormous hailstones, and they held them up to a ruler he kept in the car and took pictures. One was lumpy, more than six inches across. Judy couldn't believe it. It wasn't quite as big as the record, but it was a killer.

The sky began to clear a bit. Beneath the ragged clouds that remained, a bright, orange orb slipped into view. Judy instinctively looked back toward the east, where she knew the rain continued. A rainbow had appeared, set afire by the declining sun.

"We're getting a little of everything today," Robinson said as he saw it.

"It's so beautiful."

"Maybe we can find a better place to take a picture of it. I kind of want to see where that tornado went, too."

"Are you sure?" Judy asked. "Your car is a mess. Do you want to drive it around?"

"It's drivable," Robinson said. "Now it just has a lot of character."

"The windshield is pretty bad."

"I think I can see through it well enough for tonight. Come on. Aren't you curious?"

"Yes," she said. But a little of her childhood trauma still nagged at her.

"It'll be good therapy," he said, reading her mind. "We won't gawk. We'll just take a quick look, help out if they need it, then get going."

"Fair enough," Judy said, scraping together her resolve. "Let's go."

He smiled and gave her another quick kiss. She looked forward to more of those. They stowed their cameras and got in the car.

"Except for the windows, it doesn't look so bad from in here," Robinson said.

Judy laughed. "At least the back window is intact. Maybe you can drive in reverse all evening."

"Yeah, but I'm not sure the taillights work. At least one of the headlights still does."

He backed out slowly, crunching his wheels on the melting hailstones. Then he drove, front forward, toward the road. The car slipped a little on the hail, but before long they were back on the northeast highway, which was mostly wet.

In a couple of miles, they saw where the tornado had crossed. Some of the pavement was stripped away, rough and crunchy. Humbled, they didn't say anything. Power poles were down here, too, and Judy could see where the twister had scraped through the field on the left side of the road, on its way to Prairie Rock. In the distance, the storm was still visible. Robinson turned on the weather radio. It still had a tornado warning on it. Judy knew they wouldn't go after it, not now, but she wondered who else might be in its path.

At Prairie Rock Road, they turned left, driving past the "Come Grow With Us!" plea and then the "Home of the Pickers" sign at the town limits. There were still a few houses here, a gas station, a church. But within a half mile, they entered what looked like a war zone. Debris was everywhere. Some buildings still had a few walls of crumbling brick; others were blasted to nothing. Robinson drove slowly, trying to avoid the worst of the boards, metal, glass and odd objects in the street — clothes, a patio table and shredded umbrella, a restaurant sign, a busted television. They saw the fire trucks and a couple of police cars and ambulances.

"We don't need to be here," Robinson said at last. "The experts have got this, and we'll just be in the way. We'll come back in a couple of days, do a damage survey when the worst is over. Geez. I've never seen anything like it."

Judy was impressed by the damage, which was even worse than what she remembered of the tornado of her youth, yet she was curiously detached. They would survive, she thought. That's what people did.

As Robinson looked for a safe spot to turn around, a lone figure caught Judy's eye. A man, smoking. "Oh my god. I don't believe it."

"What?" Robinson asked.

"It's Jack."

"Oh, great."

Judy looked over at Robinson, amused at this hint of annoyance, jealousy. "He might need a ride," she said. "Especially if that's his car."

Robinson looked where she pointed. "Holy crap." A crunched mesonet vehicle leaned against a small, boxy structure, the only thing standing in the immediate vicinity. "OK," he said grudgingly, "if only to hear how he came to be in this particular spot without being dead."

As they pulled up next to the curb — at least the sidewalks were still there — Jack talked on a cell phone, a cigarette in his other hand. Judy rolled down her window. The expression on his face was priceless, pure surprise.

"Need a ride?" she asked.

"Where are you again?" Jack asked on the phone, one eye on Judy. "OK. No, you don't need to come here. I'll come to you. Bye." He holstered the phone and looked at her, then at Robinson, then took in the length of the battered car. "I'd appreciate it," he answered her.

"Get in," Robinson said.

Jack dropped his cigarette and crushed it under his heel. Then he opened the back door, sat in the middle of the seat and leaned back. He closed his eyes for a second.

"Rough day?" Judy asked.

"Looks like yours wasn't so great, either," Jack said.

"I've had worse." They exchanged a long look. She knew then that he understood what she meant. Their loss was the one thing they shared.

Robinson turned the car around and headed south. "Where were you when it went through?" he asked.

"Bank safe. No more keeping money under the mattress for me," Jack quipped.

Judy let out a little laugh, and she saw the corner of Robinson's mouth turn up. She felt a subtle breeze of relief. It had been a long day, a long year, with too much bitterness. She was ready to let it go.

They arrived at the stop sign where Prairie Rock Road met the highway. "Where to?" Robinson asked.

"Left. The professor's at an intersection about ten miles east of here, he said."

"I know it," Judy said. "There's a historical marker. There was an Indian battle there, once."

"Who won?" Jack asked.

"Nobody."

He nodded. None of them said anything as the car rolled east. The rainbow had faded as the storm moved farther off. There was no rain here, now, only a few clouds, like cotton balls stretched thin, turning pink with the setting sun. They arrived at the intersection, and Robinson pulled up next to the white van parked there.

Jack reached out and shook Robinson's hand. "Thanks for the delivery."

"No problem," Robinson said.

Jack opened the back door, then turned to face Judy again. This time, she reached out her hand. He took it, shook it slowly, his green eyes betraying nothing.

"I'm glad you're still alive," she said.

"Thank you." He gave her hand a squeeze, just so she'd notice, then stepped out and swung the door shut. He walked over to the van and got in.

Robinson turned his car around again and drove slowly back toward the west and its orange sorbet sky, surreal through the broken glass.

"So you're all right?" he asked Judy. There was more than interest in her well-being in his question. He wanted to know where he stood.

"I'm all yours."

"That's not what I asked," he said, but a slow smile crept across his face.

"I'm all right," Judy said. "Are you?"

"You bet," he said, new verve in his voice.

She looked around her, at the magnificent expanse of prairie, the fiery sky, the endless possibilities where earth and atmosphere met at the horizon. She leaned over and kissed Robinson on the cheek, a lingering kiss, a promising kiss. "Let's go home," she whispered.

The engine revved as he sped up.

"I hear there's no place like it," he said.

NOTES AND THANKS

While much of *Funnel Vision* is inspired by my experiences as a storm chaser, its characters and situations are fictional. I especially have taken liberties with geography, when it suited my story, and the methods of research employed by Jack's scientific team.

That said, I borrowed the expertise of a few people who are absolutely not responsible for any extrapolations and modifications I have made in the name of fiction, including storm chaser Keith Brown, the late hail researcher Nancy Knight, and Diane Kridler, who endured some strange questions about bank vaults.

The television show *Storm Chasers* was not even on the air when I first wrote the majority of this book, and as a writer, it's difficult to watch as reality overtakes one's inventions, including Jack's loudspeaker. From first draft to last, over what seemed like just a few years, I had to update the story's technology to accommodate even the simplest gadgets. This book, published in 2012, will remain a product of its time, though a subtle edit in 2024 has eliminated a bit of its most outdated tech.

The title "Funnel Vision" first appeared on a travel article I wrote in 1998 about storm chasing tours, and I have the clever headline writers of *The Sun* in Baltimore to thank for it.

While I usually write in silence or to lyric-free music, one song inspired me to obsessive listening as I composed the early drafts of this story: "Bad Reputation" by Freedy Johnston. Leave it to a Kansas boy to rock melancholy so perfectly.

I'd like to thank my parents, Robert and the late Gloria Kridler, for allowing me to be crazy when it suited me, and George Jenkins for not just tolerating but encouraging my passion for storms and all the inconveniences it entails at home.

I also would like to thank some of my first readers for their reactions and encouragement: chasers Cheryl Chang, Bill Hark and Mark Robinson. They and other storm chasers have been my friends, teachers and companions on the road over the years, and I owe them much.

I am grateful for the writers who were always willing to lend an ear over a martini as the cruise ships sailed by, Susan Hubbard and Dianne Marcum.

Especially, I owe a debt to the writers of the Harbaugh Literary Salon, who listened to this book chapter by chapter and gave me invaluable feedback, insight and friendship: Pam and John Harbaugh, Cathy Mathias, Annette Clifford, Kimberly Moore, Jeff Schweers and Billy Cox. Thank you.

Don't miss the next Storm Seekers adventure!

When science becomes a stunt,
storm chasers reap the whirlwind...

Just when TV shows about storm chasing can't get any more extreme, along comes a production company with the ultimate exploit: the Bubble, a manned tornado probe. As the reluctant consultant, expert storm chaser Jack Andreas must get the show's nervous star, failed tour operator Brad Treat, into a twister. But Jack is losing his customary cool as a comedy of errors unfolds. Distracting him is co-star Saffire,  a Hollywood actress who is more than she seems, and producer Wynda, who will do anything to make her documentary succeed. The daring star of another show pursues them, desperate for a shot with his own flying machine. As the disasters mount, will Jack be able to launch their device into a tornado?

The sequel to FUNNEL VISION, a Storm Seekers novel, TORNADO PINBALL delivers an unforgettable adventure with action, humor, romance and stunning storms.

Learn more at ChrisKridler.com/books

BOOKS BY CHRIS KRIDLER

The STORM SEEKERS Series

Writing as Chris Kridler

FUNNEL VISION

TORNADO PINBALL

ZAP BANG

Storm Seekers Series Boxed Set: Books 1-3

BOHEMIA BARTENDERS MYSTERIES

Writing as Lucy Lakestone

These funny mysteries star Pepper Revelle and a team of mixologists who travel to colorful events where life is a cocktail of fun — until it's shaken into madcap mayhem … and murder.

RISKY WHISKEY

BAFFLED BY BITTERS ~ *story free to subscribers*

WRECKED BY RUM

VEXED BY VODKA

JIGGERED BY GIN

BEGUILED BY BOURBON

SHOCKED BY CHAMPAGNE

WHY OH RYE?

BOHEMIA BARTENDERS COCKTAIL COLORING BOOK

¶

The BOHEMIA BEACH Series

Writing as Lucy Lakestone

Award-winning hot contemporary romance

In a beautiful small city on Florida's east coast, artists meet, create, laugh and love. Where restless hearts are fueled by secrets and imagination, romance is impossible to resist. Welcome to the seductive tropical escape that's home to drama, humor and lots of heat – Bohemia Beach.

BOHEMIA BEACH

BOHEMIA LIGHT

BOHEMIA BLUES

BOHEMIA HEAT

BOHEMIA NIGHTS

BACK TO BOHEMIA ~ *story free to subscribers*

BOHEMIA BELLS

BOHEMIA CHILLS

Bohemia Beach Series Boxed Sets:

Books 1-3 | Books 4-7

¶

ABOUT THE AUTHOR

Chris Kridler is an award-winning writer, photographer and storm chaser who lives in Florida. She travels every year to Tornado Alley in search of the perfect storm. She also writes mysteries and romances as Lucy Lakestone. Learn more about her work and travels at ChrisKridler.com.